Iris Gower was born in Swansea, where she still lives. The mother of four grown-up children, she has written over twenty bestselling novels. She received an Honorary Fellowship from the University of Wales Swansea in 1999 and was awarded an MA in Creative Writing from the University of Cardiff.

The Other Woman is the third novel in her *Drovers* series. Her new novel, *Act of Love,* is now available in hardback from Bantam Press.

Also by Iris Gower

THE LOVES OF CATRIN
WHEN NIGHT CLOSES IN

The Sweyn's Eye Series
COPPER KINGDOM
PROUD MARY
SPINNERS' WHARF
MORGAN'S WOMAN
FIDDLER'S FERRY
BLACK GOLD

The Cordwainers Series
THE SHOEMAKER'S DAUGHTER
THE OYSTER CATCHERS
HONEY'S FARM
ARIAN
SEA MISTRESS
THE WILD SEED

The Firebird Series
FIREBIRD
DREAM CATCHER
SWEET ROSIE
DAUGHTERS OF REBECCA
KINGDOM'S DREAM
PARADISE PARK

The Drovers Series
THE ROWAN TREE
HALFPENNY FIELD
THE OTHER WOMAN

The Palace Series
ACT OF LOVE

THE OTHER
WOMAN

Iris Gower

CORGI BOOKS

THE OTHER WOMAN
A CORGI BOOK : 9780552150361

Originally published in Great Britain by Bantam Press,
a division of Transworld Publishers

PRINTING HISTORY
Bantam Press edition published 2005
Corgi edition published 2006

5 7 9 10 8 6 4

Set in 11/13pt Plantin by
Falcon Oast Graphic Art

Corgi Books are published by Transworld Publishers,
61–63 Uxbridge Road, London W5 5SA,
A Random House Group Company.

Addresses for Random House Group Ltd companies outside the UK
can be found at: www.randomhouse.co.uk
The Random House Group Ltd Reg. No. 954009.

The Random House Group Limited supports The Forest Stewardship
Council® (FSC®), the leading international forest-certification organisation.
Our books carrying the FSC label are printed on FSC®-certified paper.
FSC is the only forest-certification scheme supported by the leading
environmental organisations, including Greenpeace. Our
paper procurement policy can be found at
www.randomhouse.co.uk/environment

MIX
Paper from
responsible sources
FSC® C016897

Printed and bound in Great Britain by Clays Ltd, St Ives PLC

To Peter, with heartfelt thanks for teaching me how to laugh again

CHAPTER ONE

Gwenllyn Lyons stood in the small dim interior of the church and glanced up at the man at her side. In a few minutes, when the preacher had finished his droning exhortations to them to be faithful and true, she would be married to a stranger and with her belly full of another man's child.

The preacher seemed unable to stop his sermon and Gwenllyn shifted her position, impatient to be out of the church and into the fresh air of the cold snap that had taken the early spring sunshine and turned it back to winter. Her little pony and trap would be waiting to take her home and then she would never have to see Harold Rees again. This man, this cattle drover, was marrying her for the generous bag of gold she was giving him. It was a simple bargain: a child born in the bonds of marriage in exchange for money.

At last, the service was over and Gwenllyn

escaped outside, gulping air into her lungs, fearing she would be sick. Harold was at her side, helping her towards the church gate where a young boy held the reins of her horse, smoothing the animal's soft nose and whispering soothing words.

She allowed Harold to help her into the trap and to her surprise he climbed in after her.

'Where do you think you're going?' she demanded.

'I'm coming home with you.'

He didn't look at her, he just took the reins of the horse and clucked his tongue. The trap dipped as it began to move and Gwenllyn put her hands over her swollen stomach.

'That was not part of the bargain,' she said firmly. 'I gave you money and you gave my child your name. That was the arrangement.'

'Well, I've missed the drove now; they'll be halfway to Smithfield. You can at least give me a bed for the night. That's not too much to ask, is it?' He glanced at her stomach. 'I'm not likely to be after anything else with you in that condition, am I?'

She fell silent. Perhaps it was churlish of her to want him to be going on his way, but she hardly knew him. She'd seen him once or twice going through the village, heading for the ford across the river Wye, but that was all. It was only by chance that she made her bargain with him at all.

'When I talked to you by the river,' she said, 'I

didn't say anything about you staying with me. I don't want a husband – that's the last thing I need. Don't you realize I'm in love with the father of my baby?'

He nodded. 'Aye, but you can't have the father of your baby, can you? Caradoc Jones is only in love with one woman and she's his lawful wife. Once he got over his accident and got his memory back he knew it wasn't you he wanted.'

His words were hard, like sharp, jagged stones, stones that made her tremble. She remained silent: what could she say? He spoke the truth. And yet she could not forget the long summer days when she had Caradoc in her arms, in her bed, to all intents as her husband. Looking back, he had always been uneasy, warning her he might have a wife and perhaps even children in his other, forgotten world.

'So when are you going to move on?' She forced the words, fighting the urge to cry. 'I suggest you leave first thing in the morning.'

'I don't know yet,' he said briefly. He guided the pony up the steep track that led to her home and then the cottage came into sight; tall chimneys pointed fingers at the sky and the many windows shone as the sun returned as if to mock her.

Gwenllyn was glad to get indoors. She went immediately to her bedroom, where she changed into a comfortable gown and threw a warm shawl around her shoulders. The fire had gone out and the house was chilly.

When she returned to the sitting room Harold was stretched out in a chair, his eyes closed. She looked at him with little interest, but she supposed he was quite handsome in a rough sort of a way. His long legs were spread across the carpet as though reaching for the cheerful fire that was starting to blaze in the grate. He'd made himself at home, lighting the fire and seating himself before it as though he was master of the house.

Gwenllyn still shivered. The air could have a chill in it even here inside the thick walls of the cottage. Harold seemed to be quite easy with himself and with the house. Well, he could stay for tonight but tomorrow he would be on his way, she cared not where. All that she wanted by marrying him was a name for her baby, a record of the child's birth that didn't label the poor infant as illegitimate. And he knew that had been the bargain between them, a bag of gold for his name.

Harold looked up at her as she took the seat on the opposite side of the fire.

She met his eyes. 'Don't get too comfortable: you're not staying.' She forced a hard note into her voice.

'We'll see.' Harold straightened in his chair. 'What are we going to eat? I'm starving.'

'There's bread in the bin, and cheese. If you want a meal you can get it yourself or walk down to the village inn. I'm not going to run around after you.'

He sighed, frowning in irritation. 'Have you got to be so disagreeable? I'm not asking for much: a bed for the night and a meal.' His face brightened. 'You got any bacon and eggs?'

'The food is in the cold room. Why do you want to know?'

'Well, I was thinking of cooking something easy, something to fill the ache in my belly.' He half smiled. 'This getting married lark is hard work.'

If he thought she was going to be amused he could think again. 'I don't want anything,' she said and, even as she spoke, her stomach rumbled.

'You got to think of that kid inside you,' Harold said easily. 'If you don't care much for yourself, think of the babba.'

'The baby is nothing to do with you,' Gwenllyn said sharply.

'No, but it's everything to do with Caradoc Jones.' He got to his feet in a smooth movement of limbs that reminded her of an untamed animal. 'I thought he was dead and gone. So did everyone else, even his father, but he was here all along – living with you in this cosy little nest in the hills. Looked after him well, did you?'

'That's old news. It's a new year now and a new start for me.' She shook back the curls that had fallen free of the pins. 'This is 1834 and, in case you hadn't noticed, women are able to take care of themselves now.'

He looked round the elegant room. 'Aye. Well set up here, aren't you? But I bet this is all some man's doing.'

Gwenllyn shifted uncomfortably in her chair. He was right: the house and the money to keep it well maintained was due to her grandmother's love affair with a man above her station. But old Martha was gone now, dead and in her grave, and so was her rich lover. She pressed her lips firmly together, not wanting to admit he was right.

'Ah! Hit the nail on the head, haven't I?'

'Oh, leave me alone.' She moved to the fire and stood warming her hands. She felt trapped by this man, this stranger who was invading her privacy, her house and her life. 'What do you know?' She turned on him suddenly. 'All you are is a common drover's hand. You don't own a single beast in your own right, do you?'

'Carry on with your harsh words,' he replied; 'you can't offend me. Better people than you have tried.'

'Why did I expect any show of shame from you? You're not sensitive and intelligent like other men.'

'Like Caradoc Jones, you mean?' He thrust his hands into his pockets. 'He was so sensitive that he forgot his wife, his dying child, everything about his past. Very convenient, it was too, if you ask me.'

'Don't talk like that!' Gwenllyn faced him, her hands on her hips. 'Caradoc was a real man, a good man; he loved me and I loved him. He couldn't help it if an accident took his memory away.'

Harold sighed. 'And I have taken on his woman and his child, given you both my name. I'm good enough for that, aren't I?'

Gwenllyn was silent. She returned to her seat and sat rubbing her fingers together, wishing Harold would go away and the pain and anger would leave too. She missed Caradoc so much it actually felt as if her heart was broken in two.

'I'm sorry I spoke so harshly,' he said, 'and you in no condition to be upset. I'm sorry, Gwennie.' He paused. 'Look, why don't I stay until the babba's born? Perhaps folk won't talk so much then.'

'I don't give a fig for what the people down in the village say about me. They've talked about me and my grandmother for as long as I can remember.'

'But you cared enough to want a husband.'

'No!' The word was torn from Gwenllyn's lips. 'I cared enough to want a name for the baby and now I've got one I'm satisfied and I never want to see you again. Ever. Do you understand?'

'We'll see.'

Harold got to his feet and made his way to the back of the house. Gwenllyn could hear him banging about in the kitchen and soon the aroma of bacon and eggs filled the house and she realized she was hungry.

She ate the meal with him in the large kitchen and scarcely looked at him. Harold didn't seem to want to talk, for which she was grateful. They sat together, husband and wife but also strangers. She swallowed as she realized it was going to be difficult to get rid of him.

When he finished the meal he wiped his mouth with the back of his hand and she turned away from him. He sensed her mood.

'Sorry I'm not a real gent like Caradoc Jones,' he said and stretched his arms above his head. 'I think I'll turn in. You'd better show me to my room. I take it it's not the bridal suite.'

'You can go to the top floor and sleep in one of the rooms that were meant for servants to use.' She swallowed – she was being needlessly cruel to him. It wasn't his fault she found herself in such a difficult situation. 'Take some sheets from the cupboard,' she said more kindly, 'but it's only for one night, do you understand me?'

He moved to the door before he turned and spoke. 'I understand very well. Just because I travel with the cattle it don't mean I'm as dumb as them.'

When he'd closed the door behind him, Gwenllyn put her hands over her face and felt the tears trickle between her fingers. Caradoc had returned to his wife five long months ago, and even if she'd told him she was with child it wouldn't have made a difference. Once his memory had returned there was no way he would stay with her. He was too much in love with Non, his wife.

At last she went to her room. Her spirits were low; the farce of a marriage had taken a toll on her strength. All she wanted to do was lie down in the dark and lose herself in the oblivion of sleep. That was if she could sleep with a strange man lying in bed on the top floor of the house. Was Harold honest? Would he rise in the night and steal her grandmother's silver? She rubbed more tears from her eyes. What did she really know about this man she had let into her home and into her life?

She closed the bedroom door and after a moment turned the key in the lock. She didn't fool herself into believing she was attractive to Harold, but she was taking no chances. Heavy in body and spirit, she undressed and climbed into bed, but it was a long time before she fell asleep and then it was to dream about Caradoc, about being in his arms.

Harold stared up at the patterns the moonlight cast on the ceiling. He'd been shocked when Gwenllyn Lyons said she would pay him to marry her. He realized he would be tying himself by the bonds of law to a woman he didn't even know.

But then his common sense had returned and he realized he was on to a good thing. Gwenllyn Lyons, or Gwenllyn Rees as she was now, was a rich woman, living in a comfortable house above the Wye Valley. She called the place a cottage but it was like no cottage he had ever known. Where he came from, a cottage was a small, cramped dwelling in a row of many. This place was substantially built and had large airy rooms.

He sank down on the bed. He was tired now and not thinking straight, but in the morning if he regretted his decision he could forget the marriage and go on his way. On the other hand, he could stay here as long as he pleased. He could take a rest from travelling the roads – it was hard, punishing work driving the herds of beasts over the rugged countryside, often in pouring rain.

Caradoc Jones might wonder why his head drover had disappeared so suddenly, but after a day or two he would come to the conclusion that Harold had grown tired of the journey and had stopped off at a bawdy house somewhere along the route.

His thoughts drifted to Gwenllyn, lying in bed in another room. She was a beautiful woman, even with a big belly, and she had a determination about her that appealed to him just as much as it irritated him. She felt superior just because she'd been brought up to live a privileged existence.

He wondered about the lack of servants. It was

hard work keeping a cottage this size in good order. She could certainly afford a couple of maids and a housekeeper – he could tell by the size of the purse she'd given him. She had little time for the village folk though, so perhaps they didn't much care for her either. In any case, it was none of his business.

He turned over on his side, aware of how comfortable he was in this soft bed in an airy cottage; compared with the lodgings Caradoc Jones usually found for his men, this was the lap of luxury. He would stay, he decided, until Gwenllyn gave birth and then, with a squalling infant to contend with, he'd take his leave of her.

CHAPTER TWO

The wind was rising and the herd was becoming restless at the onset of the bad weather. Caradoc Jones, the drover master, reined in his horse and stood in the stirrups to look up ahead. The road wound uphill to where the going was more rugged and where the wind would be stronger, battering the trees and shrubs. It would be foolish to press on: even the sound of the leaves shaking in the trees was enough to make the cattle skittish and inclined to run.

He gestured to the outriders to guide the cattle into a field to the left of him where the land was lying fallow. For a few moments there was chaos as the beasts milled around, not knowing which direction to take, but at last they were manoeuvred between the small stone walls into the field.

Caradoc watched the beasts settle, their heads

lowered to chew on the thin grass. He sighed. If they could have pushed ahead for another hour, he'd have reached London tonight. Instead, he would have to pay the farmer a halfpenny a head for each beast, which was both a nuisance and an unexpected expense.

The gentle clip-clop of hoofs intruded on his thoughts and he glanced up to see the smithy drawing alongside him.

'Best thing you could have done in light of the weather,' Morgan said. There was an ease between the two men now, though it hadn't always been there. Both of them had loved the same woman and for a time that had put a gulf between them, of which Caradoc was well aware, but he was the lucky man who had married Manon Jenkins. As for Morgan, he'd given up any hopes he harboured about having her for his own and had married little Flora, one of the girls walking the drovers' roads. But that had ended in Flora's tragic death and now Morgan was alone again. Still, the poor man was no longer a threat and could almost be treated as a friend.

'Ride with me while I see the farmer.' Caradoc eased his horse back onto the track. 'I'm sorry we couldn't go that last few miles and at least reach Barnet.'

'Non's waiting for you in London, then?' Morgan didn't look at him. 'I wouldn't worry about the delay. She knows all about the changing conditions of the weather, having travelled the road herself. In any case it will rain soon, so it's wise to make camp.' He paused. 'If you don't mind me saying so, you're a lucky man, Mr Jones. A good wife, a fine herd of cattle – what more could any man ask?'

Caradoc nodded without speaking and urged his horse upwards on the snaking track. He had to agree with Morgan: life had been good to him. He owned the entire herd of cattle on this drove; he was wealthy, in good health and had a wonderful wife. The only cloud on his happiness was that since Non had lost Rowan, their baby son, she hadn't conceived again.

He glanced towards Morgan, ignoring his last comment. 'You're pretty good at reading the signs that the weather is changing – better than I am, in fact.'

'Well, like you I've spent my life around cattle and horses. Sometimes I travel miles to do the *cueing* at some town or other. It's the life that I'm used to, and one that I like.'

'And you're damn skilled at shoeing the animals. Anyone can shoe a horse, but when it comes to cattle you're in a league of your own. I've seen how skilfully you make the *cues* into two separate parts to cover the cloven hoofs of the cattle.'

The farmhouse came into sight and the two men fell silent. Around them the wind was howling now, sweeping earth and leaves into rising spirals, and Caradoc's horse whinnied in fear. He patted the mare's strong neck, murmuring soothing words to the animal, when just as Morgan had predicted he felt the spit of rain against his face.

He straightened in the saddle. 'You were right again, Morgan: the weather is turning bad. Still, it'll be better tomorrow and if all goes well we'll reach London by evening.'

His heart beat faster. Soon, very soon, he would be reunited with his wife and she meant everything in the world to him. He glanced pityingly at Morgan, but he had to admit the man was a good loser.

'Come on, Morgan. If the farmer is accommodating, as I'm sure he will be, we'll have good lodgings for the night. As for tomorrow, well, that's another day.'

'Well, Non, my girl, what are you making now? More medicine for the poor folk?'

Non looked up at her friend. Ruby was the landlady of a respectable and thriving lodging house, and she could buy and sell half the neighbours in the vicinity, but to look at her now you wouldn't think so. Her hands were covered in flour and she frowned as she stared into the mortar where Non was grinding down ginger root with the pestle.

Non smiled. She could see her friend was intrigued by the aromatic smell coming from the ginger. 'Do you know you've got a streak of flour right across your nose?' she said.

'Never mind that, I'm wondering what you're doing wasting your time with that stuff. Bleedin' hell, you know that funny old woman is coming back for your cough medicine tonight and I wouldn't like to feel the sharp edge of her tongue if she finds you haven't made it up for her.' Ruby pursed her lips for a moment. 'Though how stuff made from weeds can help anyone, I don't know.'

Non was careful not to laugh at Ruby's tone. 'That "funny old woman", as you call her, is the salt of the earth. In any case, her medicine is all ready and waiting – no need for you to get bothered about it. I'll see old Mrs Glover myself.'

'Bah! How folk can swallow those weeds, I don't know.' Ruby made a face at Non. 'They stink the house out.'

'I don't use weeds and well you know it, Ruby. I use proper herbal remedies taken from Mr Culpeper's book. Anyway, you were glad enough for my elixirs when you had the toothache, as I recall.'

Ruby made a face at her. 'Aye. But I had to get the teeth pulled in the end, didn't I?'

'Well, the medicine took the edge off the pain, so stop grumbling. And if you're really interested, I'm making ginger-root beer for Caradoc. He's very fond of it and he'll be here in London soon.'

'You're an old married woman now; you should be grateful for some peace and quiet. You've only been apart for a few weeks.' Ruby smiled. 'Anyway, you always enjoy being with me, don't you?'

'Of course I'm happy to be visiting you, Ruby.' Non felt her shoulders grow tense. 'But I can't help thinking of the months Caradoc and I were separated when I thought he was dead.' She felt a dart of anger. 'And all the time he was living with that woman, that Gwenllyn Lyons, and sometimes I'm so jealous of her I could spit.' She looked at her friend. 'Is it wrong of me to resent the months she had with Caradoc? He's my husband and I feel she took advantage of him.'

'Be fair, Non,' Ruby said. 'Caradoc had lost his memory, so how was the woman to know he was married? In any case, Caradoc is a man and men have their needs. Just be glad you've got him back.'

'I know, I know, but when I think of him living near the Wye Valley with another woman it tears my heart out. I'm so afraid I'll lose him again, I don't want to let him out of my sight.'

'That's all in the past now, Non, and you know he never loved that girl with the fancy Welsh name. He didn't know where or who he was supposed to be, the poor bugger.'

'You're right.' Non tried to relax but the

thoughts kept racing in her head. 'Perhaps I'm being silly, but what if I'd never found him again?'

'Now, stop that nonsense, girl,' Ruby said sharply. 'You're looking for shadows. Those months are lost ones for you and that husband of yours, but nothing can change that.'

'You're right,' Non conceded. 'Carry on with your cooking and let me get on with my root ginger.' She smiled at her friend. 'What would I do if I didn't have you to nag me?'

'Get on with it as you always did. I loved it when you had a shop by the Thames. You made a real go of it.' Ruby laughed, showing the gaps between her teeth. 'Though the stink of the river was enough to make folk bad, no wonder you had so many customers.'

There was a sudden sound of the front door banging open and footsteps hurrying along the passageway. 'That's our little Welsh Jessie coming in.' Ruby shook her head. 'She's like a bull in a china shop.'

Non saw a flurry of arms and then Jessie was hugging her, raining kisses on her cheek.

'Non! There's lovely it is to see you. I'm sorry I couldn't come over before, but the milk business is booming. There's so many people coming to my little servery these days that it takes all Albie and I can do to keep up with them.'

'That's wonderful, Jessie.' Non held her at arm's length. 'You're looking so well and

24

you're not as thin as you were last time I saw you.'

'Well, I used to be walking the streets with my little cart full of pails, but now the London folk come to me to get their milk.'

'And she's still giving the poor folk in Cutler Street their milk for free,' Ruby said reprovingly. 'Bleedin' charity, that's what madam thinks she is.'

'Come on, Ruby, that's not fair.' Jessie sank down heavily into her chair. 'Anyway, stop talking about the milk now. I got something very important to tell you.'

'Wait just a minute. Let me make the tea and we can all settle down and listen properly to your news.' Ruby smiled wickedly. 'Though I think I can make a good guess what it is.' She turned to Non. 'Albie and Jessie make a fine pair of love-birds. They find it so hard to get off the nest, I'm surprised they sell any milk at all.'

When the kettle had boiled and the cups of steaming tea were on the table in front of them, Jessie leaned forward with her dimpled elbows resting on the scrubbed table-top. 'Guess what, Non? I'm going to have a baby!' Her eyes were alight with joy. 'Can you believe it, little Jessie is going to be a mother.'

Non felt as if her face had suddenly lost all its colour. She had longed for another child since she and Caradoc had got back together. Non looked down at the floor for a moment, trying to compose herself, and then she stretched across the table and took Jessie's hands.

'Congratulations!' she said warmly. 'I wish you all the joy in the world, Jessie, and if ever you need me I'll help in any way I can.'

'I knew you'd be pleased for me.' Jessie's face was wreathed in smiles. 'And Albie's over the moon – can't believe he's going to be a father.'

'Aw Gawd,' Ruby said, 'we're going to have a squalling brat around, but seeing as I'm never going to have a baby myself – after all, I'm not even hitched yet – I'll volunteer to mind the little thing while you get on with your business, Jessie.' Ruby smiled, well pleased. 'I'll be a sort of auntie to the little one: that's a thought to ponder over.'

Non rubbed at her eyes, trying to keep her tears at bay, and she felt Jessie glance at her with a look of compassion. Though she didn't speak, it was clear she understood what Non was feeling.

So did Ruby, who got up and put fresh water in the pot. 'Come on, I think we could all do with another drop of tea.' Non held her breath as, tact-fully, Ruby steered the conversation onto matters of business. 'I've got a full quota of lodgers again this year.' Ruby poured the fresh tea and then returned to her seat. 'I'm making a good living for myself, though I could do with a husband to share it all.' She sighed. 'The trouble is I never get out of the bleedin' house. What with all the washing and changing of beds and cooking meals, I'm too worn out to find a follower.'

'One will come looking for you one day,' Jessie said confidently. 'You're not much older than me and Non: you've got plenty of time to meet the man of your dreams. Talking of men, when will your husband be back in town, Non?'

'Any day now. He'll get to London as soon as he can and I can't wait to see him again.'

'Well, you can have the use of my parlour for as long as you like,' Ruby said warmly, 'though you and Caradoc will be too wrapped up in each other to care about your surroundings.'

'It's a very comfortable room,' Non said, 'and I realize we're giving you extra work, but as soon as Caradoc arrives we'll find some lodgings until the stock is sold.'

'No hurry,' Ruby said. 'Anyway, once this tea is finished I got to get on with the meal.' She pointed her finger at Non. 'And you, dear girl, must get on with your ginger-root beer.'

'You're a slave driver, Ruby,' Jessie leaned back in her chair, rubbing her hands gently over her stomach as though to caress the child growing inside her, 'but we all love you anyway.'

Non sat back in her chair observing the scene, knowing she was very lucky to have such good and faithful friends. She needed to count her blessings – she had a good husband and a rewarding business. It was time to forget the past and all the misery it had brought her. She put down her cup and touched Jessie's hand.

'You look so happy and I'm very glad for you and for Albie. Now, come on then, Jessie, tell us everything about this baby: when is it due and what do you want, a boy or a girl?'

Jessie's smile was radiant and Non knew she must share in Jessie's happiness and put her own grief out of her mind at least for the time being.

Barnet fair was in full swing when Caradoc arrived. He had his second in command, Josh, with him, helping to lead the ponies that were for sale.

'Take the ponies into the field: they're ready for a rest. Oh, and get Morgan to check their shoes. Some of the animals might have to be re-shod.'

He slid down from his horse, hearing the music of a fiddler against the din of many voices, and the sound reminded him suddenly of Gwenllyn Lyons. Sometimes when they had sat together in the garden on hot summer evenings, the faint sound of a fiddle had come to them from the valley below. A surge of guilt shot through him. He'd left her abruptly, so glad to be reunited with his true love, his wife Non, that he'd barely said goodbye to her.

Perhaps he should go to see her, find out if she was well. He wondered whether, in the five months since he had left, she had found herself another man to sit with her, to keep her company. Perhaps that would salve his conscience.

'Hey, boss, we got a buyer.' Josh's voice broke into his thoughts. 'Some farmer wants the ponies – the whole lot of them.'

Josh was a young man but he seemed eager to learn, and when Harold had left the drove Josh had been happy to take on the mantle of head drover. The other men didn't seem to have much time for him, but so long as Josh did his job his social life was not Caradoc's concern.

Caradoc turned his mind to business as he stepped smartly across the lush grass towards the field where Josh had put the horses. The sooner his horses were sold, the sooner he could push on to Smithfield – and there he would find a good lodging house and there he would make love to his wife again.

Non waited in the kitchen of Ruby's house, her fingers plucking at the sleeves of her gown. Caradoc would be here any minute. He would come in the door to be welcomed and she would go to him, wind her arms round his neck and hold him close.

She sighed heavily; she wished she had good news for him, news that a baby was on the way. They both wanted a child very badly, although Non knew no one could take the place of their first-born son. Rowan had been a handsome baby and a good-tempered child, but now he was dead and gone and she must try to stop grieving over him.

She heard the front door swing open and she stood up, her heart beating swiftly, although she was frozen to the spot. As soon as Caradoc came into the room, filling it with his presence, she came to life and rushed into his arms.

He cradled her against him before tipping up her face to kiss her. 'My lovely Non, how I've missed you.' He kissed her again and she clung to him.

'I've been waiting too, Caradoc. I thought you'd never come.'

Ruby bustled into the kitchen. 'Hey, you two love-birds, save the kissing and hugging for later. Now, how about a bit of game pie and a good strong cup of tea?'

'Ruby,' Caradoc hugged her. 'Now, Ruby, don't get jealous. I have some kisses for you and some ribbons from Barnet fair.'

'What am I going to do with ribbons? I've got no lover to dress up my hair for,' Ruby said. 'But it was a kind thought anyway,' she added hastily.

Caradoc delved into his pocket. 'I'm just teasing you. What I've really got for you is a pretty amethyst brooch.' He held out his hand and the trinket sparkled in the sunlight from the window.

'Ooh! That's bleedin' lovely, that is.' Ruby turned the brooch around and gazed at it in wonder. 'I've never had such a pretty present before in my life.' She beamed at Caradoc. 'Now, sit down and have a hearty meal – I'll wager you ain't had a good feed since you been on the trail.'

Non watched her husband with avid eyes. She couldn't bear it when he was away from her – and now, looking at him, she admired him anew: the strength in his shoulders, the fine line of his jaw. Her gaze lingered lovingly on his lips: how she longed to kiss them. But that could wait; her husband needed some good food inside him. There was plenty of time for loving and kissing when the streets grew dark and night covered London like a warm cloak.

'You are so beautiful, Non.' Caradoc leaned on his elbow and looked down at his wife. Her eyes were misty with desire, her hair spread around her naked shoulders, gleaming in the candlelight.

She wound her warm arms around his neck. 'I love you, Caradoc, I love you so much.'

He felt himself harden with desire. She was his wife, his beautiful wife, and he wanted her more every time they lay together.

'Perhaps this time,' she whispered, 'here in Ruby's parlour, we'll conceive a child.' She touched his face. 'And then, my love, our life will be complete.'

Suddenly, his desire faded; he hated to be reminded that he had no son. He kissed Non's warm lips and touched her sweet breasts but it was no use, he couldn't make love to her however much he wanted to. He rolled away from her.

'I'm sorry, my love, I'm just tired. I'll be all right when I've had a good sleep.'

She kissed him gently. 'Just hold me, then. Tonight we'll sleep in each other's arms, and in the morning everything will be all right.'

He hoped so, Caradoc truly hoped so, but for the last few nights he'd been dreaming about the cottage nestling in the hills above the river Wye, dreaming about Gwenllyn Lyons.

He turned over in bed, afraid to look into his wife's lovely face in case she read his thoughts in his eyes. It was a long time before he fell asleep.

CHAPTER THREE

Gwenllyn felt tired; her legs ached and her belly was tight. She was like the cows on the trail, heavy with calf. Even her mind wasn't working properly; otherwise she would have told Harold days ago to go away and leave her in peace. The truth was, even though she scarcely admitted it to herself, she was afraid, afraid of being alone.

She eased herself more comfortably into the garden seat, plumping up the cushions and leaning against them to ease the pain in her back. When was the baby due? She had no clear idea; could she have been two or three months gone when her darling Caradoc left her? She stifled a sigh: she felt bereft without him, the only man she could ever love. There had been no word from him since he left and she knew he was gone for ever.

Tears filled her eyes and ran unchecked down

her cheeks, splashing onto her hands as she clasped them together in her lap. How her heart ached every time she thought of him in his wife's arms.

'*Duw*, what's up with you, girl? Not ready to drop the babba, are you?' Harold appeared at her side, startling her, and Gwenllyn looked up into his face.

'Of course not! The baby isn't due for some months yet.' She spoke with confidence, hiding her uncertainty. 'I'd better get in and cook some food, I suppose. You're hungry again, but then aren't you always?' She addressed him as if he was a stupid child and he frowned.

'What's wrong?' He sat beside her and she noticed the tang of his skin, and of the clothing, which still smelled of cattle even though she'd seen him wash them in the stream behind the house.

'I'm tired.' She sighed heavily. 'And I'm sick of being ill and fat and . . . oh, how can I expect you to understand?'

'My mother dropped seven of us,' he said grimly. 'Not all lived, mind you. I was twelve when she gave birth to my youngest brother and I was the only one there to help her.'

He spoke without bitterness and Gwenllyn looked at him, really looked at him, for the first time since they'd met and caught a glimpse of sadness in his dark eyes.

'Where was your father?'

He smiled without humour. 'I don't even know who my father was. Me and Mam were on our own. I sent the younger children outside, told them to bring me water, as much of it as they could carry.' He shrugged. 'I did my best but the boy died anyway. Looking back at it now, I suppose my mam was a whore but I loved her all the same.'

It felt strange, talking properly to this stranger who was her husband. No wonder he was rough and ill-mannered: he'd had no one to teach him the rights and wrongs of everyday life.

'Can you read?'

The question came out baldly and he looked away, his colour high. 'No.'

'Would you like me to teach you?' He had made it clear he intended to stay with her until the baby was born and teaching him to read would while away the long days and nights when they were together and yet so far apart.

His face lit up. 'Do you think you could? Am I too old to learn letters?'

His questions came out in a rush, and for a moment Gwenllyn saw some sensitivity in Harold's face. He wore a dark beard and a thick moustache and looked, she imagined, like a highwayman. Did she really think she could teach him to read, this man who spoke in brief sentences, who gave vent to oaths when he'd been drinking? Well, she would try her best; that was all she could do.

'You're never too old to learn letters.' She spoke with far more confidence than she felt. 'I'll get out some of my books, the ones Grandma gave me when I was little; they will be easier for you to start with.'

'All right.' He held out his hand to shake hers, an incongruous gesture since they were married folk, albeit tied together by a few words and a cheap ring. His hand was rough, the palm pitted and dry, but his grasp was firm and somehow reassuring.

'We'll start this afternoon,' she said. Anything to pass the long hours when she simply sat and wondered where her life was going, when she longed for Caradoc with a pain that was fierce and unshakeable.

Harold saw to the food. He had walked down to the village and returned with fresh cheese and butter and a crusty loaf and Gwenllyn realized she was hungry. She ate with more enthusiasm than usual and Harold appeared pleased, although he never said a word. He chewed steadily, with teeth that were surprisingly white. She'd seen him take soot from the chimney and rub it against his teeth. He was a clean man at least and that was something to be grateful for.

That evening, she brought out some books for him. Slowly she pointed out the letters to Harold.

She gave him paper and made him copy the letters onto it. At first he was shaky, but then, as first one hour dragged by and then another, he began to write the alphabet with a little more accuracy.

'You're doing very well,' she encouraged, and when he shrugged, 'you are,' she persisted. 'See how your writing is firm and bold?'

'Maybe, but I don't know what any of it means.' He slammed the book shut and sat back in his chair, puffing out his cheeks. 'I'll never know what those funny squiggles stand for, will I?'

'Of course you will. You'll get used to it, Harold.'

It was the first time she'd addressed him by name and he was silent for a long moment. Then he looked up at her, twisting the pencil between his thick fingers. 'Call me Harry and I won't seem such a stranger then.'

She moved away from him: she didn't want him taking liberties and thinking she was warming to him. 'Just because I'm willing to teach you letters doesn't mean I've changed my mind,' she said bluntly. 'Once the baby arrives you can go on your way, go back to Five Saints or Swansea or wherever it is you've come from.' She sat down heavily in her chair. 'Look, I don't mean to be hard but this marriage is a bargain, bought and paid for. So long as you remember that, every-thing will be just fine.'

His eyes slid away from hers but not before she saw a gleam of pain – or was it anger?

'I'm not going to forget my place, mind,' he said flatly. 'I'm a drover and you're a lady and I'll be glad to leave here, if the truth be known.' He stood up abruptly. 'I'll go now if that's what you want.'

'Aye, I suppose it is.' She was angry now and glared up at him as though he had insulted her. 'You go on your way, join the cattle drove that's due through here any day now. I don't care where you go or what you do. You've served my purpose and been well paid for it.'

She climbed the stairs slowly, holding her belly with both hands. Let him go; she would manage without him. She'd fetch one of the wise women from the village; if she paid enough any one of them would attend her in her confinement.

As she lay on the bed, she could hear Harold throwing his belongings into his bag and, suddenly, she was terrified – what if the baby came tonight when she was alone?

'I'm off, then,' he called up the stairs. 'Goodbye, Mrs Rees, and good luck to you.'

She heard the sound of the door closing and took a deep breath. What had she done? She had formed a strange sort of friendship with Harold over the past weeks. He was good to her, kind enough too, but she found his rough ways irritating and she knew with a sinking of her heart that it was best he leave before he became too used to the comforts of her home. And yet

38

suddenly the house seemed empty, silent, and her lip trembled as she turned her face to the wall.

'I'm sorry to see you go so soon,' Ruby said.

Non smiled and gave her a hug. 'You've put up with us for long enough. We never did go into lodgings, did we?' She heard the rumble of the mail coach on the busy street, and as it approached she kissed Ruby's cheek. 'You get off home: there'll be a lot of waiting around till the baggage is packed on the coach and I know you've got a lot to do.'

'All right then, but it's been bleedin' lovely having you stay at my place.'

Non watched Ruby go and for a moment she felt sad and then she turned to her husband and leaned against his shoulder. It felt so good to be with Caradoc and heading for home.

'I've bought us a new house,' he said as they settled onto the coach at last. 'I think you'll like it. It's in Swansea.'

'A new house! But why? You've always loved living in Five Saints.'

'I thought we'd be better placed for your business if we lived in Swansea. It's a fine house, in the uplands. The air is clear of the smoke from the copper works and the sun shines like diamonds on the waves.'

Non sighed happily. Once they were home everything would be fine, she had to believe that.

* * *

The house in Swansea was beautiful, sun-filled and spacious, poised on a hill looking down into the valley. They went to bed early, and even as they lay together in the afterglow of their love-making she felt restless, somehow separated from the man she loved. She had to face it, she was still thinking about the time Caradoc had spent with that other woman. On his first night in London, when he couldn't make love to her, Non knew in her heart that he was thinking about Gwenllyn.

At her side Caradoc stirred and she realized he was wakeful too. 'I expect your friends are missing you already,' Caradoc said. 'They all seem to be doing well for themselves. Ruby's lodging house is full of guests and, as for Jessie, she's so confident, I hardly recognize her as the little thing who walked the drovers' roads with the herds.'

Non felt herself grow tense, remembering how she had once walked the drovers' roads too. She was chillingly aware of the differences between herself and her husband. Caradoc was from a rich family and he had received a superb education, while she, although educated, was the only daughter of a poor cleric.

'I'm proud of my friends,' she said defensively. 'They might have come from working stock but they are good people, ambitious people, who have made every attempt to better their position in life.'

'Isn't that what I was saying?' Caradoc sounded puzzled.

'I thought your remarks were patronizing.' Non couldn't let the matter rest. 'I suppose they pale into insignificance compared with your fine friends, like Gwenllyn Lyons!' The words were spoken before she could stop herself.

He gave her a long look but said nothing. He got out of bed and stood looking through the window even though outside there was only deep darkness.

'Will you ever forget Gwenllyn?' she asked, although she knew the question would disturb him.

He sighed and shook his head. 'I can't lie to you, Non. I don't suppose I will ever forget, but that part of my life is something separate from what we have. We have each other for the rest of our lives, so don't begrudge Gwenllyn the few lost months I spent with her.'

It was the worst thing he could have said. She forced down the sick feeling that possessed her and played with the piping at the edge of the quilt, her fingers pulling at the threads as though in some way they could untangle the mixture of sensations running through her. She wanted to cry, to scream at Caradoc that he should have known he had a wife, known somehow that he was in love. But, no, he'd settled down with Gwenllyn Lyons, chopped wood for her fires, laid with her every night in her bed. It was too hard to accept that he'd been content without her, without his wife.

'I love you,' he said gently.

'But for a time you loved her?'

He looked away. 'I don't know what to say, Non. Yes, I suppose in a way I did love her. I couldn't remember any other life except the one I was living with her.'

Non swallowed the lump in her throat, keeping silent – what could she say? Yet an icy hand seemed to grip her heart. He still had feelings for Gwenllyn. Perhaps he still loved her.

Non snuffed out the candles and lay down, but she spent a restless night, tossing and turning, and all the time aware of Caradoc at her side. He slept effortlessly, like a baby, and in a way she resented his ability to put his cares aside so easily. She was glad when daylight came and the sun began to shine into the spacious bedroom.

At first she found it strange getting used to the new house in Swansea. She'd only stayed in London for a few weeks but the comings and goings of Ruby's lodging house had filled her days. Now the overwhelming quietness of this new place made her life seem strange and empty. The feel and smell of the house was unfamiliar. The lovely views from the windows, magnificent though they were, somehow made her feel lonely for the crowded streets of London.

Caradoc came into the drawing room where she was sitting and put his arms around her, resting his chin against her hair. 'I know it seems empty now,' he said, 'but one day soon it will be filled with the shouts and laughter of our children.'

He was right, she would conceive soon, once she was settled back into a routine. She suddenly felt more secure and happy. She was Mrs Caradoc Jones and it was Gwenllyn who was the single woman living alone.

'How many children shall we have?' She cupped his face in her hands. 'Four? Five?'

'As many as you like, my love,' said Caradoc as he leaned in to kiss her.

But the very next morning her flow began and she knew that, for now at least, there would be no child.

CHAPTER FOUR

'Come on, you're not trying hard enough.' Gwenllyn pulled the book away from Harry and slammed it shut. The candles flickered in the sudden draught. 'I don't know why you bothered to come back to me if you didn't want to learn your letters.' She didn't add that she'd been happy and relieved when he'd come to her door, cap in hand, and told her he was sorry for leaving her alone that night.

'I do want to learn but it's so hard.' Harry slumped back in his chair. 'I'm used to figuring things in my head – adding the price of five bulls at seven pounds a head or the cost of a few good heifers: things like that just come to me – but letters . . . well, I just can't work them out.'

Gwenllyn sighed. 'All right, let's go over the alphabet together once again. I'm sorry I was impatient. It's just that my back is aching so much it's driving me mad.'

Harry looked alarmed. 'It's the babba, isn't it? You're going to pop it like a pea from a pod!'

Gwenllyn looked up, startled: what if Harry was right? She might be seven or eight months gone, perhaps a little more, so maybe the baby was ready to come into the world. She felt a sense of panic; how would she manage to look after it by herself? Not only had she no experience of children, she didn't even particularly like the ones she met when she went to the village. They seemed irksome creatures, noisy and ill bred.

'I don't want a baby,' she said, holding her hand to her breast where her heart was thumping fast with fear. 'I don't think I'll be able to cope with a child. I don't want to be a mother.'

Harry shook his head but there was a trace of a smile on his lips. 'Should have thought o' that before bedding with a man,' he said easily. 'Natural, it is, to fall for a babba if you lays down with a virile fellow.'

'But I didn't realize . . . I never thought of having children. Especially not on my own,' she said.

Harold sighed. 'You won't be on your own. I'll stay with you – I've told you that already.'

'But you're not the father, so why should you be bothered? We agreed I would pay you to give me your name and you've had the money, so why do you want to hang around here?'

Harry scratched his head. 'I don't rightly know.' He got to his feet. 'I feel responsible for you now I've got to know you a bit. At first I just wanted to hit the road, go back to droving, travel about, because it's what I'm used to. But I'll stay as I promised, then once the babba is safely born and settled I'll be on my way.'

Somehow his words did little to reassure Gwenllyn. She wasn't entirely sure she wanted Harry around once the baby arrived. He was a common cattle drover. He had no good manners; he drank ale every night and then came home and put his dirty feet all over her fine rugs.

She put her hands under her belly and felt a kick against her fingers. The baby kicked again, harder, and suddenly she felt hugely protective of the child. This baby was hers, hers and Caradoc's. She would have a little part of him for ever – wasn't that enough to make her happy about the impending birth?

'What is it?' Harry frowned anxiously. 'Any pains?'

'I'm not having pains, but the baby is pushing and kicking as though it's trying to get out.'

'You got a good one in there – a boy, I'd say.' Harry sounded relieved. 'Even if you drop it tonight it should be a fine healthy babba.'

'Harry,' Gwenllyn spoke his name hesitantly, 'will you really stay with me until the baby is born?' All her reservations about him had paled into insignificance at the thought of giving birth alone.

'I've said so, haven't I?' His voice was gruff and he got to his feet abruptly. 'I'm going down to the village. I'll just have a few drinks with the men and I'll be back before you know it.'

He seemed to sense her need for company. He held his hand out as though to touch her shoulder but then he moved away from her towards the door. When he reached for the door handle, she spoke to him softly. 'Harry, you will come back, won't you?'

'Aye, I'll come back.' Through the window Gwenllyn watched him walk away, down the hill towards the little village inn. It was where the cattle drovers sometimes stayed when the river Wye was too full and swift to cross. Would Caradoc stop there one day, and, if he did, would he come to see her?

Caradoc cracked his whip, forcing the cattle to negotiate the narrow road out of Swansea. It had been difficult leaving Non, especially now when she was so disappointed she wasn't yet expecting a baby. What would happen if he never had another child, never fathered a son to take over the business? He thought achingly of Rowan, his first-born, the son he'd seen so little of before he'd died. He shouldn't have been away from home so much, but then how was he to know he would be parted from his son and his wife by a freak accident? His life had almost ended as he was struck by the hoofs of a horse frightened by the swell of the river Wye. The joy of eventually getting his memory back was tainted by guilt and pain.

He thought then of Gwenllyn, of her sweet submission to him. She had been a virgin when he'd taken her and regret seared him like a burning brand. What had he given her in return? He had made a settlement on her but money didn't go any way to pay Gwenllyn back for all her love and devotion.

Perhaps when he came to the crossing of the river Wye he would call up to the cottage, see if Gwenllyn was well. But no, that was a foolish idea: to see her would be turning the knife into the wound of their parting.

And yet he missed her. He pulled himself up short. It was the first time he'd admitted, even to himself, that he missed Gwenllyn's youthful reliance on him. She had needed him in a way that Non never had. Non was a successful businesswoman; she'd grown independent and strong. She was used to taking the coach to London to look after the shops she'd set up in Whitechapel and Cripplegate. Her fame as a herbalist had spread and her remedies were much sought after. He smiled. Even now she was probably sitting at home studying her books or drying herbs: getting on with things. Very probably that's what Gwenllyn would be doing too – getting on with her life. And yet, something deep inside told him Gwenllyn wasn't complete without him.

But he must forget about Gwenllyn. He could never live with her, that was impossible, but maybe he should visit her from time to time, make sure she was all right, that she had wood chopped for the fire, that her cottage was maintained and secure. Things her husband should be doing. But then Gwenllyn didn't have a husband. Perhaps she never would. He felt a tug at his heart and he tried to reason with himself: going back to visit her would only make matters worse – if she entreated him to stay a while or to come to her bed, would he be tempted?

He held up his hand for the drove to rest a while. The cattle ambled to a stop and Caradoc slid to the ground, patting his horse's neck and making clucking sounds so that the animal was calmed. The mare's head lowered to eat the fresh spring grass. He could hear a stream near by and knew his instincts had served him well, as this was a good place to feed and water the animals before they continued on towards Brecon.

He found the source of the stream and the water ran crystal clear over the well-washed rocks. He cupped his hands and scooped up the glistering water which tasted sweet to his dry mouth.

He looked out over the fields below him. He

was unaware of the sounds of the men around him, of the cattle, of the clamour of the drove. His mind was far away, in a cottage above the river, where Gwenllyn would be sitting alone grieving for him. He sighed heavily. He must stop acting like a child wanting something he couldn't have. He had work to do and it was about time he put his mind to it instead of day-dreaming like a lovesick boy.

Non was beginning to settle well in the new house in Swansea. It was a stately, dignified building and one day she might be happy there. She was sorry that Caradoc was riding with the herd instead of sending one of the men to Smithfield in his place.

She sighed and looked round the spotless kitchen, at Cook, industriously preparing a meal, and at the kitchen maids, quiet and efficient. It was clear that Caradoc had chosen his staff well.

She stood at the end of the huge kitchen table grinding dry camomile roots with her pestle; one of the maids had a fever – the girl was tossing and turning in her bed, moaning, delirious – and she needed cooling down. Non had insisted the girl be taken to her bedroom and that the fire in the room should be damped down, much to Cook's disgust.

Mrs Irons glanced at her now. 'You not giving Beryl that funny-smelling stuff, are you, Mrs Jones?'

Non strained the juice from the roots and petals

of the flower and decanted it into a glass. 'Yes, I am.'

Cook clucked her disapproval. 'With all respect, Mrs Jones, the saying is "Feed a cold and starve a fever"; that's the rule I've always lived by.'

'Well, things are changing, Mrs Irons. We learn new things about medicine every day.'

Cook sniffed. 'That's as maybe, but you're not a doctor, are you?'

Non didn't bother to tell her that in London the apothecaries listened to her lectures on herbal remedies and often took heed of them. Once, Non's medication and knowledge had helped stop the spread of cholera, and since then her work had been recognized as having merit.

'No, I'm not a doctor, but I do know what I'm doing. Believe me, Mrs Irons, I wouldn't be giving this medicine to Beryl if I wasn't sure that it would alleviate her fever.'

As Non left the kitchen, she heard Cook sniff again and smiled. Some folk needed a great deal of persuading to accept that herbs could remedy many ills.

Beryl was still flushed, her eyes glassy and unseeing, her face twitching as if she was going through the torments of hell – and perhaps she was: a sick body often made for a sick mind. But Beryl took the liquid readily, her mouth opening and closing each time Non held the spoon to her lips.

Non spent half an hour with the maid, smoothing her hair away from her hot face, drawing the heavy quilt away from the young girl's sweating body. But at last Beryl seemed to sleep a little more easily and Non washed her hands and went back downstairs. She must fill her days with work: there were a lot of people who needed her medicine and the sooner she fell back into a well-ordered life, even a life that sometimes meant being without her husband, the better she would be.

Harry sat in the garden, his book and pencil in his hand. His reading was coming along very well after intensive teaching from Gwenllyn. He could grasp the meaning of the letters she showed him. He could write 'dog' and 'cow', two animals he was familiar with, and she had told him he could soon learn to spell more difficult words such as 'horse' and 'sheep'.

Even he could see that Gwenllyn was very clever. She'd drawn rough pictures of the animals and underneath she had written their names in large letters. He'd come, at last, to see that the letters made sense when joined up correctly. He still had a fair way to go before he could read proper books but he'd get there, he was certain.

He thought Gwenllyn was very kind in the way she'd encouraged him in his knowledge of adding and subtracting figures in his head. She soon learned he was telling the truth when he said he was good at what she called 'mental arithmetic'.

'Still working hard?' Gwenllyn came up so quietly that he hadn't heard her.

Harry looked up and nodded. 'I can't wait to read proper letters.' He closed his book and stuck the pencil behind his ear.

'Well, the longer you keep at it, the better you'll become.'

Gwenllyn was looking beautiful. Her hair was bound up in ribbons held away from her face and she was wearing a full gown of white muslin sprigged with flowers that almost concealed the fact that she was with child.

'I'd better get down to the inn,' Harry said briskly. 'I can't miss out on my mug of beer with the village men.' He was getting soft in the head, he told himself. Gwenllyn had been good to him but that was simply because she needed him, at least for the time being.

Still, the knowledge that he was needed by someone was new to him. He'd been useful on the cattle drove, it was true – his experience had saved the herd from stampede more than once, he could gauge the weather, tell the mood of the wind and rain before it came – but he'd never been needed by a beautiful young woman before.

Harry pushed aside the thought angrily and told himself he'd better watch out: he was being seduced by Gwenllyn's cottage, her wealth and her beauty. He'd been willing to give his name in exchange for money but he'd not reckoned on the feelings that Gwenllyn aroused in him. The sooner he turned his thoughts to other things the better.

He knew he'd been an asset to the Jones business and some day he might team up with the Jones drove again, even if he had left halfway through the journey to London. It was a good job, and well paid. Since the moment he had clapped eyes on Caradoc Jones, he had known the man was straight and honest.

But everywhere Jones went he caused problems. He'd lost some damn fine animals in the disastrous crossing over the Wye, and then when he'd met Gwenllyn he'd brought her nothing but a heap of trouble. The man was selfish, with an arrogance that came from wealth.

Gwenllyn sat down on one of the garden seats and spread her skirts neatly around her ankles. Her feet were small like a child's and somehow the thought brought a thickness to his throat.

'I think the baby will be coming soon,' Gwenllyn said. 'Will you come with me down to the midwife in the village, perhaps in the morning?'

Harry was silent for a long time and then, at last, he nodded. 'Aye. I suppose that's the husbandly way of doin' things.'

'You're only my husband in name,' Gwenllyn

said sharply, 'and that's the way it's always going to be.'

'All right, all right, don't get yourself excited.' He tried to laugh but his words came out like a complaint. Well, serve her right: she'd wounded him with her harsh tone.

'I'm sorry,' she said softly and Harry turned to look at her. Her big eyes were filled with tears, her lips, rosy moist lips, were parted, and in that moment he felt an aching need to make love to her.

He looked away. 'Apology accepted,' he said stiffly. 'I'll be off now. See you later.'

As he walked away from the cottage he felt as if he was leaving behind in that quiet garden all that he cared about.

CHAPTER FIVE

'Well, Albie my lovely, we've had a long, hard day but it's been worth it.' Jessie looked around at the newly furnished room of their rented house in Golden Lane and smiled. At first, she and Albie had managed with egg boxes – they had sat on egg boxes and eaten off egg boxes; the only real piece of furniture they had was a second-hand bed. Now the sitting room was looking splendid with newly made curtains hanging crisp and fresh all the way down to the floor, where the colours of the carpet gleamed brightly in the slant of late sun.

She leaned her head against her husband's shoulder. 'Tomorrow we'll get the spare bedroom ready for Non's visit.' She smiled up at Albie. 'I can't wait to see her again, though I'm quite surprised she's coming back so soon. I expect her husband is going on a drove again. The poor woman must be lonely. I hardly know why she even bothers with us though, she's so rich and successful now.'

'She's always welcome at my fireside. She's been a good friend to us both, Jess.' Albie slid his arm round his wife's shoulder and hugged her. 'If it weren't for Non I might be hanging at the end of a noose by now.'

'Don't talk of it!' Jessie said. 'I don't even like to think of you in that dreadful Newgate prison.'

'Ah well, that's all behind us now and we've got Non to thank for bleedin' trustin' in me.'

'Albie!' Jessie's tone was accusing. 'I thought I'd cured you of that awful swearing.'

'Ah well, you're a ladylike Welsh girl and I'm just a poor old cockney. I can't help the way I talk.'

'Oh, mind now! Can't help it, indeed! Remember, Albie, we're successful milk vendors now and, what's more, we got a baby on the way. I don't want my child to grow up listening to rude words, so no more swearing, right?'

He pinched her cheek. 'All right, I'll try not to forget. Come on, then,' he changed the subject with a rueful wink at Jessie, 'let's eat. I'm starving.'

'Well, what are we going to have? There's not much in the larder.' Jessie smiled up at him. 'Go and get us a pie. I could just murder a fresh hot pie. It'll be just like the old days.' She winked an eye. 'That's if a successful businessman isn't too big to go to the pie shop these days.'

Albie's face lit up. 'I ain't above sharing a pie with my dear little wife. I'll go down this minute. You get the table laid and I'll be back before you know it.'

He went to the door and then turned and came back. 'I nearly forgot to give my Jess a goodbye kiss.'

She pushed him away, laughing. 'Go on with you! We're an old married couple now.'

'Old married couple, eh?' Albie's eyebrows rose in mock indignation. 'Rubbish! We're still on our honeymoon.'

Jessie wound her arms round his waist. He bent and kissed her, not a chaste kiss but one that stirred Jessie to her roots. He kissed her eyelids and her mouth and pulled her against him so that she could feel his arousal.

Her voice was trembling as she spoke. 'I think we can leave the pie till later, Albie my lovely.'

He led her upstairs to a room half furnished but sporting a large bed. He eased her down carefully and his hand went to his belt. His eyes shone as he looked at her. 'Know something, Jess? I love you more today than the day I married you. You're my life, Jess. Don't ever leave me, will you?'

Her throat was thick with tears as she answered him. 'Albie, you are the only man I'll ever want and I promise I'll never leave you.'

She drew his head down and kissed him. He

made love to her then, gently, adoringly, and she responded to his touch as she always did with all her passion and all her love.

As Non approached the servery in Golden Lane, her heart lifted. She could see the queue for milk extending along the cobbled roadway; some people had jobs, but one or two innkeepers were there with large urns making ready for the day ahead. It was still early and Non felt as though she hadn't slept a wink throughout the night. The coach journey had been uneventful but she hated the nights spent in coaching inns. All the beds seemed to be made of stones, lumpy and uncomfortable. Her back was aching and her heart was heavy as she thought of Caradoc, out on the road again. He had been so anxious to leave her, but why? Was he planning to see Gwenllyn?

Non quickened her step. It would be good to sit down in Jessie's house and have a welcome cup of tea and a proper rest. Once she'd had a good night's sleep she would look at her recipes again to see if she could improve on them. She'd already found some new remedies for herself. She'd discovered that beetroot was good for the complexion: crushed and mixed with goose grease, it could help clear the skin of blemishes. She had also experimented with beetroot as a means of dyeing faded clothes to a nice shade that was a mixture of pink and red.

At least she had her business to keep her sane. The days spent in Swansea without Caradoc were long and lonely and she still hadn't got over her disappointment at finding she hadn't caught for a child.

Non forced her mind back to her herbs. Geraniums were good for cleaning the grime from face and hands – especially useful in London, where the town seemed to sit in an atmosphere of soot and fog. And the common onion was not only good for a sore throat but made a nice yellow colour when boiled with worn rags. It was all hard work though, when, especially as now, she visited her shops.

She became aware she was standing staring at the queue of people waiting for milk which had grown while she was day-dreaming, aware too that some of the customers were watching her with suspicious eyes. She was difficult to place, a well-dressed woman and yet with a bag over her arm like a common peddlar.

Quickly, Non made her way round to the back of the building and saw about half a dozen cows grazing on terribly thin grass. She had no doubt that the animals were taken daily to a lush field where they could eat their fill of verdant grass, because they looked well fed and healthy.

There was a shriek of welcome from Jessie as Non tapped on the back door. 'Non! My lovely, come on in and make yourself comfortable.'

Non went into the house and dropped her bag thankfully on the floor.

'It's lovely to see you back in London so soon,' Jessie said. 'You're looking so well and rosy-cheeked – is there some good news to tell us?'

Non tried to smile. 'No, not yet. Caradoc and I are still getting to know each other again. We were parted for the whole of last summer, remember?' Non couldn't bring herself to tell Jessie the truth: that these days she seemed to be failing at her duty as a wife.

'Well, there's plenty of time.'

Jessie drew Non towards the kitchen, calling to Albie as she went. 'Take Non's bags upstairs, my lovely boy. The girl is parched and in need of a drink.'

There was the sound of Albie's footsteps running rapidly up the stairs and then, in a moment, he was back. The boy he'd been had vanished and he was now a man – very tall but as thin as ever. He kissed her cheek and held her away from him.

'You're looking more bleedin' beautiful than ever,' he said, and then grimaced in Jessie's direction. 'Sorry, love. Didn't mean to swear.'

'You Londoners always swear – Ruby is exactly the same. Does she know you're visiting again, Non?' Jessie pushed the kettle onto the fire.

Non smiled. 'Of course she does. I'll go and see her later. Right now I'm dying for a cup of tea. May I sit down?'

'Sit you, Mrs Jones, though I could take you into my posh parlour if you like.'

'I like it here well enough,' Non said firmly. 'I see you're still thrifty and saving your money, then?'

Jessie looked at her sharply. 'We're always saving, mind, but what made you ask?'

'I can't see any maid around here, not even a scullery maid to do the washing and clean the floors.'

'Oh, I got a washerwoman.' Jessie spoke proudly. 'Comes in twice a week, she does. As for the servery, me and Albie do all that ourselves. The urns got to be clean or the milk will turn sour, you know that.' She looked at her swollen stomach and patted it gently. 'Once the little one comes along we'll have to take on more help.'

Jessie made the tea and then sat down with Non. She glanced meaningfully at Albie and he obediently left the room.

'Right, then, what's been happening to you, Non? Why are you back in London so soon? Is there trouble at home?'

'No, no, nothing like that,' Non said quickly, 'but my businesses are flourishing. I'm opening a new shop in Cutler Street that should do well. Lots of people there sell old clothes, as you know, but I've rented an upstairs room where folk this side of London can come for medication.'

'I know all that. What I want to know is how are you and Mr Jones getting on?'

'It's strange, Jessie,' Non said after reflecting for several moments. 'I love Caradoc dearly and I'm sure he loves me – now he remembers who I am.' Her tone was rueful.

'*But?*' Jessie leaned forward, her elbows resting on the table.

'But sometimes he seems distant from me; he withdraws into himself.' Non sighed. 'I sometimes think he misses Gwenllyn Lyons more than he's prepared to admit.'

She picked up her cup in both hands and held it to her mouth. She was giving Jessie a chance to air her views, which Jessie did without hesitation.

'Try not to think of the past, lovely girl. Your husband is with you. If it was her he wanted, he'd have stayed with her, wouldn't he, even though it was his duty to come home to his proper wife.'

Non sipped the hot tea with her thoughts racing – had Caradoc come back to her out of a sense of duty?

'Come on now, what are you ponderin' on?'

'Caradoc's got a strong sense of what is right and proper, that's true. He would have come back to run the business his father started and, I hope, to me. It's just that I don't feel sure, when we make love, that his thoughts are with me.'

'That's silly talk!'

'I wish you were right but that nagging feeling won't go away.'

'What feeling?'

'That I don't have all of Caradoc the way I used to before he had his accident – before he forgot all about his life with me, our dear son, everything.'

Jessie poured more tea. Non could see she was giving herself time to think, time to choose the right words, tactful words, and yet they didn't come from her lips.

'Men have needs stronger than ours. We want a man to love and respect us, but I think sometimes a man just needs a woman, any woman, to satisfy his lust.' She put her hand to her mouth. 'I'm sorry, Non. That must sound cruel. I think I'd kill Albie if he did anything like that. Still, you mustn't spoil what you and Mr Jones have got between you now. In any case, I'm sure it's you he loves. I think you're worrying over nothing.'

'Maybe,' Non said. 'Let's talk about our little shops and I'll stop harping on about my imagined miseries.' She saw Jessie smile in relief, glad that the delicate matter of Non's husband was over and done with at least for the moment.

Caradoc breathed in the sounds and sights of Smithfield market. The stench of filth from the animals was still there, as was the harsh iron smell of blood from the slaughterhouses on the perimeter of the field, and yet it gave him a sense of home-coming; here he was on familiar ground, talking to other drovers, admiring the beasts for sale. This was a man's world, a place where he was secure.

He needn't have come here of course. Josh Wheeler had been on the drove since he was little more than a boy and could do the selling. But the itch to travel on was in Caradoc's bones. Much as he loved Non, he couldn't bear the constant guilt that plagued him when he was with her. It was good to get away and be amongst the men for a time.

Anyway, Non had been wrapped up in her business, checking that the products she was making were fresh and up to standard. When he told her he was going on the road, she didn't seem to mind; she said his absence would give her a chance to check her London shops and visit her old friends again.

No doubt she would be going to see Jessie. She was a good girl, was Jessie, and he was proud of the way she'd shaped up. She'd once walked the trails with his drove, young and inexperienced, but now she was happily married and a successful milk seller. Non would enjoy her visit, he was sure – or was that just a sop to his conscience? He knew that he loved Non, and yet, in the back of his mind, he had to admit that Gwenllyn still lurked.

'Hello, boss. Some good beasts here this time.' Morgan the blacksmith had come to stand beside Caradoc and he leaned on the fencing round the pen of solid Black Welsh bulls. 'Yours, though, are still the best. All bought up now, I believe?'

'Aye.' Caradoc pushed aside his troublesome thoughts, happy to be talking to another man, a man who understood the importance of breeding a good herd. 'Aye, we did well to sell so quickly. Young Josh Wheeler knows what he's about.'

'Will you have a drink?' Morgan said a little warily.

Caradoc smiled, resting his hand on Morgan's shoulder. 'Why not? I've got some papers to sign but that can wait.'

Inside the Smithfield inn the air was fetid with the combined odours of cattle and pipe smoke. But Caradoc was used to it, and so was Morgan. Caradoc chose a table in the corner of the dark room; he seated himself on the wooden bench and congratulated himself on a good drove.

His beer foamed to the top of his tankard, the foam white and frothy like sea breakers, but to Caradoc it tasted like manna from heaven.

Even enclosed in the small, gloomy taproom he could still hear the sounds of the market: the calls of moaning animals, the shouts of stock-breeders, the sharp voices of farmers anxious to buy the best beasts.

'Got something on your mind, boss?' Morgan asked conversationally, and for a moment Caradoc had the absurd feeling he wanted to confide in the blacksmith, tell him of the dreams that plagued him, of the way he loved his wife yet thought constantly about another woman. It came to him that Morgan, travelling round the farms and villages as he did, might be able to give him some information about Gwenllyn. Perhaps if he made a few general enquiries it wouldn't be giving away too much.

'I was wondering how Gwenllyn Lyons was getting along. I still feel I owe Gwenllyn something now that she's on her own.'

'She's not on her own.' Morgan looked at him. 'Haven't you heard the talk on the trail? But then, I suppose everyone else was too frightened to tell you.'

'Tell me what?'

'Gwenllyn is married, by all accounts, and with a babba on the way.'

Caradoc felt as if he'd swallowed a hard chunk of ice and it had stuck in his throat. He took a mouthful of beer and tried to keep his voice steady. 'No, I hadn't heard. Who did she marry?'

'Harold Rees. That's why he left the drove so suddenly.'

'And she's having a child?'

Morgan nodded. 'Yes, she's having a child, though how far on she is, I don't know. I'm sure Harry is looking after her,' he added, hoping to reassure Caradoc as the conversation suddenly seemed very strained.

'Is he though?' Caradoc said flatly. 'He was a good drover and he loved the roads, but I'm not sure what sort of husband and father he'd make. I didn't think he was the type for settling down.' It goaded him to think that he was living in Gwenllyn's cottage. It goaded him even more to think the allowance he was giving Gwenllyn might be used to support Harold Rees.

He put down his tankard with deliberated slowness; he suddenly couldn't see anything but a red mist. Another man tasting Gwenllyn's sweet lips, sitting in *his* chair, eating victuals that he, Caradoc Jones, provided.

Suddenly he realized this had nothing to do with money. Gwenllyn had her cottage and was provided for by her grandmother's estate: she didn't need his allowance. She may even have considered the gesture he'd made as a mark of his guilt, which of course it was. He was angry because he'd thought of Gwenllyn as his own. She still inhabited his dreams at night; she was almost part of him. How could she be with another man?

He became aware that Morgan had risen to his feet, obviously uncomfortable with the sudden silence.

'I'll be seeing you, then, boss,' he said awkwardly. 'You and your wife travelling back on the mail coach?'

Caradoc didn't reply. He just waved Morgan away and stared down into his drink. He slumped back into his seat, realizing that he was in a roomful of people, and yet he was alone.

CHAPTER SIX

Gwenllyn relaxed her back as she sat in a chair in the kitchen. Her stomach had become even more rounded now as her time drew near. And yet, as she studied her features in her hand mirror, she looked healthy and well, almost blooming. Her mind was settled now. Harry had kept his word and was staying with her.

She heard a knock on the door and put down the mirror. It was probably the midwife, the old woman who would deliver her child. No one else would be calling on her. She walked heavily across the hall and opened the door. Suddenly her heart leapt and her hands began to tremble. She staggered and almost fell with the shock of seeing the man she loved standing on the doorstep.

'Caradoc! What in the name of all the saints are you doing here?'

'It's true, then.' His voice was bitter; his eyes as

they took in her swollen belly were shadowed. 'It didn't take you long to find another man to replace me.'

Caradoc pushed past her, making his way into the house. He went unerringly to the drawing room, but then why shouldn't he? He'd lived here with her long enough; he knew the layout of the cottage as well as she did.

'You're married, I hear.' When he turned to face her his complexion was ashen. 'Married to a drover. A man who can't even write his own name.'

For a fleeting moment Gwenllyn wanted to go into his arms, to tell him the truth, that the baby was his and that she had never slept with another man. But she remembered his life as it was now: respectable, with no hint of shame attached to his name.

'When your memory returned you left me without a backward glance. Have you conveniently forgotten that? In fact, how is your wife?' Her voice was heavy with sarcasm. She was glad Harry had gone out – he would either have blurted out the truth or punched Caradoc on the nose.

'Leave my wife out of this.' Caradoc sank into a chair, his head in his hands. 'How could you forget me so quickly?' he said pleadingly. 'I thought you loved me.'

'And I thought *you* loved *me*.' She was suddenly angry. 'How dare you come here passing judgement on me? You're a married man, try to remember that! I had no future with you, did I? Why are you here harassing me?'

'Gwenllyn,' he said more gently, 'I left the drove for two days to ride here, just to see you. I had to know the truth.' He got to his feet and took her hand, observing the thin metal band on her finger. 'I see now I was wrong to dream about you, wrong to think the only man you'd ever loved was me.'

She turned away from him, her eyes blinded with tears. 'Will you please go?' She managed to keep her voice steady. 'My husband will be home at any minute.'

'How could you do it, Gwenllyn? Marry a common man like Harold Rees? You must have been desperate.'

'Harry is a fine, honest man,' she said defensively. 'He is happy to stay with me, to look after me. I need him. It's as simple as that.'

'So you're happy with your lot, are you?' Caradoc said harshly.

'As happy as you are with yours, I dare say.' She lifted her chin and met his eyes. He looked away and she knew he had no answer. 'Well, now you've seen me, you might as well go back to your wife.' Her tone was sharp. 'At least she loves you and I don't. Perhaps I never loved you.' She was lying but he had no way of knowing that. She watched as he turned and left her; then, standing at the window, she felt the tears run down her face as he mounted his horse in one easy movement. She stayed there until he was out of sight, then she sat heavily on one of the curved armchairs and let her hot tears flow unchecked.

Caradoc urged the pony into a gallop, for the sooner he put distance between himself and the cottage, the easier it would be. At the moment he felt like a fool. He'd no right to visit Gwenllyn because, as she'd reminded him, he had a wife. The life they had lived together had been like a dream and one day he'd woken up to the fact that he had another life and a wife waiting for him at home.

Gwenllyn was right: once his memory returned he'd not hesitated to run home to his Non. How could he blame Gwenllyn for finding a substitute so quickly? And yet he did blame her and he felt an appalling sense of loss, as though something very precious had been taken away from him. Was it possible to love two women at the same time? He wasn't sure but all he knew was that Gwenllyn's trust in him had been absolute. By leaving her so hurriedly he'd broken that trust. He'd longed to take her into his arms, to hold her as he used to, and to taste the sweetness of her lips. But now she belonged to Harold Rees and that was perhaps the worst part of the whole sorry mess. He glanced back once but all he could see was a spiral of thin smoke rising from one of the chimneys in the cottage and he'd never felt so alone in all his life.

'What was Caradoc Jones doing here?' Harry came into the kitchen and dragged out a chair. Sitting astride it, he was groaning and Gwenllyn knew he was angry. She paused from cooking the evening meal, drawing the pot onto the hob at the side of the fire. 'There's no good denying it. I saw him riding away from here, sitting high in the saddle as if he owned the whole of the Wye Valley.'

When Gwenllyn didn't answer him he went on with his tirade. 'He needn't come sniffing round here: he's not wanted – not least by me at least. What about you?'

She glanced at him, her eyes large in her pale face. 'I didn't ask him to come here and if you must know I sent him away with a flea in his ear. I've got some nice stew for our tea. Do you want some bread and cheese to start with?'

The shadow across his face lifted. She was aware that he was looking at her more kindly and she knew then that he was jealous of Caradoc.

'Aye, a bit of bread and cheese will stay my stomach. I've been working down on old Dai Beesley's farm all day and I'm starving.'

'Wash your hands, then, and I'll put the food out.'

He nodded. 'You're good to me, girl. You've been taking good care of me since I've been working on the farm and I do thank you for it.'

'Think nothing of it.' She forced a smile. 'Once the baby comes, you'll have to wait on me a little.'

'I know.'

Gwenllyn watched as he washed his hands in the water barrel near the door and rubbed them dry on his trousers. He stood for a moment looking up at the dying sun and she almost knew what he was thinking. She knew he'd planned to have a drink of beer tonight, but once he spotted Caradoc he'd come rushing home to her. Somehow the thought warmed her heart.

They sat at the table and Harry ate hungrily, but she simply tasted a spoonful of the rich liquid and put down her spoon.

'You're not hungry?' Harry looked at her anxiously.

'I'm just a bit upset.' She bit her lip, regretting her words as soon as they left her lips.

'What did he say, fancy man Caradoc Jones? He's upset you, hasn't he?'

'He'd heard from someone that we got married, so God knows why he came here.'

'And the babba, did he ask about it?'

'He assumed it was your child.'

'And you didn't tell him the truth?'

Gwenllyn could see that Harry was pleased but he simply grunted and continued with his meal.

He ate heartily and when he'd almost finished he took his last slice of fried bread and wiped it through the thin smear of gravy left on his plate. He caught Gwenllyn looking at him.

'Sorry. I know you don't like me doing that.'

Gwenllyn sighed. 'I suppose I should take it as a compliment: it's obvious you enjoyed your meal.'

It was clear that Harry felt uncomfortable: his colour had risen. 'Look, I can never be a gentleman, like Caradoc Jones.'

'You're doing fine,' she said comfortingly.

'You're right. I'm the one sitting here in your kitchen. It's my ring you got on your finger.' He paused. 'Look, I'll wash the dishes.' He got to his feet. 'Is there some hot water?' He shook the blackened kettle and nodded. 'Aye, there's enough.'

Gwenllyn looked up at him. 'Thank you, Harry. I am a bit tired. Perhaps I'll have an early night. You go down to the inn if you like. I'll be all right.'

'Na. I'm too tired to walk back down to the village. I'll just sit here for a bit, have a little drink of wine, ease the ache from my bones.'

'Try studying your reading,' Gwenllyn suggested. 'You're coming on so well with it and I'm proud of you.'

He blushed with pleasure and, emboldened by her praise, took her arm to help her up the stairs.

She shook his hand away. 'Don't forget our

bargain.' Her voice was stilted and she didn't look at him. 'There's nothing more to it than that. Once the baby is born, we go our separate ways.'

'Well, aye, that's what I want as well.' His voice was thick when he spoke. 'You don't think I want to stay by here with a woman and a brat that's not even mine, do you?'

'No,' she said dully, 'of course not.'

'Soon as the brat is born, I'll be off like a streak of lightning.'

'All right,' Gwenllyn said wearily. 'I won't try to hold you against your will, Harry, I promise you that. I'll have the baby soon and then you'll be free to go wherever you please. Good night.'

Harry stood watching her make her ungainly way up the stairs. When he heard the bedroom door close, he returned to the kitchen, the only room in the house where he felt comfortable. He filled a glass with wine and sat before the fire, his legs stretched out before him. He would forget he was married to Gwenllyn, once he was away from this place. Back on the road again, he would be a free man. That's what he'd always wanted. Somehow the words rang hollowly inside his head and impatiently he swallowed the wine in one gulp and refilled his glass.

Gwenllyn took off her clothes with hands that shook. She was feeling lost and lonely. What would she do when the baby came? Harry would leave then, and she wanted him to. He was uncouth; his manners were those of a pig. If she didn't nag him to wash himself, he'd go round smelling like a pig too. Well, no, that was unfair; Harry was a clean man.

Well, he needn't get any foolish ideas about staying here with her. Once the baby came he could up sticks, and good riddance to him. A man like Harry was built for the road; he wouldn't be happy staying in one place for any length of time.

When she was washed and undressed she sank onto the bed, feeling utterly weary, tired of Harry, tired of cooking for him and washing his clothes, tired of her swollen stomach. And then she thought of Caradoc, standing in the doorway of her house, his face set and angry. He hated her now, thought her a trollop. That hurt her and yet perhaps it was all for the good: he wouldn't come to see her again. That was what she wanted, wasn't it?

She tried to curl up in the bed but her belly was like a huge weight, her legs ached, her back ached, everything ached. Suddenly, Gwenllyn began to cry bitter tears that soaked her pillow and racked her body. How had she come to this? Married to a man she didn't love and fear curdling her blood every time she thought of giving birth to a baby she didn't want. She turned her face into the pillow and wished she was dead.

* * *

Caradoc couldn't explain even to himself why he was so angry with Gwenllyn. He had no claims on her. She was free to marry whoever she wanted, and yet to think of her with that ruffian Harry was almost too much to bear.

He'd booked a room for himself in the village inn and decided he would drown his anger and outrage in a few mugs of good dark beer. Then he would go to bed and sleep off all his foolish ideas.

The taproom was filled with smoke and voices and the secure feeling of being in a masculine world was reassuring. He got his beer and sat down next to a farmer who had a dog lying at his feet.

'You're the drover man,' the farmer said – 'the one who lost his brains in the river.' He smiled a toothless smile. 'It was a miracle that you lived at all, mind, what with a terrified horse trampling your head to a pulp.'

Caradoc nodded. 'Aye, I was lucky all right.'

The old man smoked his pipe and absent-mindedly stroked the dog's ears. He seemed to have lost interest in the conversation and that suited Caradoc, who wanted to be quiet, to try to sort out the confusion of thoughts and feelings that plagued him. He would go to bed early, he decided, try to get some sleep, and then he'd start for London at first light. How would he face Non without her seeing his pain and anger? Non was sensitive to his every mood; she would know something was wrong. Well, he would have to lie, tell her a deal had fallen through and he was not worried about anything except work. He put down his mug.

'Good night, then.' He tried to stroke the dog's head but the animal bared his teeth and almost took a piece out of his hand. Caradoc walked away. This was a day of days. Everything had been bad from the minute he opened his eyes that morning and now even a dumb animal was turning on him. If he'd been in a better humour he would have laughed at himself; instead, he went upstairs to bed feeling as if all the demons of hell were inside his head.

CHAPTER SEVEN

Non looked around at her comfortable surround-ings. She was alone; Jessie and Albie were both out working. She knew the Jones drove had reached London but Caradoc had sent her a message saying he had to spend a few days away on business. Exactly what business he'd failed to tell her, which caused her a now-familiar stab of apprehension about where he might be going.

She was impatient with herself for harbouring suspicions about her husband, aware she'd be better occupied going out and looking after her shops. She got to her feet. She would go to the new premises in Cutler Street and see if the young woman she'd put in charge was doing a good job. Anything was better than sitting around, moping.

It was a lovely spring day and as soon as Non stepped outdoors, she felt better, more positive. Of course Caradoc wouldn't be visiting Gwenllyn

Lyons, why would he? As Jessie had pointed out, once his memory had returned he'd chosen to leave Gwenllyn immediately and return to her.

Cutler Street was as crowded as ever. Garments were hung on the shop fronts, inviting inspection by prospective buyers. Non noted with pride that the sign for her shop was already prominently displayed over the narrow doorway, with her name written large and an arrow pointing towards the dark stairwell that led to her rooms above.

Carrie Mayhew was a tall, thin girl with glasses perched upon her nose, which gave her a studious look. And indeed she was a good student; she learned quickly and was now adept at making up remedies herself.

'Mrs Jones, this is a nice surprise.' Carrie had the manner and speech of a well-educated girl, though Non knew she was almost entirely self-taught. Carrie could read well and write a good hand and her command of figures was masterly.

'How is the trade, Carrie?' Non peeled off her gloves and sat in one of the old chairs strategically placed for customers who found it an effort to climb the stairs.

'Very good, Mrs Jones. I've had a good number of customers already and, just today, two ladies and a gentleman came in for some foot balm.'

Carrie delved into a cupboard and brought out the accounts book. 'Have a look for yourself, Mrs Jones. I think you'll be well pleased.'

Non opened the book and nodded approval at the clearly written lists of goods with the correct price of each item written at the other side of the page. Carrie's neat and accurate accounting was a pleasure to behold; she had a great future ahead of her. One day she would realize that and move on, but in the meantime Non was very glad to have her services. 'You're doing a good job, Carrie. Have you had any problems?'

'Nothing to speak of. A few cheeky ragamuffins came in yesterday and tried to steal some mint leaves.' She smiled – a rare event for Carrie. 'Goodness knows what they thought they could do with them. Anyway, I slapped their hands and sent them off.'

Non nodded. Carrie was a strong character; though she was young she had an air of authority that even Non found a little intimidating. 'I'm very pleased with you, Carrie,' she said. 'I think you're doing a splendid job here and once the shop is established I shall certainly give you a pay rise.'

Carrie's cheeks turned a little pink. She must have been pleased but she hid her feelings so well that Non could not be sure.

There was a sound of feet clattering on the wooden stairs and Non rose and nodded at Carrie. 'I think you've got customers, so I'll leave you to it. I'll pop in and see you again before I go back to Wales.'

Two men accompanied by a quartet of giggling, chattering women came into the shop and at once it seemed crowded. Soon, if business continued to do well, she would have to find larger premises for Carrie.

Having made her way back out into the sunlight, she stood on the roadway, wondering what to do with her time. She didn't want to go back to Jessie's house and sit alone but she could go to the servery to chat with Jessie.

Non hailed a cab, watching as the horse snorted to a stop and dipped his head to allow his big fleshy mouth to search the ground for titbits. Soon she was being driven along the riverside towards Jessie's servery. The smell of the Thames was as bad as ever but Non was used to it now. She glanced up at the sky. A thin drizzle had begun and the clouds were hanging low over the forest of smoking chimneys. London sometimes showed an ugly face but it was as dear to her as her home in Swansea.

Jessie was at the back of the building, bent over the milk pails with a cleaning cloth in her hand. She looked up and smiled when she saw Non.

'Glad to see you,' Jessie said. 'You'll have to wait for a cup of tea until I have washed these damn pails out. It's hard work but it's got to be done. Don't want the fresh morning milk to go sour just for the lack of a bit of elbow grease.'

'You shouldn't be doing that in your condition.'

Non frowned. 'Surely you could employ someone else to do it?'

'Don't want to waste money, Non.' Jessie straightened. 'Though when I gets bigger, I'll have to hire a young lad to do it for me, I suppose.'

Non took off her coat and pushed up her sleeves. It was a long time since she'd done any real work. Her day was occupied with making herbal remedies or poring over her accounts. She cleaned the pails with gusto, surprised to find she was actually enjoying herself.

When the work was finished, Non stood back, pleased with her efforts. 'No sour milk tomorrow, Jessie,' she said – 'not with all the scrubbing I've done. See: the pails are gleaming.'

'Well, what the bleedin' 'ell is going on yer, then?' Ruby appeared at the back of the servery and stood, arms folded across her chest, looking at Non with raised eyebrows.

'Mrs Bloody Rich Man's Wife doing real work for a change. I never thought I'd see the day.' She winked at Jessie. 'What's come over our Non, then, Jessie? What you think?'

'Aw, don't tease like that,' Jessie said. 'Make yourself useful and dry this last pail for me – my poor back is starting to ache now.' She straightened up and rubbed her back. 'Then we'll close up for the night and go back home for a cup of tea and a bite to eat.'

There was the sound of horse hoofs outside the door. 'Albie!' Jessie called, 'is that you?'

Albie came in from the drizzle of the day, untying the spotless apron he wore when serving milk. With his hands on his hips, he stared at the three women. 'Here's a pretty kettle of fish! All these women sitting about and the poor man earning the living.'

'Never mind the chit-chat,' Jessie said, 'go and fetch the horse and trap. We're all going back to the house to have some tea.'

'Don't mind me,' Albie said. 'I'm only the poor muggins who does most of the work around here.'

As he retreated into the dimness of the servery Jessie threw her cloth at him and he turned just in time to catch it neatly.

'How did I see that coming?' he said. 'Because I got eyes in the back of me 'ead, Jess, and you should know that by now.'

'Can anyone join in this conversation?' Non laughed out loud. 'It's like a Punch and Judy show in here and I'm tired now. I just want to sit down in comfort.'

'Aye,' Jessie said. 'I'll shut up shop and we'll all be off home. Coming for a cup of tea, Ruby?'

'Well, I ain't going to leave you lot to chat about me once my back is turned. Of course I'm coming for a cup of tea.'

A little while later, when she was seated with Jessie and Ruby in the well of the trap, Non watched as Albie clucked his tongue at the horse, urging the animal forward, making his way cautiously out of the narrow section of road off Golden Lane.

The gentle jogging of the horse and the sound of the wheels along the cobbles seemed to soothe her and with the dying light throwing leafy shadows over the streets and buildings she felt that everything in her life was going well after all. Her fears about Caradoc and Gwenllyn Lyons evaporated. She was simply being foolish, allowing her imagination to get the better of her. Caradoc was entitled to take care of his business just as she was hers. Did he wonder where she was when she visited her shops? He trusted her and she should trust him in return.

Jessie shifted in her seat. '*Duw*, I swear my bum has got bigger already and me only five months gone.'

Non's happy feeling vanished; she faced reality. Her worries were very real because her husband had lived with another woman, had loved her and slept with her. Even though they were reunited, Non was afraid he wasn't truly back with her. And looking at Jessie now, seeing how her small waist was a little thicker, seeing the happiness in her eyes, Non felt that Jessie had the most precious things in the world: a husband who loved her and his child growing in her womb. And in that moment, Non envied her.

* * *

Gwenllyn stepped out into the sun-splashed yard. It was a good fine day but it might as well have been pouring with rain for all the joy she felt. She'd been having niggling pains in her stomach since early morning, probably caused by something she had eaten.

She became aware of a masculine voice singing, out of tune, accompanied by the sound of splashing water. She walked towards the bushes at the edge of the garden and parted the branches with her hand.

She took a deep breath. Harry was bathing himself in the small stream that ran along the perimeter of her land. He was naked except for his cotton underdrawers, which, he being thin, clung to his legs and outlined his manhood as he stood up and began to walk up the bank towards her. She couldn't help but notice what a fine figure of a man he was. And then she hurried away, feeling as if she'd been spying on him. She scuttled into the kitchen, opened the door of the cold larder and took out a jug of fresh lemon water. She poured some into a glass, hesitated for a moment, and then took another glass and poured a drink for Harry.

She averted her eyes as he came into the kitchen. He was still wearing only his thin cotton drawers.

'You should get dressed,' she said at once.

'Don't go all red now, Gwennie.' She heard the laughter in his voice. 'It's not the first time you've seen a man in his underdrawers, is it?'

'That's none of your business and I wish you wouldn't call me Gwennie.' Her tone was sharp.

'Look, Gwennie, while we're living under the same roof you have to get used to my ways. In any case, you're my wife, so there's no need for modesty.'

Gwenllyn was about to make a scathing reply, when a pain ripped across her belly and spread round to her backbone. She gasped and held her swollen stomach, as if she could gain some relief by holding the weight of it with her hands, but the pain grew stronger and she felt as if her bones were being pulled apart.

'What's wrong?' Harry came close to her and even through her pain she smelled the clean scent of him and reached out for him.

'Fetch someone, Harry – the woman from the village. I think the baby's coming.'

He looked down at her. 'Will you let me look at you?' he asked uncertainly. 'I helped my mam – remember I told you about it?' She nodded, too much in pain to care what he did. He felt her stomach carefully and after a moment he nodded. 'Aye, it's coming, all right.'

Even as he spoke, her waters broke and she stared at the puddle on the floor with mounting fear. 'What's happening to me, Harry?' The words came out in a sob. 'Am I doing to die?'

''Course you're not going to die! Come on, let me get you upstairs to your bed.' He lifted her and she closed her eyes at the indignity of it all. Harry didn't seem to care that her gown was soaked, he took it all as a matter of course, and that reassured Gwenllyn a little.

He put her down on the edge of the bed and pulled back the patchwork quilt. 'I'll get some paper to put under you. Now, don't you move. I'll be back in a minute.'

'Harry, are you going to fetch someone to help me?'

He shook his head and sighed. 'It's too late for that. You got no one but me.'

'But, Harry, you can't see me naked . . . I mean, it's not right for you to . . . well, you know what I mean . . . it's all so embarrassing.'

Another pain caught her and he held her until it had passed. 'Hold on. I'll fetch some things up with me – water, towels . . . you know.'

Gwenllyn didn't know and she called after him to come back. She was so frightened as she clung to the post of the bed that she wanted to fall into a heap on the floor.

Then Harry was back. He spread the paper on the bed and gently lowered her down onto it. 'Let's get this damned gown off you.' He pulled at the neck and the material split. It was one of her best gowns but Gwenllyn no longer cared. He dropped the soaked gown to the floor and put a clean sheet over her. 'Now, knees up, there's a good girl.'

Gwenllyn's every instinct told her to press her legs firmly together, but nature had other ideas. She began to grunt, low in her throat, and obediently bent her knees and pressed her feet against the bed.

'It's going to come out before long.' Harry's voice was cheerful. 'From the way the little bugger is kicking in your belly, he'll be out with us before another hour or two have passed.'

Gwenllyn began to cry. How could she stand the pain for a whole hour or more? She felt Harry's hands on her belly and it seemed he was pushing with her, helping the baby to come into the world.

It should be Caradoc here helping her, not a strange man she'd married as a bargain. Caradoc would have known she was in labour and called for help long before now. But she was being unfair: she scarcely talked to Harry and hadn't told him about her pains, so how could he have done anything differently?

He sat with her, bathing her face with cold water, and soon she forgot her dignity. All she wanted was relief and peace.

The time seemed to pass with agonizing slowness, but at last Harry nodded at her encouragingly. 'I can see the head,' he said. 'Try to bear down now, there's a good girl. Push with all your might.'

Gwenllyn found she had no choice in the matter. Her womb contracted fiercely and she had an overwhelming urge to force her child into the world.

'Just a little bit more now, there's a good girl, push once again and we'll soon have this little one born.'

She found that Harry had been optimistic. Her labour continued for almost another hour and then, miraculously, the baby found its way out into the world and bawled with loud frantic cries.

'*Duw*, you got yourself a fine boy!' Harry sounded jubilant. 'He's built like a bull: big shoulders and big head. No wonder he took so long to be born.' He wrapped the baby in a towel. 'Here, Gwennie, meet your son.' He carefully laid the baby against Gwenllyn's breast and for a moment she was afraid to look at her child. 'Go on, he won't bite you,' Harry urged. 'You admire your son while I see to the rest of this business.'

Gwenllyn looked down then and her breath left her as she saw a minute version of Caradoc: his nose, his ears, his bright hair. 'It's a miracle,' she breathed, touching his soft cheek with her finger.

She was dimly aware of Harry drawing something from her. He quickly took it and wrapped it in paper. 'That's a good job done. I'll put it on the fire when I go downstairs.'

'What is it?' Gwenllyn imagined she'd had another baby, a dead one, and Harry was too afraid to tell her.

'It's just what comes out after the baby's born – the afterbirth, it's called, and you're well rid of it. Now let's get you washed and covered up, shall we?'

She looked up at him, her eyes brimming with tears. 'Thank you, Harry. I don't know what I would have done without you.' She reached up and touched his cheek. 'Thank you from the bottom of my heart.'

CHAPTER EIGHT

The new-born infant seemed to disrupt everything in Gwenllyn's life. The boy cried only when
he was hungry, but she found it difficult feeding
him at the breast and this morning was no
exception.

It was a bright morning, with a little chill in the
air, and when she got up from her bed she saw
that Harry had, as usual, lit the fires. The baby
was a sweet weight in her arms as she carried him
downstairs and sat in her chair, cuddling him,
hoping his frantic crying would stop. She tried to
put her nipple in the small puckered mouth, but
the child turned his head away from her. 'What
am I doing wrong?' Her voice was anguished and
the next moment Harry peered round the
door.

'Can I help?' He was half afraid to look in her
direction and her instinct was to refuse point

blank for him to see her with her bodice all awry. But the crying became more insistent and after a moment she turned to look at Harry.

'What would you know about feeding a child?' She knew her tone was truculent but she was agitated, not knowing how to soothe the baby and make him take her milk.

'I helped you with the birthing. Perhaps I can help you now.'

He had a point and she nodded. 'All right. Come in and tell me what is wrong.'

'If you'll excuse me, Mrs Rees . . .' He took a firm hold of her breast and squeezed it so that the nipple stood out proud. 'Now tip your . . . er . . . your teat into the boy's mouth and let him clamp on.'

'It's worked!' Gwenllyn watched in triumphant amazement as the baby began to suckle. The pull of his mouth was strong and she felt as if her womb was contracting inside her. It was a most strange feeling and yet a satisfying one and she smiled up at Harry in triumph.

'I'm doing it, Harry, I'm doing it!'

He nodded and stood up, then moved slightly away from her. 'See, I'm not so useless, am I?'

Gwenllyn felt ashamed. 'Harry, I don't know what I would have done without you these last months.'

He frowned, obviously embarrassed by her praise. 'I'm going out now to shoot some rabbit.

We'll have a good meal tonight, you'll see.'

She heard the front door slam and the sound of his boots growing fainter as he went down the path and she was left alone. She'd come to rely on him far too much, she told herself sternly: she'd decided he would go once she had the baby and yet here she was taking his help and giving him nothing in return. But that was nonsense! She was giving him a comfortable living, a roof over his head, and her money paid for the food they ate. But then he'd taken time off from his job on the farm to look after her, so she had no one to blame but herself if he brought in no money.

The baby pulled at her breast and she looked down at him, seeing Caradoc's features with a desperate feeling of regret. Why couldn't it be Caradoc here helping her, Caradoc teaching her how to feed the baby? But he was back in his old life now. When he had come to her house he'd been so eager to think she didn't love him any more. He'd taken one look at her swollen belly and assumed she'd taken another man to her bed.

She smoothed the fair hair away from the baby's eyes and looked down at the tiny crumpled face. 'What am I going to call you?' she said softly. 'I'll have to give you a name.'

The baby's eyes opened and he seemed to look at her with an arcane wisdom.

'I think you've been here before,' she whispered. 'You're like a wise old man there.

'Are you a Richard or a David? Yes, David is a good name, it's the name of our patron saint. I'll call you David and woe betide anyone who dares to call you Dai or Dafydd or any other such name.'

She leaned back in her chair, feeling relaxed and warm and at peace with her motherhood. And that, she reluctantly reflected, was all because Harry Rees had been there to help her. She had a great deal to thank him for.

It was good to be back in Wales. Non had enjoyed her trip to London – she was pleased that Carrie was doing so well and that her other two shops were drawing more and more customers – but now she was tired and just relieved to be home with Caradoc so that they could talk, really talk. She still didn't have any explanation for his disappearance on 'business'. He was evasive whenever she asked him about it and she could hardly cause a scene when she was a guest in Jessie's house. But now they were home she could speak more openly.

She felt a dart of apprehension when she heard his step in the hall. She looked down at her hands – they were trembling. But why was she so anxious? Did she really believe he'd go off to see another woman on the sly? That was not the Caradoc she'd married.

He came into the room. His hair was ruffled by

the breeze and he looked tanned and handsome and somehow a little aloof. He came to where she was sitting and kissed her cheek. 'You shouldn't be sitting indoors on a beautiful day like this,' he said. 'It's so warm in the sun, I'm sure a walk would make you feel better.'

'Why do you think I need to be made "better"?'

Caradoc shook his head. 'I can see something is wrong. Is it the shops or have you fallen out with Jessie or Ruby? You've been quiet ever since we came home.'

She took a deep breath, looking for the courage to talk to him honestly. 'It's those lost days that worry me,' she said, her voice low.

He sat down opposite her and he looked so calm, so relaxed, that it seemed a shame to talk to him about anything unpleasant. Still, it had to be done: she had to know the truth.

'Do you mean when I lost my memory?' he asked. 'Those are the only lost days I can think of.'

'You know it's not that, I'm not stupid. What I want to know is what business was it that kept you away from me for three days when I was staying with Jessie?'

He looked away and she knew by his frown he was troubled, but she persisted – she couldn't stop herself now.

'You went to see *her*, didn't you?'

He didn't insult her by pretending not to know

who she was talking about, but it was a shock when he nodded. 'Yes, I went to the cottage to see how Gwenllyn was getting on. I do feel a certain responsibility towards her.'

Non felt as if a knife had been thrust into her heart. It was bad enough suspecting he'd seen Gwenllyn, but to know the truth was much more painful, much more than she could have imagined.

'And how was Gwenllyn Lyons? In good health, I trust?'

'Being sarcastic won't get us anywhere,' Caradoc said quietly. 'I can't forget I lived with her for months. She cared for me, brought me back to health, and I'll always be grateful to her for that.'

He got up and walked to the window and she knew he wasn't seeing the lush gardens or the green of the trees against the sky: he was remembering Gwenllyn, her beauty, her kindness to him.

'In any case, none of us needs worry about her now. She's married and she's having a child.'

Relief sped through Non and she relaxed. Looking down, she saw that her hands had been so tightly closed that marks of her nails were embedded in her palms.

'She didn't waste any time.'

Non regretted the words as soon as they were spoken. Caradoc turned, gave her a long hard, cold look, and walked away, out of the room and out of the house – and, for all she knew, out of her life.

Gwenllyn stood in the window, cradling David in her arms as he slept, his small face crumpled and his little fists curled like the petals of a flower. He was a beautiful child and her heart filled with warmth as she looked down at him.

She glanced up at the clock. It was Harry's first day back at work. He'd be home soon and it was time she put the supper on to heat. She wondered at herself accepting her strange way of life. She was married but without a husband in the real sense of the word: she and Harry could never be more than uneasy friends. She still loved Caradoc Jones and would always love him.

Gently, she settled David into his crib and set it swinging. His hands punched the air as if he was afraid he was falling. She leaned over him, her finger touching his soft cheek. 'I love you, little David. You're Mammy's sweetheart and you'll always be safe with me.'

Harry was late returning home that night and Gwenllyn felt uneasy about him. Had he got into trouble down at the local inn? He was a man to speak his mind and was often too blunt for his own good. But it was silly worrying about him: he was a grown man and didn't need her to look out for him.

She went to bed and lit the candles in her room.

The fire had gone out and with a feeling of surprise Gwenllyn realized that these days she left that sort of chore to Harry. She took the baby in her arms for his last feed of the day and prayed he would sleep a few hours through the night. As she cradled him in her arms she felt all her protective instincts rising within her. The boy had a right to know who his father was and she must see to it that when the time was right she told David the truth, whatever it might cost.

She was awakened by the sound of the front door banging and she sat up, her heart beating swiftly with fear. She heard Harry's voice calling her. 'Gwennie, where are you? Where's my little wife?'

Angrily, she pushed aside the bedclothes and took up a candle. She peered into the crib and saw, with a feeling of relief, that David was still asleep. She hurried down the stairs and found Harry sitting in the middle of the kitchen floor, a mug of ale in his hand.

'You're drunk!' she said accusingly. 'How dare you come home like this! I won't have it, do you hear me?'

He laughed and drank more of his beer before lurching to his feet. 'You sound like a wife.' He flung his arms wide, spilling his drink over the floor. 'But then you are my wife, I was forgetting that.'

She sighed and pushed the kettle onto the

embers of the fire. 'I'm going to make you a cup of tea to set you right,' she said wearily. 'I don't know, if it isn't the baby disturbing my sleep it's you. Why do you do it, Harry?'

'Don't want no tea,' he said. 'I like being drunk. It helps me to forget.'

'Forget what?'

'Forget that I'm bought and paid for, a married man and not a married man. I can't make any sense of it all. Why did I get myself into this mess? What with a nagging woman and a screaming baby, my life is like living in hell.'

'Well, you don't have to stay.' Gwenllyn was suddenly angry. 'You have it easy, Harold Rees. You live very fine, if you ask me. You have a good roof over your head, plenty of food to put in your belly – what more do you want?'

'I work for a living when you'll let me.' He met her eyes and she saw the fog was clearing from his brain. He got to his feet and put his mug on the table very carefully, every movement measured.

'When you earn money what do you spend it on? Drink! Your paltry pay wouldn't keep you for a day in this sort of house.' She knew she was being cruel but she couldn't stop the tirade of words that poured from her mouth.

'I work for you, Gwennie,' Harry said quietly. 'I see to the fires, I catch rabbits for our dinner. I know I don't earn much by your standards but I do my best.'

His words made her stop and think. Perhaps she was being too hard on him. He was used to working hard on the drove, being in authority. She was about to say something conciliatory, when Harry thumped the table with his fist.

'I'm fed up of this!' he said loudly. 'I've done my best for you but it's never no good, is it? I could crawl on my bare knees over cinders for you and it wouldn't make a bit of difference, would it?'

Gwenllyn stared at him, aghast. 'I never promised you anything, Harry, remember? I gave you a bag of money in exchange for your name, that's all.'

'And you never stop reminding me of it. Ask yourself, what have I given you? Just ask yourself that, Gwenllyn.'

'Oh, just go away and leave me alone.' Gwenllyn suddenly felt near to tears. 'I don't need a drunken man in my house. I'd be better off without you.'

He became very still and Gwenllyn could see how much her words had hurt him. She lifted her hand, but Harry, galvanized into movement, brushed past her. He hurried up the stairs to the top floor and she knew what he was doing, he was packing his few possessions into a bag, and it was not the first time her harsh words had turned him away from her.

She waited for him to come downstairs and she didn't have to wait long. He passed the kitchen door and made straight for the hallway. She hurried after him.

'I didn't mean you had to leave tonight, Harry. Don't be so silly. Where will you go?'

'That's my affair,' he said, 'so keep your nose out. You don't rule my life, Mrs Rees.'

'But, Harry, it's late, the inn will be closed. Where will you sleep?'

'I've slept rough before and I can do it again.' He didn't look at her but she thought she detected a note of sadness in his voice.

'Harry, would it help if I said I'm sorry?'

'It's too late for that, Gwenllyn. You want me out, and as for me I'm fed up to the back teeth with you and your selfish ways and that baby of yours crying the place down every night.' He paused. 'Come to think of it, I'd be better off without you.'

She heard him go round to the stables. His horse whinnied a little and she could imagine him putting on the saddle, strapping the girth round the horse's round belly and fastening it tightly. But what if he was made careless by drink? What if he made mistakes with the saddle? It could cost him his life.

Her outdoor boots were near the back door but even as she struggled to pull them on, her long nightgown hindering her progress, she heard the sound of galloping hoofs and knew she was too late to do anything to stop Harry leaving. She waited until the sound faded away and then she cast her boots aside savagely. Harry was gone and all at once she felt stifled by the lonely silence of the night.

CHAPTER NINE

Caradoc was glad that he had a new drove to lead. The constant tension between him and Non was almost unbearable. He felt the need to get away from his wife, from the hurt in her eyes.

Non had not mentioned Gwenllyn, but the accusations were there every time she looked at him. He knew she dreaded the thought of him being away, wondering if he would be seeing Gwenllyn again. But hell would freeze over before he went back to the cottage resting above the river Wyc.

Gwenllyn was no longer his concern; she had more than enough money on which to live comfortably, she had a husband of sorts and no doubt by now she'd had the child. She wanted nothing from him, needed nothing except to be left alone to get on with her life. Perhaps he should feel happy for her but somehow he couldn't.

The cattle were restless; Caradoc heard the strident calls from his herdsmen and dragged his thoughts back to the task in hand. He looked round him at the field where his stock were penned, ready for the move on the trail to London. He was proud of his stock, Welsh Black beef, worth a great deal of money, profit on the hoof providing he arrived in Smithfield on time with a herd in good health. He was almost ready to begin the journey but Josh had not reached Swansea with the herds from Carmarthen. If the man didn't come soon, the drove would have to start without him.

Caradoc checked his saddle-bags and his gun and went at last to look at the supply wagon. That should have been Josh's duty, but in his absence Caradoc had to see to it himself. Still, he had a good team of men riding with the drove and five young women. Most of them had worked with him before and knew all about the hardships on the road.

The girls were dressed in plain gowns, a turnover of Welsh wool and an apron of sacking. Right now with the excitement of travelling to London, the girls were smiling, quipping and making eyes at the men, but by the end of the journey they would be so weary they'd be glad to sleep in a barn or even in the open fields. The newcomers soon learned how hard it was on the trail; the girls would be required to weed the fields when the animals were resting, as well as knitting hosiery along the way which was destined for the big London markets.

It was a hard life but all his workers would be well paid when they reached Smithfield and afterwards they could travel home or, as some of them did, spend some time in London working at the markets.

An hour later the drove began, without Josh. Caradoc gave his horse a soothing pat on its strong neck and sounded the horn, and gradually the men pushed the cattle into place on the road, prodding them with sticks until a slow but sure pace was set.

Caradoc was exhilarated, feeling, as he always did at the start of a drove, that there was an adventure awaiting him on the road. He urged his horse into a trot ahead of the herd and he stood up in the stirrups, staring ahead, his hand shading his eyes. Soon they would be on the outskirts of Swansea, following the narrow meandering road on the first leg of the journey towards Brecon.

Then, in a few days, he would have the river Wye to contend with. If there was even a hint of rain or the slightest brush of wind he would avoid the river crossing and pay the toll to cross over the bridge. Caradoc had tangled with the river once and he'd been the loser. He relaxed into his saddle. All he needed now was to get the herd to cover between fourteen and sixteen miles a day as that would mean good progress.

A few miles outside Swansea, as the drove headed through the hills thick with trees, he heard his name being called. He turned to see Josh, red-faced, his horse foaming at the mouth, ridden hard to make up the distance.

'Sorry I'm late, Mr Jones,' Josh gasped: 'family problems.' He took off his hat and rubbed the sweat from his forehead. 'Mam's sick again, gone to stay with my auntie, so I've had to bring my sister with me, but Emily's a good girl and used to hard work.'

Caradoc frowned. 'I do the hiring and firing around here, Josh,' he said. 'I don't want an inexperienced girl on the drove. Is she used to walking long distances?'

'Aye, she is, sir. She's eager to learn the weeding and, as for the knitting, she's done enough of that to make a stocking that would stretch from Swansea to Newport.'

'Well, when we stop I'll speak to her. If I think she's suitable, well and good. If not, I'm afraid it's the road back to Swansea for the both of you. Where's the herd you were supposed to be bringing from Carmarthen?'

'The farmer changed his mind about sending the beasts on the road. They were scrawny animals anyway – no loss.'

Caradoc nodded. The boy knew his cattle and

if he said they were inferior stock he was probably right. 'All right. Fall back now, follow at the rear of the herd, and make sure none of the cattle stray off the roads and into the fields.'

Josh tipped his hat and obediently fell back. Caradoc rode up the steep rise in the hill knowing that the cattle would slow up, sometimes slipping when the metal shoes touched a stone.

He rode the herd steadily for several hours, making good distance with no trouble, but by now man and beast would need a break. Caradoc lifted his arm, signalling to the men to bring the cattle to a halt.

While he sat in the grass, watching the girls rest, skirts billowing around their legs like fallen flower petals, he remembered he needed to talk to Josh's sister. Even as he thought about Josh, he could see him striding up the slope, with a young girl behind him, the hem of her gown lifting to reveal her tiny feet as she ran along.

'Mr Jones, sir.' Josh looked anxious. 'This is Emily, my sister.'

Caradoc could see the girl was very young, not more than fifteen years of age. She was beautiful too, with long sunkissed hair and deep-blue eyes fringed with heavy lashes. All that youth and beauty was bound to unsettle the men. He'd almost made up his mind to send her home when she spoke.

''Scuse me, sir,' she said softly. 'I'm young but

very strong. I won't be a drag on the rest of the drove, I promise. Anyway, if you was to send me home there'd be no one to take care of me. Please, Mr Jones sir, don't send me back to Swansea.'

Caradoc saw the pleading in Emily's eyes and softened. 'All right, Emily, you can come to London with us but you have to behave yourself – no idling away the time or getting into trouble with the men.'

She blushed. ''Scuse me, sir, but I'm a well brought-up girl. I don't bother with no men – don't even talk to them 'less I know them.'

Josh added his own plea. 'I'll watch out for her,' he said.

Caradoc nodded. 'And I'll have a word with the men myself. Some of the older ones have daughters of their own back home.' But even as he spoke, Caradoc knew that the men on a cattle drove saw only a pretty face and didn't think beyond that. Daughters or no, they would all be trying to please little Emily.

The drove got on the road again after resting for little more than an hour and Caradoc was glad to be on the move again. They would reach the Lamb and Flag inn by nightfall, all of them ready for a good meal and a jug or two of beer.

As he rode along, hearing the familiar sounds of the herd, the drums of hoofs against the dirt road and the intermittent, plaintive noise of the animals, he felt more at peace than he'd been in a long time. Here on the trail, he could forget his wife's pleading, questioning eyes, and put Gwenllyn and her new family out of his mind. All he needed to do was lead the drove safely to London.

It was lonely without Harry, for as much as she hated to admit it Gwenllyn was missing him badly. In the morning, she had to light the fires before she could make a cup of tea and she realized that Harry had been spoiling her. He had even found a job, determined not to be dependent on her for his keep. Perhaps she had been unjust to him: most men took a little too much ale from time to time. And he wasn't the scoundrel she'd first thought him. His table manners had improved and even his reading was quite good now. He could read from the Bible and although he stumbled over some of the longer words she had to admit he'd been quick to learn.

As she looked out of the window, at the path leading away from the cottage, she wished she could see a figure approaching, a man, and the man she truly wanted was Caradoc Jones. But no, he would never come back, not now that he had learned she was married to Harry. How could Caradoc know it was an empty union, bought and paid for, a name for a bastard child in exchange for money?

The baby began to cry and she picked him up

and cuddled him close to her. He could smell the milk and his rosebud mouth sought her nipple. She opened her bodice and held her breast towards the baby's mouth the way Harry had taught her. At once David clamped his mouth onto her breast and began to suckle contentedly. She should feel relief that her baby was safely born and Harry gone out of her life, but all that she felt was an overwhelming sense of loneliness.

As the weeks went by, Non waited anxiously to see if she had conceived Caradoc's child on one of the few nights they had spent together in the same bed. She had lost the Caradoc she'd fallen in love with but the urge to make her marriage work was strong. In any case she longed for a baby, not one to replace Rowan, her first-born – he could never be replaced – but another son or even a daughter, and a child might bring them closer together. Caradoc would have the family he desired.

The date of her courses came and went with no sign of blood and her excitement was difficult to contain. She was with child this time, she had to be. She had been taking her herbal remedies: mint to stay the courses and columbine to ensure a safe and speedy delivery when the time came for the child to be born. She had made a preparation of mixed berries steeped in water and honey and took a measure of it every day, a good potion for expectant mothers.

Non felt hope rise within her. Soon Caradoc would come home again and she would be eager to tell him the good news. She imagined it now: Caradoc taking her into his arms, kissing her, telling her that he'd forgotten all about his lost summer and knew his place was with her and their baby.

But there was to be no baby. One morning, Non woke to find her courses had begun. She couldn't bear it and she had no one to talk to about her disappointment because the only other people she ever saw in the Swansea house were her staff of cooks and maids.

She must put the need to have a baby out of her mind – there was such a thing as being too eager. It was time to occupy herself with other things.

Perhaps she would take the mail coach and go up to London. Ruby would understand her fears and comfort her. A thought struck her: it was her husband who should be there for her in her time of need. In a rush of anger, she picked up the cup of berry juice and threw it across the room. As it shattered and fell to the floor, the juice seeped out across the carpet, red as blood.

'So, I don't want anyone playing the fool over Josh's little sister.' Caradoc was seated at the table in the Lamb and Flag inn. It was the first chance he'd had to talk to the men. 'Emily is still a child and anyone found bothering her will be whipped and then dismissed and I'll make damn sure he never works a drove again.'

'And I'll be waiting behind a tree to stab any man who hurts my sister,' Josh added for good measure.

Caradoc looked at him. He was young, a little hot-headed maybe, but he'd grow out of that in time. Caradoc smiled. 'No need to go that far, Josh. I think everyone knows Emily is a pure young girl and as such has a right to be treated with respect.'

The men murmured in agreement and Caradoc noticed that Josh settled back, the tension leaving his face. He was a good hand and would make a fine head drover one day; when he was a little older he could be trusted to lead the way to London on his own. Somehow the thought didn't please Caradoc. He enjoyed the open road and the freedom of the hills and the excitement of the market in Smithfield. In short he relished the life of a drover and the urge to travel the road would always be in his blood.

Later, he went across the open land to the barn where the glint of lanterns showed through the wooden doors. He knocked before entering and saw that the women were settled round a brazier and the smell of rabbit stew rose enticingly as he drew nearer.

'Something smells good,' he said, his eyes resting on little Emily. Her cheeks were rosy from the heat of the fire and her eyes were filled with excitement. She would be quite a beauty when she was older.

He turned to the head woman of the drove and smiled. 'How about me sharing a bit of that rabbit stew, Carmel? The food at the inn isn't half as good, I can tell you.'

She filled a tin bowl and held it out to him, bobbing a curtsy. Even here in the primitive surroundings of the barn he was still treated with respect. He sat silently eating his food for a few minutes, listening to the amiable chatter going on around him, and as he looked up from his platter of stew he caught Emily's eyes on him.

'How are you managing, Emily?' he said. 'Is the drover's life to your liking?'

'It is, sir.' Emily blushed in embarrassment at being singled out. 'I don't know much about the weeding, mind, but I'm learning, and then there's the knitting – I'm a fair hand at that.'

'Good. And are the men respectful to you?'

'Yes, sir. No one's been anything but kind to me. I feel as if I'm part of a family again. I do miss home and my mother, mind, but I'm well looked after by all my friends here.'

Caradoc finished his stew and got to his feet. 'Well, ladies, thank you for the tasty dish, and if you're all settled I'll leave you to have a good night's rest.'

A chorus of 'good nights' followed him as he

left the barn and he smiled; his people were good people and Emily was right: on the drove they became like a close family.

He took his time walking back to the inn. The moon was bright and the stars twinkled against the velvet darkness of the sky. He stood for a moment hearing the cattle shifting in the fields. One of the heifers let out a mournful cry and Caradoc walked over to the fence and peered at the shapes of the animals like shadows in the darkness. He was grateful that the weather was staying fair. Tomorrow he would take the herd across the Wye, and once that hurdle was over he could enjoy the rest of the journey.

As he neared the inn, a figure detached itself from the darkness of the doorway. 'Mr Jones, sir.'

The man's tone was gruff but Caradoc recognized it at once. 'Harold, what are you doing here?'

'I want to join the drove, sir. I don't like being stuck in one place for too long.'

'I thought you had a wife and child to deal with,' Caradoc barked. 'Surely your place is with them?'

Harold beckoned Caradoc away from the inn. 'I'm not asking to be head drover, sir, I know that place is taken, but I am used to the roads and I have a way with the animals. As for my wife and child, perhaps it's time you knew the truth about that.'

'What are you talking about, man? Come on, out with it. Plain speaking or shut your mouth.'

'The marriage, it was a business arrangement. Gwenllyn was already with child when I wed her – she didn't want the baby being branded a bastard. She paid me, sir, I won't hide it: I took the money and gave her my name. The boy is the spit of you. She's called him David.'

At once Caradoc knew, deep in his bones, that the child must be his. His mouth was dry and his voice when he spoke was hoarse. 'The boy – you're saying he's my son?'

'Yes, sir, that's what I'm telling you. Gwennie is a good girl. Only took one man to her bed and that man was you.' He paused and coughed. 'If I could change places with you, sir, I would like a shot.'

Caradoc caught Harold's arm. 'Would you swear that you've never touched Gwenllyn, never went to her bed? You married her – how could she say no to her husband?'

'As I said, it was a bargain marriage and I kept my part of it.'

The truth began to dawn on Caradoc. He had a son, a son he'd never seen. He could hardly believe it. Perhaps he would have many sons, perhaps even now Non was with child, but this baby, born out of his lost days, was so very important to him.

'Thank you for telling me the truth, Harold,' he

said. 'You're hired for as long as you want to work the drove.' He could hardly keep the excitement from his voice. 'I'll catch up with you later. But for now I've got more important business to see to. I've got to meet my son.'

CHAPTER TEN

Jessie climbed out of the trap, patted her pony Polly reassuringly on her arched neck and handed the reins to one of the street boys.

'You look after my horse for me now, Billy – properly, mind. No riding poor Polly when my back's turned or there'll be no more free milk for you ever again.' She smiled; she knew young Billy would guard the horse and trap with all his might. He beamed, honoured to be entrusted with such an important task, and Jessie bent over him. 'And there might even be a penny in it for you, if you keep the other kids from feeding Polly bad apples, right?'

She pushed open the door to Ruby's boarding house and called out cheerily as she made her way through the dimly lit passage to the kitchen. Ruby could usually be found there, making bread and baking cakes; she always said being a landlady meant being chained to the kitchen for ever more. She loved it all really. The lodgers had become like the family she'd never had.

To Jessie's delight, not only was Ruby making a brew but she was entertaining a visitor too.

'Non! There's a nice surprise. Lovely to see you again. And where's Caradoc?'

'I don't know where he is – still on the road, maybe. I've just arrived myself from the mail coach.' She rose and hugged Jessie. '*Duw*, you're getting bigger by the day! That must be a boy you're carrying or maybe even twins!'

In spite of her cheerful greeting Jessie thought Non seemed out of sorts. Her face was pale, her eyes shadowed.

Ruby frowned at Jessie. 'Sit down, will you? We can't have an expectant mother standing around getting varicose veins. Here, put your feet up and have some tea.'

Jessie ran her hands over her belly. 'I don't expect to get varicose veins,' she said; 'in any case, I'm not far gone enough to start fussing about myself. Still working in my servery, I am.' She rested her hand on Non's shoulder. 'And what about you, Non? When are you going to start a family?'

'Soon, I expect.' Non spoke rather stiffly and Jessie cursed herself for being a tactless fool.

'Sorry, love, it's none of my business. In any case, you and Caradoc are still having your second honeymoon, aren't you?'

'I don't know about that,' said Non quietly. 'He doesn't seem to be in a hurry to get back to me these days. I think he cares more about the cattle than he does about me.'

There was an uncomfortable silence which Jessie was unable to fill. She fiddled with her spoon, stirring the milk into her tea, watching it, careful not to meet Non's eyes.

She realized that her visit could have been better planned. It looked as though Non had come to London to talk to Ruby about her problems. Though what problems did she have? She had a fine man for a husband, a rich man at that, she was beautiful enough to eat and with a lovely nature that no one could fault, so what was wrong?

'Have a piece of my plum pudding, Jessie,' Ruby said, 'and, talking about husbands, where's that bleedin' man of yours got to? Albie shouldn't let you roam the streets by yourself. Someone might run off with you, you being a rich business-woman an' all.'

Jessie laughed. 'Who'd want to run off with me? I look like a pig's bladder and I got a way to go yet.' She caught the slight shake of Ruby's head and dropped the subject. 'I think Albie's gone over to the market. He said we needed some fresh meat for our supper.'

'How is Albie? Keeping well, is he?' Non asked. She was making polite conversation but anyone could see her mind was on other things.

'Look, I can't stay long,' Jessie said. 'I'll have this cuppa and then I'd better get back to the house or Albie will be sending out the street boys to find me.'

Non turned to her and took her hand. 'No, Jessie, don't go – you might as well be in on the conversation. I was just telling Ruby how unhappy I am not to have another child yet.' She paused. 'I still miss my darling Rowan. I suppose I'll always miss him.'

Jessie looked closely at Non. Having a baby was not the only thing worrying her: she seemed thinner now and her face was gaunt even when she smiled. 'But you and Caradoc got plenty of time to have children. You're young yet.'

'That's as may be, but why haven't I fallen for a baby, then? Another thing, Caradoc isn't as eager for me in the bedroom as he used to be.'

She fell into a glum silence and Jessie searched her mind for something to say but she couldn't think of any words of comfort. It was Ruby who broke the hush.

'You've got to get used to each other all over again, lovey. Lord above, Non, you've only been back together for a short while.'

'Long enough to catch for a baby,' Non said bleakly. 'I was sure that I'd be expecting by now.' She sighed. 'I've been taking my herbal remedies but the courses came this month as they always do. I don't think I'm meant to have a child, not after losing my Rowan.'

'Look, love,' Ruby said, 'you can be too anxious and you get all riled up waiting for a baby. Just rest easy, enjoy being back with your lovely husband – isn't that enough for now?'

'It might be,' Non said, 'but I know that Caradoc has been to see that awful Gwenllyn Lyons and I can't bear it.'

'She's not Miss Lyons any more, she's married now,' Jessie said. 'At least, that's the gossip going round Smithfield. She's now Mrs Harry Rees. Do you remember Harold, who was the head drover for Caradoc's herd? Well, the gossip is he just left the drove one day and went off on his own.'

Non sat up straight and Jessie saw a sudden look of relief brighten up her face. 'So she's really married some other man, then? Does Caradoc know who she married?'

'I don't know, Non. Some of my customers have men working at Smithfield, tell me all the gossip, they do, but they haven't always got the full story – just the juicy bits.' Jessie smiled. 'I learn a lot in my little servery.'

Jessie could see relief writ plain on Non's face. Were things really so bad between them that she couldn't trust Caradoc to be faithful to her? Jessie hesitated and Non looked at her steadily.

'Come on, what else is there?'

'Well, only that Gwenllyn's got a baby. That

Harold Rees didn't wait long getting her in the family way.'

Non put her head in her hands and Jessie stared at her in alarm. 'You're not going to be sick, are you?'

'No, I'm all right.' Non spoke quietly but it was clear she was under a great strain. 'But I think I'll go back to my lodgings.' She took Ruby's hand. 'I know you'd have me here but I must have time to think things through on my own.'

Jessie glanced at Ruby, who was shaking her head sadly. 'Well, Non, my girl, no jumping to any silly conclusions – not until you know the truth of all this.'

Non met Ruby's eyes. 'I'm not jumping to any conclusions. If Gwenllyn has a child, Caradoc must be the father.'

Jessie put her hand to her mouth. Why hadn't she just shut her mouth instead of blabbing every-thing to Non? Still, she meant well, but then remembered something about the road to hell being paved with good intentions. She put her arm around Non's shoulders.

'Come on, then. You look as if you could do with a little rest. Let's get you to your lodgings. You can kick your shoes off and lie on the bed – you'll soon feel better.'

The street where Non was staying was in a respectable area of London, a little way from Smithfield but near enough to keep an eye on the drovers as they came and went. Jessie reined in her pony and watched as Non stepped down onto the pitted road

'Will you be all right?'

Non managed a smile. 'Of course I will. I'll rest for an hour and then I'll go to get some fresh herbs ready to make up some more medicine. I should probably go to see Carrie – you know, the girl who works in one of my shops? I'll see if she needs any more herbs.' She stood on the pavement, looking to her left and then to her right as if she wasn't sure which way she was going.

'Well, rest for now, there's a good girl,' Jessie said. 'You look fair washed out, you do.'

She watched until her friend went inside the lodging house. Non seemed to have lost all her spirit; even when talking about her precious herbs there was no joy in her face. The door of the lodging house swung shut and then Jessie guided her pony out into the traffic and headed for home.

Outside the cottage, Caradoc stood in the sunlight, letting the memories wash over him – the memories of days of sun, of chopping wood, being close to Gwenllyn, living life out of time, a life that now seemed to have been little more than a dream. A baby started to cry, and the sound was carried on the clear air. It was a pitiful sound and the calm shattered.

He saw that the door was open and he walked

into the hall. It was dim after the brightness outside but it was so familiar to Caradoc that he could have made his way blindfolded to the sitting room, where the sound of crying was coming from.

He pushed open the door and saw her, Gwenllyn, feeding her child, his child. As he looked at her it was as if his bones melted.

'Gwenllyn,' he said softly.

She looked up, colour washing her face. She tried to hide her breast from him but the baby, unsettled, began to cry again.

'What are you doing here?' she said. 'You should be home with your wife.'

'Harold told me about the baby. I had to come.'

'I don't want anything to do with you.' Gwenllyn stared up at him defiantly. 'If you've seen Harry, then you'll know he married me, gave my baby a name.' The accusation hung in the air.

'I couldn't give the baby my name, could I?' Caradoc said. 'If I'd been free I would have married you, you know that.' He sat beside her. 'We always knew I might have a wife and children, didn't we?'

'Well, that doesn't matter now. Harry is my husband and everyone thinks the baby is his, so just go away and leave me in peace.'

Caradoc slipped from the chair and knelt beside her, looking at the baby's small pink face. His lips were rosy; beads of milk dribbled down his small chin. Caradoc felt such a surge of protective love that he was overwhelmed. He bent his head to hide his sudden tears.

'Please don't, Caradoc,' Gwenllyn said softly. 'No good can come out of you being here. What if your wife found out?'

'Non will understand,' Caradoc said, 'and anyway I couldn't hide the truth from her if I wanted to. Harry's probably told everyone in the drove about the boy.' He hesitated. 'What have you called him?'

'David. His name is David and he's my son. Never, ever, believe you'll get him from me.' She caught his chin in her hand and made him look at her. 'Is that what you want, Caradoc? To take my baby away from me?'

'I wouldn't be so cruel.' He took her hand and kissed her soft palm and she leaned against him, her head on his chest, while in between them the baby suckled noisily.

'Promise me I can see him, though,' Caradoc said, 'that I can pay for him to have a good education – the best I can afford.'

'We'll see what David wants, when the time comes,' Gwenllyn said firmly. 'Now, you'd better go.' She moved away from him. 'What about Harry? Is he staying with the drove?'

'He's riding with my herd,' he said, 'and along with my main hand, Josh, he'll see the cattle safely to London.'

'Oh.' She looked at him, her eyes filling with tears. 'He's been wonderful to me. I don't know how I would have managed without Harry. He helped me through the birth . . . Do you know he actually brought David into the world?' She swallowed hard. 'He even showed me how to feed the baby.'

'Have you fallen in love with him?' Caradoc asked. With a feeling of relief, he saw Gwenllyn shake her head.

'No, but I've a great respect for him. He's been nothing but kind to me.'

The baby had finished feeding and Gwenllyn buttoned up her bodice.

'I'll see Harold is rewarded, don't you worry,' he said.

Gwenllyn shook her head. 'He's a proud man. He'll only take what he's entitled to, so I wouldn't go offending him if I were you.'

She wrapped the baby in a shawl and moved towards the crib.

Caradoc intercepted her. 'Please, Gwenllyn, let me hold him, for just a little while.'

Reluctantly Gwenllyn handed him the child and Caradoc felt a warm glow in his chest as the baby's tiny fists waved protestingly.

'He's a handsome boy,' Caradoc said proudly. 'He's got a firm grip and his eyes are so knowing.'

'Perhaps he follows his father, then.' Gwenllyn took the baby from Caradoc's arms and settled him in the crib. 'I suppose I can't stop you from seeing him, from paying towards his education when the time comes, but I want you to know you have no rights to him, no moral rights anyway. Is that agreed?'

He nodded. He knew she was right: it would only be down to her goodwill that he would have any say at all in his son's life.

'Another thing: any love that was between us is gone, dead and buried. You have a wife and I have a husband and we must never forget that.'

Caradoc didn't know if he could keep such a promise. His whole being urged him to reach out and take her in his arms and make love to her in the sunlit bedroom as he'd done so many times before. But now there was a barrier between them and perhaps that could never be breached.

There was a long silence and then Gwenllyn spoke again. Her tone was firm. 'You'd better go. If you want to catch up with the herd, the sooner you make a move, the better.'

She saw him to the door and Caradoc wondered about the new strength she possessed.

'Thank you for allowing me to see David and to hold him. You don't know how precious he is to me.'

'I think I do.' Gwenllyn looked away from him. 'But once your wife has children, things will be different. They will come first in your heart then.'

'I have room in my heart for a dozen children.'

His voice was hoarse. He longed to add that there was also love enough for two women. He knew he was being foolish but he wanted both women: Non, his dear wife, and Gwenllyn, the girl he'd lived with for a summer, who'd borne him a son and who even now was looking beautiful and dignified as she stood in the doorway, waiting for him to go. He hesitated and Gwenllyn stepped back into the hall.

'You'd better go at once. It wouldn't do to keep your wife waiting, would it?' She spoke without spite or emotion and Caradoc nodded. She was right – even now, Non would be waiting for him to return home.

'I have to get to Smithfield first,' he said, 'to see to the sale of the animals.'

'And then?' Gwenllyn asked.

'And then I'll go home to Swansea and tell her all about you and the baby. I can't keep the truth from her. She must hear it from me.'

Gwenllyn sighed. 'You don't know your wife very well, do you?'

'What do you mean?'

'I mean she's already in London.'

Caradoc frowned. 'How do you know?'

'Have you forgotten that men returning from the droves bring all the news? They tell all the gossip to people in the village and gradually it all filters through to me.'

'But you don't mix with the village people.'

Caradoc didn't want to believe what she was telling him.

'I have to go to market, I have to buy food.' She smiled wanly. 'And the villagers seem to have softened towards me now I'm married and have a baby. So, as I said, you'd better make haste to London, and save your marriage.'

She closed the door then and Caradoc stood outside the cottage, looking up at the tall chimneys, wondering how he'd come to make such a grievous mess of his life.

CHAPTER ELEVEN

Harold was glad to get the last leg of the journey to Smithfield over. His boss must still be on his way. Or maybe Caradoc Jones had stayed with Gwennie. The thought hurt him deeply but as he headed the cattle along St John's Road towards the market, he felt a sense of relief that now, with his task completed, he could decide what to do with his life. Perhaps even return to that cottage by the Wye.

The droving no longer appealed to him. Once it was fine to ride the roads to London, but then he'd been a free man. Now he'd had a taste of being part of a family and he liked it.

Harold guided his horse into the market with the herd slowing up behind him, the drovers keeping the beasts under control. Whenever the beasts arrived at Smithfield they instinctively showed reluctance to go into the pens and the drovers had to goad them with a sharp stick, not a practice that Harold was in favour of.

'What a stink!' Josh rode up beside him. He was scowling, his nose wrinkled in distaste. 'I always knew cattle on the trail reeked to high heaven but this smell is enough to kill off any man.'

'You get used to it.' Harold was so accustomed to the smells and sounds of market that he hardly noticed the stink of hide, the filth underfoot or the heavy fog that seemed to hang permanently over the square. His horse slipped in the slime and Harold held the reins more firmly.

'What pens have we been allotted?' Josh asked. 'The place seems full of beasts already.'

'Over there.' Harold pointed with his whip. 'See Mr Jones's name on the wall there?'

'Oh, aye. I didn't notice that.' Josh shrugged. 'But there, you've been acting like head drover, you might as well take all the responsibility.'

He would have turned his horse away but Harold caught the reins. 'I am not head man, but if you take that tone with me again I'll give you a good leathering. Now get the men rallied round and get the beasts penned before someone else's drove takes our place.'

Josh threw him an ugly look but did as he was told. Harold suddenly felt tired. Was this what he strived for all his life – to carry on another man's business for him? And a stinking business it was too. He'd been better off labouring near the river

Wye, going home at the end of the day to a woman who was his wife. It might be in name only but the status of married man appealed to him. When he bathed, Gwenllyn would put out fresh towels for him, and when he was clean and dressed there would be a meal ready for him to eat.

He smiled, remembering his first days as Gwenllyn's husband when she'd vowed she would never wait on him, but, to be fair, once he was a working man she looked after his needs very graciously. All except his needs in the bed-chamber, and he was too wise to think he would ever be offered that honour.

He stood up in the stirrups and looked around for any sign of Caradoc Jones, hoping he'd already arrived in London. He would know then that Gwennie had sent him away with a flea in his ear. In any case, he should be here, attending to the sales himself, not leaving it to his head man. He looked round. There was no sign of Josh.

Harold knew he could take charge of the sale. He had the confidence to stick out for a good price for the beasts. A good bull would bring in seven or maybe eight pounds. The best of the cows would be kept for milk and the fine bull that came with the Jones herd would sell with no trouble. The Welsh Black bulls were good breeding animals, and though smaller than some of the other bulls they were sturdier, with deep chests and broad shoulders.

Harold gestured to one of the men to stay with the herd. 'I'm going to see if I can find Mr Jones,' he said. 'He must be round here somwhere.'

The sounds of the market seemed magnified, penetrating his brain, as he guided his horse between the pens. As usual the beasts were crowded into spaces too small to hold them, but it didn't really matter: some of them would soon be in the charnel-house, being slaughtered ready for sale.

Harold couldn't see Caradoc anywhere. He patrolled the perimeter of the market one last time and then tied his horse to one of the Jones pens. Josh was there, looking tired and cold. 'I'm going across to the King's Arms to see if Mr Jones is there.'

'What if he isn't?' Josh seemed determined to be unhelpful. 'I can't deal with the bidding and all that nonsense.'

'I'll be back, and if needs be I'll do the selling myself.'

The doors of the inn were open wide and the big taproom was crowded with men in good clothes, mostly the herd owners. There were a few head men but none of them was dressed in shabby trews and patched jacket as he was. The atmosphere was heavy with pipe smoke, rivalling the fog outside. Several men turned to look at him but Harold folded his arms across his chest.

'I'm dealing in the Jones cattle sales,' he said

loudly. 'In the absence of Caradoc Jones, I'll be doing the selling.'

The effect of his words was immediate: he was drawn into the crowd of men, someone handed him a tankard of foaming beer and one fellow patted him on the back. 'Anyone who works for the Jones herd is welcome in here.'

Once, Harold might have been pleased and flattered by the words but not now. At this moment all he wanted to do was get on his horse and ride back to Gwenllyn as quickly as he could. He'd been silly to leave – they'd just had a small quarrel, nothing really, and he'd walked out like the fool he was.

He sighed. He'd been even more of a fool telling Caradoc Jones about Gwennie's baby. Why hadn't he kept his trap shut? He drank his beer and stared through the smoke at the businessmen, who laughed and bragged about the deals they'd made or were going to make: happy, enthusiastic talk, but then they were getting something out of the cattle droves. All he was getting was a load of responsibilities and a sore arse.

In that moment, ambition was born in Harold. What was wrong with buying his own stock and taking them to market – local markets at first, and then perhaps a drove to Smithfield, where he would find himself with a bagful of money all of his own? His skills at reading were fair now, thanks to Gwenllyn, and he'd always been able to work out figures, so what was he waiting for?

He put down his tankard and without bothering to say goodnight he left the inn, his head buzzing with ideas. He would be paid once Caradoc deigned to come to London, and in the meantime he would try and push up the prices of the stock. The higher the prices, the more bonus he could expect from the boss.

And then he could go to Gwennie as an equal; he would be a businessman, a man of honour.

Caradoc was still at the inn. He was impatient to be back on the road, but he'd caught some sort of fever and the last few days had been hell. If only Non were with him, she'd soothe him with her herbal mixtures. At the thought of his wife, he closed his eyes in pain. How could he do this to her? How could he betray her by going to see Gwenllyn?

The serving maid tapped on the door and came into the room with a bowl of water for him to wash with. 'Feeling better, sir?' she asked. 'You look better, that's for sure. *Duw*, you should have had the doctor to call. You had a real bad fever and I don't mind telling you I thought you was a goner when you started to talk a lot of silly nonsense.'

'What sort of nonsense?' Caradoc asked cautiously.

The girl waved her hand in a vague gesture. 'I

dunno. Bits about a babba and then you was calling for your wife and . . .' she hesitated, 'and another lady, sir.'

'What lady?'

'Gwenllyn Lyons, sir, but she's married, mind: Mrs Rees, she is called now. Though they do say her husband has gone and left her. Poor girl and her only lately had the little boy.' She looked up at him from under her lashes. 'Will I bring you a bit of breakfast, sir?'

'That's a very good idea,' Caradoc said, wondering how much she had really heard, 'and don't take too much notice of what I said in a fever. It was probably just nonsense.'

'Yes, sir, righto, sir.'

When she left the room Caradoc stood naked at the table and washed the sweat from his body. He felt better but was he well enough to ride up to the cottage and talk to Gwenllyn again? But he couldn't do that: he'd be risking her health and that of the baby's too.

He enjoyed his breakfast and when he'd finished eating he began to dress. He wondered how Harold was getting on. He would have the drove in Smithfield by now. He could trust the man to do his job even if he now hated the guts of him, hated the thought of him living with Gwenllyn, seeing the boy, holding him. But what right did he have to complain? He'd left Gwenllyn and gone back to his wife; he should be with his wife now, patching up his marriage. The thought came as a shock. Did he really think of his marriage in terms of 'patching it up'?

He pushed the tray aside, took up a pen and began to scratch out a letter to Non explaining that he had fallen ill of a fever and had stopped at the inn to recuperate. But it was all an excuse and Non would see through his lies right away. He crumpled the letter into a ball and dropped it onto the floor.

'I don't know what we want to take on another girl for anyway.' Jessie heard the peevish note in her voice as they walked along the narrow lane leading to the house off Cutler Street, but somehow she felt peevish. 'Emily is too young. She knows nothing at all about the business. She can't even milk a cow properly.' Josh's sister had decided to stay in London for a time, after finishing her first drove.

Albie punched her cheek. 'You can show her how, love; you'll need to rest. You're having a baby, remember?'

He was right: the job was hard and the standing about in the servery was getting too much for her. But Emily was too pretty by far.

'Why did Ruby send the girl to us?' Jessie opened the door and slumped into the nearest chair. 'We're not a charity, mind.'

'Aren't we, Jess? Then, how come we give milk

away to the poor people in Cutler Street? Anyway, when Emily went to Ruby, looking for lodgings, Ruby had no vacant rooms so she thought of us.'

'I suppose Ruby thought she was doing us a favour.'

'Well, Jess, you've been talking about getting help for a few weeks now. Look at you, you're exhausted. You shouldn't be cleaning out pails, not when your belly's growing by the day.'

Jessie stared at him. Her hands were bunched into fists as she planted them firmly on her hips. 'So you're saying I'm fat and ugly now, is that it?'

'Don't be silly, Jess. I love you whatever you look like, you know that.'

'Oh, so you don't think I'm fat and ugly?'

He put his arms around her. 'I love you, my dear wife, so there's no need to be jealous of poor little Emily – she's just a child.'

'I'm not jealous and Emily's not a child, she's a young woman, and I'm not sure I want her working here, especially when I have the baby and you're alone in the servery with her. What would folk say?'

'You're not in Wales now, Jess. You're living in London, it's a big bugger of a place, and no one's interested in what we're doing. So long as the local people get their milk they don't mind who does the work.'

'But we're respected round here, Albie. I don't want any loose talk about us.'

'You're not getting too big for your boots, are you, Jessie?'

Jessie heard his tone, heard the way he said her name, and she felt ashamed. 'I'm sorry, love, but I suppose I am jealous, just a little bit.'

'Well, there's no need. Why would I look at any other girl when I've got my lovely Jess by my side?'

Jessie felt ashamed. She'd needed help when she first came to London and she'd found willing friends like Ruby who'd given her a roof over her head and then Albie had come along and, well, he was hers now, her husband, and why should he be unfaithful to her? He'd never even looked at another woman.

'All right, we'll give little Emily her chance.' She rested her hand on Albie's arm. 'And I do trust you and I love you. Come on, give your missis a kiss.'

Albie knelt beside her, put his arms around her and gently kissed her mouth. 'I love you, my Jess, and I'd never do anything to hurt you.'

'Well, I'm not daft, I know that.' She changed the subject. 'Tell you what, why don't you go and fetch us a pint of ale, treat ourselves for a change?'

'Like the old days.' Albie's voice held a smile. 'But then again, what old days? We're still young lovers and of course I'll buy you a pint – anything to keep my sweet wife happy.'

It was quiet once Albie had gone. There was still the low drone of voices from the street outside but the day's business was almost over. The customers who frequented Cutler Street looking for good, second-hand clothes would be heading for home – those folk who had homes.

Jessie got slowly to her feet and walked over to the window. The panes were covered in grime; no matter how hard she worked cleaning them, the fog and the dirt seemed to mingle and cling to her windows.

Was the idea of having Emily working for her such a bad one? Jessie trusted Albie with her life; as he said, he would never do anything to hurt her. And yet, at the back of her mind, there was a little voice telling her that she would rue the day when she agreed to take the young girl into the business.

CHAPTER TWELVE

Non was in the little shop near Cutler Street. She was busy making an infusion of mint leaves and she pressed the pestle into the mortar, grinding the herbs with rather more force than was necessary. Her hands were busy but her mind was not on her work. Instead she thought of her husband.

She'd met Morgan the blacksmith at Ruby's lodging house. He told her Caradoc had left the drove at Wye and her heart ached at the news. Harold Rees was staying at the lodging house too and he barely nodded to her when they happened to meet. Judging by the closed look on his face, Harold clearly knew that his marriage was in sore jeopardy. Didn't Caradoc realize that people were being hurt by his actions?

Carrie came into the room in the discreet way she had, her feet making little sound on the stone floor. 'You shouldn't be working so hard, Mrs Jones.' Carrie spoke softly. Even when she was rolling dried herbs she hardly seemed to make a sound.

Non paused. Looking into the mortar she saw that her herbs had turned to pulp. 'I suppose you're right. I am tired and I could do with a little time off.' She untied her apron and folded it as carefully as if it was precious silk, not a piece of well-washed sacking.

'Are you troubled, Mrs Jones?' Carrie asked. 'You've seemed out of sorts for a few days now.'

Non sank into a chair and stared at her hands. Her fingers were stained green from the herbs but she hardly noticed. 'I'm waiting for news of my husband,' she said. 'He should have reached London by now; he should be selling the stock at market, not leaving things to his men.'

'He might be riding up to Smithfield right now,' Carrie said. 'If his drove has reached the market, then I'm sure he wouldn't be far behind.'

Carrie spoke reasonably but she didn't know Caradoc, didn't know he had another woman tucked away in the Welsh hills that ranged above the broad river Wye.

Suddenly Non's mind was made up: she'd go to Smithfield, find out if Carrie was right. Perhaps Caradoc had reached the market by now. 'I'll leave you to carry on.' She glanced ruefully at the pulped herbs in the mortar. 'You'd better throw those out and start again, Carrie.'

Carrie nodded. 'The pony and trap is around the back. I've nearly finished the deliveries and those that are left can wait until morning.' She looked into the mortar. 'It isn't often you make mistakes, which is why all your customers trust you. I wish I could be like you.'

Non put her hand on Carrie's arm. 'Thank you, Carrie. You're a good girl and I'm sure you'll make a name for yourself with or without my help.'

Carrie gave her a strange look but said nothing.

Non stepped outside into the narrow cobbled lane and made her way to the small stable at the back of the shop. The pony lifted his head, his soft mouth touching her hand, searching for treats. Non fondled the pony's ears. 'Sorry, girl: no apples or carrots today.'

She climbed into the trap and carefully guided the pony around the side of the shop and onto the roadway. Her heart lifted. Perhaps even now Caradoc was there at Smithfield, in charge, just getting business sorted out before he came to find her. It was a slender hope but right now hope was all she had.

Harold faced the crowd of men who were gathered around the pens holding the Welsh Black cattle. These men were shrewd but he could handle them – he would bloody well have to.

'Who is going to start the bidding?' He hoped his voice carried to the edges of the crowd. 'Come on now, don't be shy. There's some fine Welsh beef for sale here – good for breeding and good for eating. See this sturdy black bull? He'll sire plenty of calves, mark my words. Take a heifer as well, do the job properly, and you'll have a herd of good beasts before you know it.'

One of the men in the crowd moved forward for a closer inspection and Harold, encouraged, spoke again. 'A good investment, this randy bull is, so who will open the bidding at six pounds?'

No one spoke. 'Well, say, five pounds to start me off.'

One of the men raised his crop and Harold nodded. 'There's five. Who will give me six pounds? See the chest and shoulders of this fine beast.' He felt his heart sink as no one spoke. 'I could take the animal back to Wales and get more than five pounds for it any day of the week. Good stock, this is. He's already sired more calves than I can remember.'

'I'll give you six pounds,' one of the men called from the centre of the crowd, and all at once the bidding became brisk.

Harold's heart swelled with pride. He was going to do as well as Mr Jones at selling the animals, perhaps even better. He'd show Caradoc Jones that he was just as good a man as him any day of the week.

By the end of the afternoon Harold was tired and his voice had grown hoarse, but he had cleared the pens of all the animals. He was staying for a night or two at Ruby's boarding house, but once Mr Jones arrived on the scene he'd go home to the cottage on the hills above the river Wye.

He had a fierce longing to see Gwenllyn and hear her soft voice. He missed the care she took of him even though he was a bought-and-paid-for husband – he missed everything about her. He realized Caradoc Jones was doing his best to get into Gwennie's good books, but he guessed she would send him away.

All he wanted was to be home, back in Wales. Not selling stock to make another man rich, but to work on his own. She would be proud of him then; perhaps in time she might even develop a fondness for him. That was Harold's dearest wish.

Gwenllyn stared out of the window, remembering when she'd last seen Caradoc. When he'd come to the cottage he'd been so humble, almost begging her to let him hold the baby, and she'd been cold, distant, unwilling to let him break her heart again.

And yet the ache was there inside her. She knew he would never be hers: he had a wife, who would bear him more children one day, and then Caradoc would forget all about David. But somehow she didn't truly believe that. Caradoc was no philanderer; he was a good man and he wanted to love his son, to care for him. But he didn't belong with her: he should be with his wife. She was blameless and even now Gwenllyn knew that Non's heart was probably breaking.

And yet Gwenllyn longed to have his arms around her again, longed to kiss him, to make love to him. He'd awoken her to womanhood and there was no forgetting that. She felt desire keenly, felt the sweet weight of him, felt again the passion, remembering how his body had possessed hers.

She turned away from the window, impatient with herself. She must forget Caradoc, try to make a new life for herself. She was married now and though she didn't love Harry she owed him her loyalty.

Later in the afternoon, she wrapped the baby in a shawl in the Welsh fashion, winding the shawl around the baby to pinion him to her, and tucked the end of the material under the tiny body. She needed to go out to distract herself from her thoughts.

It was a warm day and the market in the village was crowded with shoppers. Gwenllyn bought some honey and a loaf of freshly baked bread and put them in her basket; she had no great appetite these days but she must keep up her strength to have milk for her baby.

''Afternoon to you, miss.' One of the stall-holders leaned across her barrow. 'Can I tempt you with a nice piece of fish? Fresh caught this morning, mind.'

Gwenllyn shook her head. She had never been able to face gutting a fish. The very act of slipping a knife into the soft belly of the fish turned her stomach.

'No, thank you, Mrs Berry,' she said. 'Not today but maybe I'll have some at the weekend.' By then perhaps Harry would be back. Gwenllyn harboured a secret hope that, as before, he would return once he had thought matters over. And if he did return he would be in charge of all the unpleasant tasks, such as killing a chicken or gutting a fish.

'How's the babba? Doing well, is he?' She didn't wait for a reply. 'You've been having visitors, I see, and is your husband back yet from his travels?'

Gwenllyn knew what was behind the question. The woman was a notorious gossip. She must have seen Caradoc riding towards her cottage.

'Harry's up in London with the drove,' she said defensively. 'He's working for Mr Caradoc Jones, you know.'

'Aye. I thought I saw Mr Jones the other day. Here on business, was he?' Mrs Berry folded her arms across her ample bosom.

'That's right.' Gwenllyn quickly moved away. She didn't want to offend any of the villagers but she didn't want to answer any more awkward questions.

As she stopped at the flower stall she saw an array of herbs and turned away quickly. That's what Caradoc's wife did: she made medicine out of herbs. She had a great reputation and was a successful businesswoman. How could Gwenllyn even begin to match up to the famous Mrs Jones?

Suddenly the day was ruined for her. She had tried so hard to keep thoughts of Caradoc at bay, to lock away her grief at losing him deep in her heart while she got on with the mundane tasks of everyday life. But not now, not when she'd seen him so recently, been close enough to touch him. And, what with Mrs Berry reminding her of his visit, she was near to tears.

Gwenllyn turned towards home. She needed to be indoors where everything was familiar to her, where Caradoc had been close to her. It was the only place she could feel him near. And suddenly the tears began to flow as she walked blindly up the hill towards the cottage.

It had unsettled him, seeing Gwenllyn again, and Caradoc remembered her in his arms, smiling up at him, her eyes full of love. Now she was subdued, no longer the innocent young girl she'd been when he first saw her. Guilt was like a heavy weight inside him as he rode the trail that led him towards London and his wife.

Non must be aware of his reasons for handing

over the drove to Harold; she must have known when he didn't ride into Smithfield with the cattle that he was seeing Gwenllyn.

He felt torn in two. When he'd set eyes on Gwenllyn, seen her with his son in her arms, he'd wanted to hold her, reassure her, tell her he would always be there for her. And yet the thought of Non haunted him. What was wrong with him? How could a man be in love with two women at the same time?

The trail ahead of him was deserted. The only sound was the beat of his horse's hoofs against the hard ground, echoed by the pounding of questions in his head. In a few days' time he would be with his wife again. How could he look into her trusting eyes, knowing that part of him wanted to be with another woman?

He spent that night under the stars. The nearest inn was still miles away and as he lay looking up into the velvet of a summer sky he thought of the first time he'd lain with Non. Like Gwenllyn she'd been young, innocent; she had given herself to him trustingly, and by going to see Gwenllyn he'd betrayed her.

Non had tried to understand why he'd lived with Gwenllyn. She accepted he'd temporarily lost all knowledge of his past and she had taken him back believing in him, knowing that he wanted to be with her. But how could he explain the days he'd remained near the river Wye longing to see Gwenllyn again and yet dreading it at the same time?

He heard the rustle of an animal in the under-growth and turned impatiently, unable to sleep. At last, he packed up his belongings, saddled his horse and as dawn washed the countryside with colour he continued on his way towards London.

Non knew as soon as her husband stepped into the shop; she knew he had a guilty secret. Did he believe he could keep it from her? She had not found him at Smithfield. Instead she'd seen Harold selling the beasts and her heart ached. Caradoc's visit to Gwenllyn had not been a brief one.

Caradoc embraced her and she clung to him for a moment, with one last prayer that she was wrong. But, leaning away from him, and looking into his eyes, she knew she had guessed the truth.

'You've seen her, haven't you?'

He released her and turned to look out of the window of the small shop. 'Yes. I won't lie to you, Non.'

Non put her hand over her mouth. She wanted to scream, to slap his face, to hurt him as he was hurting her. But she stood quite still, waiting for the pain of jealousy to subside.

'She's got a son,' he said, still looking away from her: 'my son.'

'I know,' Non said. 'I've spoken to Harold; he

told me all about it. She's married now, though, isn't she? She's Harold's wife.'

'In name only,' he said quickly, and Non felt a rush of pain at his swift interjection.

'Does that make her any less married? And you too are married, or have you forgotten that small point?'

He turned then to take her in his arms again, but she pushed him away.

'Tell me the truth, Caradoc. Did you sleep with her?'

'No!' He sounded angry.

She looked at him, trying to read his expression, and after a moment she gave a sigh of relief, knowing he was telling her the truth.

'But you wanted to, didn't you?'

He hung his head and she knew he couldn't bring himself to lie to her.

She sank down into a chair, pressing her hands together to stop them trembling. 'You saw the baby?'

'Yes,' he said softly. 'But, Non, we'll have babies too. We're both young – we can have a nurseryful of children.'

'But there will always be another woman's son in this world,' Non said heavily. 'You'll always feel guilty and resentful about another man bringing up your child. Won't you?' Her voice had an edge to it.

He shrugged. 'I don't know how to answer that, Non.'

She watched as he rubbed at his eyes; he was distressed, she could see it in every line of his face. He hated hurting her, she knew that, and yet she had to keep asking questions.

'What's his name?'

'David.' The word was dragged from him.

'And did you hold him?'

'Yes.'

'And did you promise *her* that you would provide for him?'

He shook his head. 'Please, Non, no more. My head is full of questions for which there seem to be no answers. How can I explain my thoughts to you when I can't even explain them to myself?'

'So you still have feelings for her.' It was a flat statement. He refused to look at her. Still she probed. 'Tell me, Caradoc, do you love her?'

'I don't know.' He moved towards the door. 'I'm going to the lodging house. I'll wash away the stink of horse and then I'll speak to Harold, find out if he's managed to sell all the beasts. I'll talk to you later.'

She let him go without another word being spoken. She already had her answer. Caradoc did love Gwenllyn – not perhaps in the way he loved her, but there were feelings he couldn't hide.

Non packed away the goods from the counter and took off her apron. Thank goodness Carrie had left early to deliver medicines to some of the customers. She didn't have to put on a brave face in front of her.

Non brushed the floor and sprinkled sawdust over the boards, trying to keep her mind from thinking about Caradoc and Gwenllyn and the child they shared together. It hurt so much, the pain was almost physical, and yet she couldn't cry.

At last, she closed the shop and stepped out into the dying light. There was nothing for it now but to go back to Ruby's and face Caradoc and see the guilt in his eyes. The thought was like a dagger piercing her soul.

CHAPTER THIRTEEN

Harold looked down at the ragged urchin who'd brought him a message from Caradoc Jones.

'That rich man, that Mr Jones, 'e says you're to meet him in the taproom of the Butcher's Arms, sir.' The boy stuck out a grimy hand and Harold put a few pennies into it.

'Did he say when?'

The boy shrugged and darted away into the crowd, disappearing into one of the narrow streets.

Harold crossed the almost empty market, holding his breath against the stink of cow dung and dead meat that permeated the place.

The Butcher's Arms was full of cattle men, drovers, farmers and a handful of butchers. Harold saw Caradoc Jones at once. The man was unmistakable. He was tall, for a start, and his bright hair shone in the pale streak of sunshine that managed to penetrate the grimy windows.

Harold pushed his way through the crowd. 'Mr Jones, sir, I've brought the money from the sale.' He resisted the urge to catch Jones by his shirt collar and punch him on the nose. He slipped his arm into the deep pocket of his jacket, but Caradoc stopped him.

'Not here.' Caradoc caught his wrists and guided him to a corner where it was more private. 'You never know who could be looking on and I don't fancy having a beating and being robbed as soon as I step foot outside this place.'

Harold slid the bag under the table and Caradoc took it, then deftly put it away in his own pocket.

'I haven't taken my wages out, Mr Jones,' Harold began hesitantly. 'I wondered if we could come to an agreement on a bargain.'

'What sort of bargain?'

Caradoc's tone was cold; his resentment of Harold was plain to see. Harold could understand it – Caradoc wanted Gwenllyn – but it was he who was married to her. The thought gave him a small glimmer of comfort.

'I want to start a herd of my own,' he said. 'Gwenllyn's place has a lot of land going waste and I could put it to good use.'

'So?' Caradoc said coldly. 'What's that got to do with me?' Caradoc was so jealous of Harold that he now viewed him as a bitter enemy.

Harold realized there was only one way Jones could be made to give him what he wanted and that was to play on his conscience. 'It's like this, sir,' Harold said boldly. 'You know I've got a family to support and I don't want to be on the road all the time, leaving my wife and child alone.'

'David is not your child.' Caradoc's eyes sparked fire.

'I know that only too well,' Harold said in a harsh voice, 'but I want to do my bit to bring up the boy in a way Gwenllyn would be proud of.'

Caradoc slumped back in his seat. 'All right, I get your point. Well, you'll need a couple of heifers and perhaps a milking cow. Once we get back to Wales, I'll see what I can do.'

'I want a good breeding bull too,' Harold said. 'Heifers are no good without a fine breeding bull to serve them.'

Caradoc nodded. 'All right. In the meantime, there's the matter of your wages.' He held up his hand as Harold attempted to speak. 'It's not a favour, it's only what's fair. You did a good job of leading the drove and of selling the beasts, and for what it's worth I think you'll make a fine owner. I suppose I ought to wish you luck.'

'Thank you, sir.' Harold sat back a little as Caradoc leaned across the table towards him.

Caradoc seemed to be struggling to find the right words. 'Have you and Gwenllyn resolved your differences?'

'I don't know what you mean, sir.'

'I'll put it more plainly then. Do you intend to start a family with Gwenllyn at any time in the future?'

Harold knew what the boss was really asking. 'It's early days yet, but once I'm set up, earning a good living for us, I think maybe we'll make a go of our marriage in spite of everything.'

'So she hasn't let you into her bed yet?'

Harold frowned. 'I don't think that's anything to do with you, Mr Jones. For better or worse, Gwenllyn is my wife now and whether I'm allowed my husbandly right is a matter we have to settle between us.'

'You're right, of course.' Caradoc slipped some money under the table.

As Harold's hand clasped the bag he felt a surge of triumph. 'Thank you, Mr Jones.'

Caradoc rose to his feet. He seemed more relaxed and for a moment his hand rested on Harold's shoulder. 'You are a good man, Harold, an honest man. You'll look after them well, won't you?'

Harold felt a lump in his throat. Mr Caradoc Jones had swallowed his pride enough to speak gently.

'I'll look after them, don't you fret. They are my family now, all I've got or will ever want.' He could see his words pained Caradoc but the man had to realize he was not welcome to intrude any further into Harold's private life.

He watched as Caradoc made his way through the crowd, flung wide the door and vanished into the night. He suddenly felt sorry for the boss, though he dismissed the feelings at once. Caradoc Jones was rich and he had a fine wife, a woman who had proved her worth. He'd had Gwenllyn too for a short while; he'd had more luck than any man could expect.

As Harold left the taproom and stepped out into the night, he looked up at the sky. The fog lay heavily over the houses and he could see no stars. Well, tomorrow he would be on his way home to where the stars shone brightly and Gwenllyn, his wife, was the brightest star of all.

Gwenllyn put the baby down for his afternoon sleep and buttoned up her bodice. Her face softened as she looked down at her sleeping son: he was so perfect, so wonderful.

She heard the sound of horse hoofs on the road outside and her heartbeat quickened. She hurried to the door and swung it wide, but the smile of welcome died on her lips as she saw not Caradoc but Harold reining in his horse and slipping from the saddle.

'I'm home, Gwenllyn, where I belong,' he said. 'I'll take the horse to the stable and then I'll wash myself down. If you'll be so good as to put the hot water ready, I'd be obliged.'

Gwenllyn nodded. He smelled of horse and cattle and she felt, in spite of everything, it was her duty to look after him. 'I'll put the big pot over the fire right away. Leave your clothes by the tub. I'll wash them later.'

'No need,' Harold said. 'I'll wash them myself. I'm used to doing my own chores.'

He looked at her and wanted to touch her. She smelled of baby milk; her bodice was partly un-buttoned, and it was damp where the milk had flowed. Desire flared in him. He wanted her so badly, wanted to strip her of her clothes to love her and kiss her and make her his wife in more than name. She must have read some of his thoughts in his eyes because she turned abruptly and went indoors.

Later, when they were seated at the long table in the dining room, Harold, feeling properly clean for the first time in weeks, told her of his plans for building up a herd of his own.

'As part of my wages I'm getting a pair of heifers and a breeding bull.' He heard the pride in his own voice and saw Gwenllyn smile for the first time since he'd arrived home.

'I've made a bargain with Mr Jones for the beasts and he agreed because of you, I don't fool myself about that.'

'It's good to have plans but you needn't feel you have to work. I've enough money, more than enough, to keep us all in comfort.'

'I want to be my own man,' Harold said. 'I don't want to be the sort who lives on his wife's money. No, I'll build up a good herd and then I'll be a drover myself.'

'So you'll be on the road a great deal then?'

Was that relief he heard in her voice? 'At first I will; later, I'll employ a head man and he can do the travelling for me.' He sighed. 'All this is going to take a long time, maybe even a few years, but one day I'll be as good as Caradoc Jones and then perhaps you'll think more of me.'

Gwenllyn got up from the table and began to clear the dishes away. 'By the way,' she said, changing the subject abruptly, 'I've hired two girls – one to work in the kitchen and one to see to our meals. They'll start at the beginning of next week.'

Somehow the idea didn't please Harold. He'd grown used to them being alone, Gwenllyn, the baby and him.

'I thought the villagers didn't get on with you.'

'They're not so bad now I'm married.' She looked away from him. 'They think David is your child, and I'm glad. It's easier to let them think that. Do you mind?'

''Course I don't mind.' He straightened in his chair. 'Perhaps one day we'll have children of our own, Gwenllyn.'

'Harry, don't forget this is a bargain, nothing more.'

'So I'm to live like a monk for the rest of my life,

is that it?' Her words had hurt him and his tone was sharp.

'You can take your fill of girls from the village. Some of them are only too happy to accommodate a man – for a price.'

Harold stood up and pushed back his chair. 'That's not what I want, Gwenllyn.' His voice rose. 'I want a wife, a woman I can respect and love. Is that too much to ask?'

She faced him then, her eyes fixed on his. 'I paid you for your name, Harold, nothing more. You can count yourself lucky that I allow you to live here with me as though we are a proper married couple.'

He sighed, feeling suddenly weary. 'I suppose you only let me stay here to keep the gossips quiet.' He moved to the door. 'I'm going to bed. We'll talk more in the morning.' As he left the room, he could hear Gwenllyn's sigh of relief. Did she find it so difficult even being in the same room as him? Well, perhaps by morning his brain would be clear and he could talk to Gwenllyn again, put over his position more tactfully. He hoped then she would see things his way but somehow he doubted it.

Gwenllyn couldn't sleep. She hated to hurt Harold but he couldn't be allowed to think she would ever love him. Her heart still ached for Caradoc. The baby sleeping in the crib beside her stirred in his sleep and she leaned over to look at her son. The moonlight was shining through the window, catching the bright colour of the baby's hair, turning it to a halo of soft gold. She sighed. What was to become of her? She couldn't have the man she loved – he wanted her, but wanting was no good without honour. Harold's words came back to her: he didn't want to live his life as a monk; and did she want to live out the rest of her life like an old maid?

Perhaps she could make the best of it with Harold. She would never love him but she could come to care for him. He had proved himself loyal, he'd looked after her when she had the baby and it was good to have a man about the house, she couldn't deny that.

She lay back and closed her eyes, feeling the ache of desire. She was young and healthy, she'd known Caradoc's love, known his lust and loved him for it. She tried to think kindly about Harold. He was tall, good-looking in a dark, swarthy way. Why couldn't she lie with him, make their marriage real and perhaps even have more children? If she didn't she would never have another child and David would never know the love and security of family life.

At last she fell asleep, but her dreams were filled with restless thoughts and when she woke in the morning she felt too weary to get out of bed. The baby cried and Gwenllyn tried to get up. As soon as she was on her feet her knees buckled and she slumped to the floor. She didn't know how long she lay there but in a daze she heard Harold come into the room, lift her up and put her back in the bed.

Hazily, she looked at him through eyes that felt as though a lace curtain covered them. 'David . . . I must feed him,' she mumbled. 'Help me, Harry.'

'You're not well – you must have a fever. I'll get somebody.'

'No. Put the baby to my breast. I'll have to feed him.'

She was aware that Harold was opening the bodice of her nightgown and then she felt her baby's soft mouth close around her nipple. She tried to hold him but her arms were without strength and it was Harold who held the baby in place, crouching beside the bed, waiting patiently until David was content. Then he put him back into the crib.

'I'll wash you in cold water,' he said. 'It'll help bring the fever down.'

He gently took off her nightgown and she was too weary to protest. She shivered as she felt the coldness of the water against her burning skin, but soon she was dried and dressed in a fresh clean nightgown.

'I'll take the baby to the kitchen, where I can keep an eye on him.' He looked back into the room. 'I'll leave the door open and I'll be back to see you in a little while. Just try to sleep now.'

Sleep: the thought was a welcome one and, feeling clean, and comfortable in the knowledge she wasn't alone, she closed her eyes.

'I'm sorry, Non,' Caradoc said. She didn't look up when he spoke; instead she busied herself packing the bags for the journey home. 'I love you, you're my wife, but . . .'

'But what, Caradoc?' She still didn't look at him. She was afraid of what she might read in his eyes.

He shrugged. 'I just feel a sense of responsibility, that's all.'

'She has a husband to take care of her now. Good heavens, how many times do I have to say that?' She was fighting the anger and tears that threatened to overwhelm her.

He sighed heavily. 'I'm sorry.'

'Why did you have to go to see her?' She'd asked him the same question time after time and there never was an answer that reassured her. 'I know, Caradoc,' she held up her hand, 'you went to see your son. Are you trying to make me feel guilty because our first son died and I haven't conceived another child?' She changed her tone and spoke more softly. 'We've only been back together for a little while. We're getting to know each other all over again. We'll have children of our own soon enough, you'll see.'

That night they fell asleep in the same bed but to Non it felt as though they were miles apart. In the morning they caught the mail coach and she sighed with relief. Everything would be all right once they were home again.

The coach had stopped at the little inn beside the river Wye. Non couldn't help looking up at the house perched far above the village, the place where the other woman in Caradoc's life lived.

'Step down, if you please,' the driver called. 'We'll be changing horses here and you might as well stretch your legs.'

Non was impatient to be away from the place. She could see Caradoc's eyes straying to the hill and she wanted to hit him. She seated herself on the wooden bench outside the inn, praying that the delay wouldn't be a long one.

'Mrs Jones, Mrs Jones!' A voice called and Non turned to see Harold running down the path from the hill. He stopped beside her. 'Oh, Mrs Jones, thank the Lord you're here. It's my wife – she's been laid low with a fever these past few days. Nothing I do seems to help her.'

Non looked up at him. Surely he didn't expect her to help?

He stood before her, his face red from running. 'Please, Mrs Jones, if you would only give Gwenllyn some of your medicine, I know she'd get better.'

Non turned to Caradoc.

He met her gaze and nodded. 'We can catch the next mail coach instead,' he said.

'But that won't be here for a few days yet. We have to get home.' Her voice rose. 'Surely, Caradoc, you can't expect me to nurse the woman you were unfaithful with?'

'She's in need,' Caradoc said. 'If you can't think of her, think of the baby.' He touched her shoulder. 'You've too much compassion to ignore a cry for help.'

He was right: how could she walk away from a sick woman? Her job was healing people; she must do her best to help Gwenllyn, whatever her personal feelings.

'Get my bag from the coach,' she said briskly and Caradoc nodded. The driver argued with him at the top of his voice but Caradoc ignored him and took the bags from the rack.

'I'm obliged to you, Mrs Jones,' Harold said. 'Come this way. The going is easier if you follow the path.'

By the time she reached the cottage Non was breathless. She looked back into the valley and saw the silver snake of the river winding away between the folds of hills. She paused for a moment to gather her wits and then she took a deep breath and stepped inside the cottage.

Gwenllyn was very sick, Non could see that at once. 'I'll need the angelica elixir,' she said as

Harold put her bag on the table. He looked at her, his eyes beseeching her to help, and she felt the icy knot of pain and anger fade away. Gwenllyn was just a woman who needed help.

'Your wife will get better, Harold,' she said fiercely. 'She'll get better even if I have to nurse her night and day.' And somehow Non knew she would do her utmost to help the woman who had stolen her husband's heart.

CHAPTER FOURTEEN

Jessie was impatient with herself: she was so slow and awkward these days. Her feet were swollen and her back ached every time she leaned over to clean the milk pails. The worst of it was that Albie hardly seemed to notice. Jessie straightened up and rubbed at her aching back, glad that the cleaning of the pails was nearly done.

'Let me finish that for you, Jessie.' The girl Albie had taken on was young and not used to the milk trade, but she was willing and she'd proved to be a hard worker, ready to tackle any job, however menial.

'Is your brother coming to see you tonight, Emily?' Jessie sat on one of the milking stools and eased her wet shoes off her feet with a sigh of relief.

'Josh thought he'd like to work in London but he's changed his mind. He's going to travel back with Morgan the blacksmith. He'll be leaving for Wales tomorrow.' She smiled and her teeth were small and dimples appeared in her cheeks: she really was going to be a beauty when she grew up.

Jessie sighed. She'd been quite pretty herself before she'd fallen for the baby. Now she was fat and ungainly like the cows she milked.

'Josh likes the open road too much to stay in one place for too long,' Emily said, 'and he's happy to see me settled in a good job. He knows I'm safe here with you and Albie.'

'So you'll be on your own in London, then. It's a hard life for a young girl – are you sure you're up to it?'

'I'll be all right,' Emily said. 'To be sure, I'm fine now that Albie has asked me to live in with the two of you. If it suits you, I'll be over tonight with my things.'

The news was a surprise to Jessie. She felt piqued; it would have been nice if Albie had consulted her before making such a decision. She looked at Emily with new interest. The girl was slim and young; her skin was pale and her hair, escaping now from under her linen cap, was thick and dark. 'Did he now?' Jessie's tone was sharper than she'd intended.

'Is something wrong, Jessie?' Emily looked concerned. Her beautiful, bright blue eyes, which were fringed with heavy dark lashes, became huge.

Did Albie see her beauty too? Jessie took a deep

breath to steady herself. The girl was little more than a child. She was being foolish even to imagine Albie would be interested in anyone else. 'No, he did the right thing,' she said. 'It isn't safe for a young girl like you to be alone. We'll look after you, me and Albie.'

'Well, I'll be able to look after you when the little one is born.' Emily smiled. 'I'm that grateful to you both for taking me in, so I'll do all I can to repay you.'

Jessie rubbed her back. 'Well, I've done enough for today. I'll leave the rest to you and Albie.'

Even as she left the yard, she felt uneasy – the situation was so similar to one she'd once been in herself. She remembered when she had first arrived in London, fresh from the country. Fred Dove had given her a job, taught her all she knew about the milk trade. Fred had a wife and a baby but that hadn't stopped him falling in love with her. She remembered the swift rush of attraction she'd felt for him, a man older and more experienced than she was, with a successful business. She knew the temptations of two people working together and she was afraid.

That evening, as she and Albie sat in the comfortable parlour, she tried to voice her fears to him, but it was difficult. The name 'Emily' stuck in her throat.

'Want a nice little tipple of brandy to settle you

for the night?' Albie asked. He got to his feet and looked down at her and she saw that, unnoticed, he'd changed from a boy to a man. The skinny youth she'd fallen in love with was now broad in shoulder, strong and confident.

'Just a little drop, then,' Jessie said. 'It'll warm my stomach.'

He brought the drinks and then moved to the door. 'I'd better see to the fires – we don't want the house getting cold.'

Jessie listened to the sound of his footsteps as he went upstairs and she bit her lip, worrying, wondering if he would stop by Emily's door. The girl had arrived after supper and already Jessie felt that the comfortable and intimate lifestyle she'd shared with Albie was gone for ever.

She heard his footsteps overhead and wondered if Albie was whispering to Emily the way she used to whisper to Fred Dove. When Albie returned to the room, Jessie looked up at him. 'Is Emily still awake?'

He shook his head. 'I don't know. She's got a bucket of coal in her room so she can see to her own fire.' He looked ruefully at his dusty hands. 'I'll go and wash and then look over the books and tot up today's takings.'

Jessie relaxed. Of course Albie wasn't interested in young Emily. 'Albie,' she said softly, 'I do love you.'

He smiled warmly at her and as he left the room

he said, 'And I love you too, my lovely Jess. I love you too.'

Non sat beside the bed, a bowl of cool water on her lap and a cloth in her hand. Gwenllyn's fever was still high, her cheeks were flushed and her eyes roamed around the room unseeingly. It was time for another dose of angelica. Non put down her bowl, took up the spoon and gently tipped the liquid between Gwenllyn's lips. Once, the girl looked up at her, eyes focused, and Non realized that her days of patient nursing were paying off: the fever was beginning to break.

She wondered how she had coped with it all, being in the house where Caradoc had once lived with Gwenllyn, seeing his son grow more like him with every day that passed. She'd seen the yearning look in Caradoc's eyes as he held the boy and her heart seemed to die within her.

Harold was affected by the situation too. He came and went like a shadow, fetching and carrying, doing everything that Non asked of him. He was so grateful that he couldn't do enough for her.

That night, contrary to Non's expectations, events took a turn for the worse. Gwenllyn was very sick, the words pouring from her mouth making no sense. She tried to sit up, to go to her baby, but her eyes were glazed, seeing nothing but demons.

Non sat with her all night, while Harold came

and went, his face pale with worry. The long night hours seemed to stretch into infinity but she would not give in.

'I won't let you die, I won't!' Non peeled the bed-clothes back from Gwenllyn's slight body. 'I know you feel cold, but this is the best thing I can do for you.' She opened the window wide and returned to the bedside.

All night Non bathed Gwenllyn with the cool water. Every few hours she administered the herbal elixir. She was exhausted – she'd had very little sleep in the past few days. She almost gave in and admitted defeat, and then in the early hours of the next morning Gwenllyn opened her eyes.

'Non Jones!' Her voice was thin and reedy. 'What are you doing here?'

'I've been looking after you,' Non said softly. 'Thank God the fever has broken at last. You're going to be all right now.'

Gwenllyn tried to sit up. 'The baby – where is he?'

'He's being cared for,' Non said. 'Your husband brought a wet nurse in from the village to look after him, so don't worry. Come on, let me change your nightgown. You'll soon feel fresh and comfortable.'

'How long have you been here?' asked Gwenllyn, obediently lifting her arms as Non took off her nightgown.

'Several days,' Non said. 'Your husband caught

us in the village as we were on our way home.'

'And you agreed to look after me? Are you a saint, Non?'

Non looked at her with steady eyes. 'I'm not a saint, but I couldn't ignore a cry for help when my past years have been devoted to helping the sick.'

'Well, I'm grateful,' Gwenllyn said. 'Could you please call Harry for me? He must be so anxious.'

When Non returned to the kitchen, Harold looked at her, his face a mask of anxiety.

She smiled at him. 'You can go and see her now. The worst is over.'

He caught both her hands in his. 'I can't thank you enough. God bless you and yours for ever more.'

Non looked around for Caradoc and found he was out at the back of the house, chopping wood for the fire. She watched him through the window and saw how comfortable he was on Gwenllyn's property. It was as if a knife stabbed her heart.

She went outside and sat on the edge of a fallen tree. 'She's going to be all right.'

Caradoc didn't stop working. He lifted the axe and brought it down with such precision that the wood split cleanly in half. 'I never doubted it,' he said. 'With you nursing her, she had to recover.' He put another piece of log on the block.

'Stop that, for heaven's sake!' Non said. 'You needn't pretend you don't care, because I know you do. Look,' she said more quietly, 'can we just go home?'

'There's a mail coming through the day after tomorrow,' Caradoc said tersely. 'We can be on that.'

Non fell silent. She had lost her beloved Caradoc once; she didn't want to lose him again. She wanted to rail at him, to demand he tell her he'd got over Gwenllyn, but the words remained unspoken.

Caradoc put down the axe and came to sit next to her. 'I know all this has been hard on you, Non. You've been wonderful – so generous and forbearing; not many women would stop to nurse . . .' His voice trailed away.

'Her husband's mistress?' Non heard the words but she couldn't believe she'd said them out loud. She was aware of Caradoc getting to his feet. 'I'm sorry,' she said quickly. 'That wasn't fair of me.'

'You're tired.' Caradoc rested his hand on her shoulder. 'You've hardly had any sleep – no wonder you are feeling edgy.'

'This is so difficult for me,' she said. 'I can't help thinking of you and her together, of Gwenllyn having your baby. Oh, Caradoc, I'm so frightened.'

He drew her to her feet and took her in his arms, kissing her hair. 'I love *you*, Non, you are my wife, but I can't be indifferent to Gwenllyn and I'm sorry if that upsets you but I'm just a man and I don't know how to deal with all this.'

'Would you marry her if it wasn't for me?' Non hated herself for the pleading note in her voice but she needed reassurance.

He moved away and rubbed his eyes wearily. 'I don't know.'

'Tell me the truth, Caradoc. Don't insult me with lies.'

'How can I tell you what I don't know myself? I'm married; she's married; soon we'll go our separate ways. That's all there is to it.'

From inside the cottage, Non heard the crying of the baby and the sound pierced her heart. 'I just want to go home,' she said quietly. 'I just want everything to return to normal.'

'Be patient for just another day,' Caradoc said. 'We'll catch the mail and when we get back to Swansea everything will look different, you'll see.' He took her hand. 'Come on, let's go inside. It's getting chilly out here and I don't want you going down with a fever too.'

She leaned her head against his shoulder, taking comfort from his nearness. He was so dear to her, so very dear. Soon they would be back in their own home, out of sight and mind of Gwenllyn and the baby. Then everything would be as it was before. But would it? Would life ever be normal for her again?

* * *

Gwenllyn smiled as Harry came quietly into the room, his face anxious. 'It's all right, I'm not asleep,' she said.

He sat beside the bed and took her hand in his. She stared at him, wondering at the tears in his eyes. He cared about her, Harry really cared about her, and a flood of pity swamped her. She was too weak to deal with emotions at this moment.

She took her hand away. 'The baby, Harry: will you bring him to me?'

'Just rest tonight,' Harry said. 'David is being well looked after and you don't want him catching your fever, do you?' He took her hand again. 'Thank God you're on the mend,' he said softly. 'Non has done wonders she's made your fever go away. No one will ever poke fun at her funny remedies again, not in my earshot anyway.'

'I can't help feeling guilty,' Gwenllyn said sadly. 'I suppose I'll always love Caradoc. I thought we would be wed one day.' She saw Harry wince and regretted her words instantly. But then she couldn't go through life pretending to Harry that she'd never loved Caradoc.

'Don't take any notice of me.' Her voice was choked, tears were welling in her eyes and she felt so helpless. What a mess she'd made of her life. Would she ever be happy? Suddenly she felt very tired.

'I need to sleep,' she said softly, turning away

from Harry's pleading eyes. 'I'm so tired, so very tired.'

He pulled the blankets up over her shoulders. 'You'll feel better in the morning. Just rest now.'

Gwenllyn heard Harry creep out of the room, and when she was alone she turned her face to the wall. She wanted Caradoc, longed to be in his arms, to feel his lips touch hers with passion and, yes, with love. He did love her once, she was sure of that, but now? Well, now he had his wife back and that seemed to be enough for him. Then the tears came, hot and heavy, and she gave herself up to her grief.

CHAPTER FIFTEEN

Caradoc and Non had left for home and the place seemed unusually quiet even though the two maids were working downstairs. The wet nurse had fed the baby and was sitting quietly in the nursery, sewing. The sun was streaming in through the bedroom window and the baby's hair shone like a halo around his face. Gwenllyn studied his features as he lay in her arms. In the few days she'd been ill, David had changed: the contours of his face were more pronounced and his little fingers curled like petals in her hand. Love ached through every fibre of her being.

The door opened and Harry came into the room, a big smile on his face.

'Mr Jones has been as good as his word. The beasts have been safely delivered to me – three heifers and a fine strong bull.'

'What are you going to do with them, Harry?' Gwenllyn asked and he smiled broadly at her.

'What do you think I'm going to do with them? I'll breed them and when my own cows are with calf I'll hire the bull out for stud.'

'I suppose that was a daft question.'

'Maybe, but then you're a lady, not used to dealing with beasts.' He bent over the sleeping baby. 'He's growing into a bonny boy. You must be very proud of him, Gwennie.'

She looked up at him, knowing how much it must have cost him to say such kind things about the baby, but then Harry had changed since she'd first met him. Now she found him to be a generous, kindly man. How he must have hated having Caradoc under the same roof, and yet he'd thought only about her health, patiently waiting for a miracle to make her better, and if her salvation came in the form of Caradoc Jones's wife so be it.

'Well,' his voice broke into her thoughts, 'I'd best get to work. I've a lot of planning to do if I'm to be my own boss.' He looked at her questioningly. 'You'll be all right, will you? The nurse will give you a hand if you need it.'

'I'm all right. Don't you worry about me. Go and see to your business and good luck with it, Harry.'

When he'd gone, she lay back against the pillows, revelling in the sunlit silence. Soon she would get up and go downstairs; it was time she resumed her normal lifestyle.

Gwenllyn didn't see Harry for the rest of the day but she knew he was busy setting up fences and organizing his animals. There were several outbuildings on the land and no doubt Harry would make use of them for housing the heifers. Her knowledge of farming was sketchy but she imagined the bull would be kept separate from the cows until it was breeding time. She shuddered: good thing Harry was used to riding the trail, used to managing beasts.

It was strange to be downstairs. The sun still shone through the tall windows and outside a soft breeze lifted the heads of the daffodils. There was a knock on the door and the nurse came in, pressing down her already pristine apron. 'Shall I feed the boy now, Mrs Rees?'

'Yes, if you please, Betty. David has just woken up and he'll be ready for a feed.'

She lifted David out of his crib and Betty immediately took him from her arms. 'You need rest, if you don't mind me saying so, Mrs Rees. You're not over your sickness yet, not by a long chalk.'

Gwenllyn nodded. 'I think you're right. I'll just sit outdoors for a while and enjoy the sun.'

It was warm in the garden and Gwenllyn settled on a bench and closed her eyes. It had been strange seeing Caradoc and his wife together. There was a tension between them that was impossible to miss and Gwenllyn knew it was because of her. Now that she'd had the opportunity to learn more about Non Jones she realized how kind and good she was, a fitting wife for a man like Caradoc, and she felt even more guilty about the past.

She pushed aside the feelings of guilt. She couldn't do any more to make things right: she'd let Caradoc go without protest, she had made a new life for herself, she'd become a wife and a mother and all her memories of summer days spent with Caradoc were put to the back of her mind.

She must have slept a little because when she opened her eyes again the sun was hidden behind a cloud. It was time to return indoors. Soon, Harry would come in from the fields for his meal. She sighed; time to face reality and somehow the thought was wearying.

By the time Harry returned, Gwenllyn had hot water ready for him to bathe in. He smelled dreadful; his clothes were covered in mire.

'Out there,' Gwenllyn said firmly, pointing to the back yard, 'and don't come into the dining room until you're presentable.'

Harry did as she told him without a murmur of protest and when at last he came to the table he looked well scrubbed and rather handsome.

'The outdoor work suits you, Harry.' She pushed the tureen of potatoes towards him and indicated the bowl of green vegetables and then sat back in her chair, feeling she'd done her duty and more by Harry. Her gloom of earlier had faded; for some reason she felt rather pleased with herself. Harry had a goal in life now, soon he would be taking to the roads and, in the meantime, they were going to get along just fine, she was sure of it.

'I'm glad to be home.' Non walked into the familiar sitting room and sank into her favourite chair. The window in front of her was large and outside she could see the green rolling hills and, below, the sea glittering in the evening sunshine.

'You did a wonderful thing.' Caradoc wasted no time on polite talk. 'It was good of you to look after Gwenllyn the way you did.'

She met his gaze. 'It wasn't easy.' The words fell into the silence and hung there and after a moment Caradoc turned away from her.

'I know it wasn't easy, I'm not a fool.'

'Well, that's a subject for debate, isn't it?' Non's voice was edgy; she was tired and downhearted. 'It isn't often that a wife cares for her husband's mistress, is it?' Her voice was cold.

'Don't let's argue over it,' he said wearily. 'You did what you thought was right. No one forced you into it.'

'How could I refuse to help a sick woman? I've

spent years making my medicines, I'm known and respected for my skill with the herbal remedies, so how could I refuse to help?'

'So it was your reputation you were worried about, was it?'

'No, not just that.' She looked down at her hands. 'I'm sorry, Caradoc, I shouldn't go on about it. I just feel very tired, that's all.'

He came to her side and kissed her cheek. 'I'm sorry. If I could turn back the clock, perhaps I'd do things differently.'

'You sound doubtful.'

'I *am* doubtful. How could I have changed anything? I'd lost my memory, Non. I thought I needed to make a new life for myself.'

'And you wasted no time doing that!' She took a deep breath. 'I'm sorry, I shouldn't be blaming you – but, Caradoc, do you realize how hard it was for me to see her with your son?'

He pulled her close. 'We'll have sons together and daughters. You must rest more – stop running back and forth to London for a start: the business up there is in good hands and you trust Carrie to look after things, don't you?'

'Yes, of course I do.' She fell silent. What would her life be without her work? She needed badly to fill in the time when Caradoc was away on business because she was so very lonely then, but Caradoc was right: once they had a family everything would be different. She would revel in her children, she would treasure every moment they spent together.

She had loved her son, Rowan had been a joy to her, but he was gone now and she needed to start afresh. She smiled and touched Caradoc's cheek. 'Let's take ourselves to our bed, my love.'

'Good idea.' He took her hand and drew her towards the stairs in full view of one of the footmen, who was putting away the travelling bags. Caradoc closed the bedroom door and suddenly Non felt absurdly shy of him. Caradoc was her husband, he had made love to her many times, but she trembled like a maiden with her first kiss as he undid the buttons on her bodice.

Caradoc took her with some of the old zest he'd once possessed and Non's senses swam with the joy of it. They were in love, they were still passionate with each other. She must concentrate on the here and now for otherwise she would spoil the loving relationship she and Caradoc were trying to build together.

Non clung to him, kissing his naked shoulder, then his neck and finally his mouth. For the first time since he'd come back to her, Non felt pure joy at their coupling. Caradoc was with her, possessing her; it was not Gwenllyn whom Caradoc was embracing, but her, his wife.

It was a few days later when Caradoc announced he intended to head the next cattle drove to London.

'Why do you have to go?' Non was fearful, knowing he would need to cross the Wye, knowing he would pass near the cottage where Gwenllyn lived. 'Are you going to call on your other woman and see your son?'

'I've got to go – I've no experienced head drover this trip,' he said reasonably. 'I have to find someone I can rely on as I relied on Harry. He was a good drover: he knew exactly what he was doing and I could trust him.'

'No doubt you'll be seeing him too while on the road?' Her voice trembled and Caradoc, sensing her distress, took her in his arms.

'Please, Non, don't be fearful. If I do see Harry it will be to check the stock I've sent him, that's all.'

'And *her*? Will you be seeing *her*?'

'I don't know, Non. How can I say?' He kissed her lips. 'It's you I love. You are my dear wife; I don't need any other woman.'

'No, but you need your son, don't you?' She pulled away from him, imagining him with Gwenllyn, both of them cooing over the baby boy, and it broke her heart.

'I'll not go to see her, then.' He sounded resigned. 'I'll keep away if it distresses you so much.'

'Of course it distresses me!' She looked at him and saw the weary look in his eyes and was sorry. Then, 'Don't take any notice of me,' she said, forcing a smile. 'I shouldn't be nasty to you – not when you're about to embark on a hazardous journey.'

'Don't worry so much. My accident was a rare occurrence; usually the trail is as safe as a row of houses.'

Non made an attempt to relax. She knew her constant nagging would ruin their marriage in the end and yet jealousy possessed her; it would not let her be at peace.

Caradoc had lived another life and there was nothing she could do about it now. She must enjoy what she had here and now instead of harking back to the past. But it was difficult, so difficult. She put her arms around Caradoc and held him close. 'I love you, my darling,' she said softly and she hoped he didn't see the sudden tears that misted her eyes.

Caradoc breathed a sigh of relief as he headed the drove from the Carmarthenshire fields on the route to London. It was good to be on the trail again, good to feel free. He loved his wife dearly but lately things had been so tense between them. He couldn't blame Non for the way she felt, but she was a changed woman, so anxious and sad.

He was weary of trying to reassure Non, to impress on her that he loved her, when she seemed unable or unwilling to let his past go. There was a rift between them now that might never heal. He didn't blame Non and yet how could he blame himself for something that had happened without his will or consent?

He headed up the trail with the stink and noise of the herd behind him. The hoofs of the animals sent up the dust in the roadway, the beasts protesting as the drovers chivvied them along with a swish of a slender stick.

He congratulated himself that he'd managed to assemble a good team of drovers, stalwart men used to hardship and well versed in the ways of animals. The women were stoic country folk, who would walk uncomplainingly all the weary miles to Smithfield market, doing their knitting and weeding along the way. The day was fine and dry; he should put his worries out of his mind and think of the job in hand. He glanced up at the sky. There were few clouds and no rain in the air, so they should make good progress today.

He missed Harold, though. The man had been with him for a long time and he was well able to head a drove himself. He'd been a dour man, not given to talking much, but he had an inner strength that Caradoc admired.

Inevitably, thinking of Harold led him onto thoughts about Gwenllyn. Was she happy married? She certainly seemed to bring out the best in Harold: he was a changed man – clean and tidily dressed, and more articulate than Caradoc had ever given him credit for.

It took a strong man to be father to another man's child, even though he had been paid a bag of gold. He could have hit the trail again once he had the money but he'd stayed with Gwenllyn, and helped her with her labour and with bringing up the boy.

At the thought of his son, Caradoc felt a tug on his heart strings. The child was so beautiful, so healthy, he would doubtless grow up into a fine man. And then what would he think of the father who abandoned him at birth?

The first few days of the drove passed without incident. The cattle were well behaved, walking steadily along the narrow roads with docile stoicism, and the cows were more settled without the distraction of a bull among them.

With this drove Caradoc had opted to bring ponies as well as the cattle to the market. The horses usually sold well – they were fresh and young, broken but still spirited enough for the most daredevil rider.

On the third day into the drove the rain came down heavily and the track was turned into mud, with large pools of water gathering in the ditches. The cattle plodded on, heads lowered, but the women made a fuss, wanting to spend the worst of the weather indoors.

This trip Caradoc had no intention of using the river crossing at the Wye, he'd no intention of stopping anywhere near Gwenllyn's cottage, but with the weather turning even more stormy, he knew it would be foolhardy to go on past the village.

He called a halt at last near a farm on the out-skirts of the village and he watched as the women gratefully went into the barn. They would light a fire and dry their clothes and then they would cook a good meal.

He saw the provision cart draw up and he nodded to the driver. 'I'm going to settle up with the farmer,' he said. 'We'll stay here for the night and pray that the morning brings us better weather.'

'Oh, I don't know about you going off and leaving us alone.' The drover, a big man with a red beard and new on the road, spoke up loudly. 'There's not one sod here who could manage the cattle if anything went wrong.'

'Look, I'll be half an hour at most. I'll come back with a head drover, so there's no need for anyone to panic.'

Caradoc realized he'd been foolish to set out on the trail without a second in command. He would need to leave the herd several times on the trip to find accommodation for the night; he couldn't manage without a good man in charge.

He knew what he had to do: he would offer Harold the job, pay him over the odds; the man could ride back on his own once the cattle were safely delivered. At most, the trip would only take him a little short of two weeks.

As he rode up the hill that led to Gwenllyn's home, he felt a twinge of guilt. He'd told Non he wouldn't go anywhere near the cottage and yet what was the alternative? Had this been in the back of his mind all along? Was he determined to see his son whatever the cost?

It was Harold who opened the door to him. 'What do you want?' His tone was brusque.

'Can I step inside?' Caradoc asked. 'It's raining cats and dogs out here.'

Harold stepped aside reluctantly. 'Aye, come in, if you must.' He led the way into the kitchen. 'What can I do for you, Mr Jones?' His tone was a little more civil and Caradoc took advantage of the small window of hope that this offered.

'I need a head man,' he said. 'I'm desperate, Harry.'

Gwenllyn came into the kitchen. 'Who is it, Harry?' She stopped in her tracks when she saw him and Caradoc saw the rich colour come into her cheeks. And he knew he still wanted her.

'Good evening, Gwenllyn. You're looking a little better. Are you over the worst of your fever now?' His words sounded ridiculously terse; it was as if he was speaking to a stranger.

'Yes, I'm very well. What are you doing here?'

'I've come to ask Harry to be head man for the rest of the journey. I really need him and I assure you I will send him back with a good horse to make his journey easier and quicker.'

'What do you think, Harry?' Gwenllyn looked at him and Harold shrugged his shoulders.

'Please help me, Harry,' Caradoc said. 'I wouldn't ask if I wasn't pushed to it.'

'What about Josh?' Harold said. 'I thought he was shaping up to be a good drover.'

'I don't know where he is. He didn't join the drove, so he must have found some other job,' Caradoc said. 'I repeat, I'm really desperate, otherwise I wouldn't be bothering you.'

'Perhaps you should go, Harry,' Gwenllyn said gently. 'If it will help Mr Jones out of a fix I think you should do it.'

'And what about my own beasts?' Harold said. 'I don't want to leave all that work to you.'

'I'll manage,' Gwenllyn said grimly. 'I'll get one of the local farmers to help. In any case, I'm not useless, you know.'

'I realize that but . . .' His words trailed away and he shrugged his shoulders in resignation. 'Well, all right. If you really need me I'll come along.' He stared long and hard at Caradoc. 'But only this once. I won't feel obliged to help you out another time.'

'Good man,' Caradoc said. He looked at Gwenllyn. 'How is the baby?'

'He's well. I've just put him to bed; he'll be asleep, so I'd prefer you not to disturb him.'

Caradoc felt a deep sense of disappointment, but after a moment he nodded. 'I understand.' And he did. He knew that Gwenllyn was worried he might try to take the boy from her. In any case, it eased his conscience a little: he could tell Non in all honesty that he hadn't seen his son.

'Right then,' Harold said. 'I take it the herd are down by the riverside?' He didn't wait for a reply. 'You go on ahead. I'll join you when I've got my things together.'

Caradoc found himself dismissed, and without another look in Gwenllyn's direction he left the house. He mounted his horse and in spite of his predictions a heavy rain was falling, driving stinging darts into his face. He brushed at his eyes, not knowing if the mist in his eyes was rain or tears.

CHAPTER SIXTEEN

Carrie counted out the day's takings as efficiently as she did everything. She put the money into a bag but kept back half for herself. Quietly she was amassing a good amount of savings; soon she would have enough to set up a shop of her own. She knew as much as Mrs Jones did about the business and she wasn't such a soft touch. No one had free medicine from Carrie Mayhew – if they didn't pay they went without. In the morning she would collect all the takings from the other shops; some of that would be hers too. Soon, when the time was right, she would make her next move, and one day in the not too distant future the whole of the business would belong to her. Carrie smiled in anticipation: she would be rich and famous and soon everyone would forget Mrs Manon Jones had ever existed.

She went to her rooms above the shop, where

the fire was burning low. It was the devil of a job carrying coal up to the third floor but she'd made the small rooms her own sanctuary, a place where she could keep the books, both sets, and work on them at her leisure. So far, Mrs Jones had not learned the truth that Carrie was creaming off most of the profit for herself.

Mrs Jones would find the discrepancies one day, it was inevitable, but at the moment she spent most of her time in Wales mooning over that husband of hers. She was so trusting, so painfully honest, that it was easy to lull her into a false sense of security. Well, Mrs Jones would have no one to blame but herself when the customers stopped patronizing her shops. By then Carrie would have feathered her nest and be ready to open her own shop and it wouldn't be in the poky back streets of London either, oh no. She'd had enough of the stink of poverty. She had her eye on the more affluent areas of the town. Still, this place would do for now, but one day soon she would be out of here and Mrs Non Jones could whistle for her money.

Gwenllyn found she was missing Harry's company. She missed teaching him his words, hearing his voice, sometimes faltering as he attempted to read the books she put before him. And since he'd gone, she realized what a great help he was in the house. He lit the fires every day before she'd even got out of bed so the kitchen was always warm when she brought David down from his crib. Now, for the first time, she felt the house lacked warmth and cheer.

For months Harry had been her trusted companion. She'd turned to him for help, little realizing that she was becoming dependent on him.

Now, in the morning, she had to spend precious time watching the maid coax the fires into flame before she allowed the wet nurse to come and give David his feed. This morning, having gone home to her own family for the night, the nurse was late.

It was quiet in the house and Gwenllyn admitted to herself that she was unbearably lonely. She also knew she would always be alone unless she took Harry as her husband, let him into her bed and into her life.

She heard David cry and hurried up the stairs to the nursery. There was still no sign of the nurse and Gwenllyn picked David up, holding him close, her lips against his downy head. He was a good child but today he was fretful. She put her finger into his mouth and felt the beginnings of a tooth and smiled. She knew what remedy she could give him to soothe his pain. Mrs Jones had left some camomile medicine for her in case the fever came back.

Gently, she rubbed some of the liquid along the baby's gum. It seemed to soothe him almost at once. Gwenllyn smiled at the irony of the situation: Mrs Jones had nursed her husband's mistress and now, without knowing it, she was helping his child.

Gwenllyn stopped smiling. She should be ashamed: she knew in her heart that Mrs Jones was a good person, only too willing to help anyone in pain, and the thought twisted like a knot inside her.

She acknowledged that she was jealous of Caradoc's wife. Why couldn't she be nasty and wicked so that Gwenllyn could hate her? But instead of hating her she had a grudging admiration for Mrs Jones. Gwenllyn reaffirmed her vow to put Caradoc out of her mind for ever – after all, she was a married woman herself and it would pay her to remember that. She should stop wasting her time pining over another woman's husband and be a proper wife to Harry.

He was a good man and more than she deserved. She had had plenty of time to think while he was away and she decided that her future was going to be a difficult and lonely one if she didn't make the right decisions now.

There was no sign of the maids. Breakfast should be on the table by now but she had plenty to do while she waited; in any case, she wasn't really hungry. She pulled on her boots, bunched up her skirts and headed for the outhouse where the bull was penned.

Already, she hated the animal. He had frightening-looking horns and an evil gleam in his eye and she stayed well clear of him except at feeding times.

She carried the bucket of animal feed to the outhouse and pushed open the door. The bull was staring at her with head lowered and she hastily thrust the fodder into the trough. The beast didn't even bend his great neck to look at it; he pawed the ground and snorted, his nostrils flaring, and Gwenllyn felt her heart begin to beat hard in fright.

Carefully, she retreated a step at a time, putting as much distance between herself and the animal as she could. Dozens of frightening thoughts flashed through her mind. If she was injured by the bull what would happen to David? What would Harry find when he came home?

She quickly stepped outside and tried to close the gate, but the bull was too quick for her. With a snort he charged and she flattened herself against the wall, too terrified even to cry out.

The bull seemed not to notice her; he plunged towards the byre where the heifers were kept, charging the gate, cruel horns tearing at the wood. For a moment Gwenllyn stood frozen to the spot, and then she began to run across the yard, her heart thumping, expecting any moment to hear the pounding of hoofs behind her. At the back door she turned to see the bull demolish the gate completely and then she slammed the door shut and leaned against it, breathing heavily.

She couldn't cope with this situation; she'd been foolish to try. Why hadn't she called in one of the farmers to help her?

'Harry, please come home,' she said softly. 'I need you.' The kitchen was silent and empty, the fire burning low in the grate. She frowned. Where were the maids? She put on more coals and pushed the kettle onto the flames, her hands shaking. She didn't know what to do next. What if the bull ran away? What would she say to Harry when he came home? Her heart was racing: the animals were loose now and there was nothing she could do about it.

She forced herself to be calm but she was still shaking as she made the tea and sat down at the kitchen table.

She looked round the empty room and suddenly it occurred to her that the gossips had been busy again. Harry had gone with the drove, so the villagers must think he had left her. She knew the women in the market gossiped about Caradoc visiting her so often and Harry's absence added fuel to the flames.

The silence closed in around her. She felt so frightened: she was alone, how could she manage? She couldn't even feed her son. Her milk had dried up when she was sick with the fever. She felt tears burn in her eyes and brushed them away impatiently – where had her spirit gone?

She looked down at the baby. He was sleeping soundly, looking even more like his father now that his little features were in repose. But his father was not here; nobody was here to help her; she was alone.

Harry came home a few days later, days when she'd searched endlessly for the animals, days when she'd eked out the milk in the cold larder to feed her baby. Harry was smiling as he came through the door.

'I've had a good trip.' He looked at her carefully. 'I've earned a bit more money – that'll go to fodder for the animals – but something's wrong, isn't it? I can tell by the look on your face.'

'Come and sit down. I've got something to tell you.'

'You're not sick. Is it the little lad?'

'No.' She rested her hand on his arm. 'It's the animals . . . the bull, well, he got out, chased the heifers . . . They're all running amok, for all I know. I haven't seen hide nor hair of them for the past few days.'

Harry smiled reassuringly. 'Is that all? Well, don't worry too much about it – they'll come back home when they're good and ready.'

She looked at him doubtfully. 'I'm sorry, Harry. I couldn't do anything. The bull charged past me, making straight for the shed where the cows are kept.'

He smiled, then: 'Well, we'll be having a few calves in due course,' he said. 'Better sooner than later.'

'Are you sure they'll be all right? You're not angry with me?'

'Of course I'm not angry. I should have been here by your side. You're too little a lady to care for that huge brute of a bull.'

She sighed in relief. 'Hungry? Shall I make you something to eat?'

'I'm starving, but where are the maids? Aren't they busy cooking food in the kitchen?'

'They left suddenly. I think they see me as a scarlet woman without a husband to care for me.'

Harry's face softened. 'I'm so sorry, Gwennie. I wouldn't have gone on the damn drove if I'd known you'd be left alone.'

'Never mind that. I'll make a fry-up for us. You must be exhausted.'

'I'll have a wash first.'

She nodded. 'The kettle's boiling.'

She smiled as Harry went out to the scullery. She could hear him stripping off his clothes: he was like a child with no false pride. From outside she heard the splash of water and her heart warmed. Harry was a different man now from the one who'd sold her his name for a bag of gold.

After he had bathed and changed, Gwenllyn

made him a meal, wondering if he would go as usual to the village inn. She hoped not; somehow she felt the need for his company. He seemed to sense her loneliness, because he helped her clear away and then sat in the chair near the kitchen fire.

'How have you managed, Gwen?' he asked quietly. 'Were you afeared of being here alone?'

She was about to tell him she'd coped just fine, but the words died on her lips. 'I missed you, Harry.' She stood, one hand on the mantelpiece, looking down at him.

His eyes met hers. 'I won't be going away again – not in a hurry, anyway.'

'But you'll have to run a drove when you have the stock.'

'I know, but that won't be for a long time yet.' He smiled. 'After all, I haven't even got the makings of a herd just now, have I?' He frowned. 'Sit down, Gwennie, you look worn out. Been working too hard, you have. It's a good thing I came home when I did or you'd be falling sick again.'

'I'm just worried about the animals, that's all.'

'Well, don't fret. They've probably wandered into one of the top fields. They'll come down soon enough when they want warmth and shelter and fodder put in front of their mouths.'

'You're taking it all very calmly.' Gwenllyn was puzzled. 'Do you really think the beasts will come back of their own accord?'

'Aye, I do, and if they don't I'll go looking for

them. Everything will be all right, so don't worry your pretty head about it.'

She glanced at him. He didn't often pay her compliments. 'What is it, Harry?' she asked suspiciously. 'Why are you so calm about the animals breaking loose?'

He didn't answer for a moment and then he looked up and met her eyes. 'It's because of you. When you said you'd missed me, I was over the moon.' He held up his hand. 'Now, don't worry, I'm not going to take advantage of you or anything silly. It's just good to know that someone on this God's earth cares about me, if only a little.'

Gwenllyn felt tears choke in her throat. 'I meant it, I did miss you.' Tentatively, she put her hand on his arm. 'I really did, Harry.'

He looked up at her with a light of hope dawning in his eyes. He took her hand and raised it to his lips. 'You're a beautiful woman, Gwenllyn Rees,' he said, 'and I hope you're not playing games with me.'

She released herself and moved to the door. 'David is already asleep,' she said, and as if it was the most natural thing in the world she smiled at him and added: 'Are you coming to bed?'

Gwenllyn's heart was beating fast. Would her courage desert her when she reached the bedroom? She heard Harry follow her up the stairs and into the bedroom. She lit the candles and turned to face him. Harry looked at her with such longing that her fears melted away. She turned her back to him.

'Harry, will you undo my buttons for me?'

She held her hair aside and felt his hands tremble as they touched her neck. Her mouth was dry; a mixture of emotions swamped her. She was beginning to feel aroused, she'd been so long without love. But this wasn't Caradoc, her love, her wonderful darling, touching her, it was Harry Rees, the man to whom she was married, she reminded herself.

Clumsily, he undressed her and watched as she slipped under the blankets. He turned his back as he took his clothes off and she realized with surprise that he was just as awkward as she was.

He sank into bed beside her and she stiffened for a moment as his leg touched hers.

'It's all right,' he whispered: 'I won't hurt you. I won't do anything you don't want me to do.'

For a moment she felt real terror that she would fail him; at the last moment she would jump from the bed and run away. But she didn't; she stayed still while his hands moved over her breasts, tenderly and lovingly.

She had been so long without the love of a man that when he raised himself above her and moved inside her, she was no longer afraid. Whatever the future might bring, after tonight there would be no turning back. Harry Rees would be her husband for good or ill.

CHAPTER SEVENTEEN

Gwenllyn woke to the early-morning sky aware
that someone was standing beside the bed. Then
she remembered the night before and the way
she'd responded to Harry's passion. She would
never love him – her heart would always be with
Caradoc Jones – but she would hold firm to her
marriage vows; she would cherish Harry and be a
proper wife to him, which was no less than he
deserved.

'Thank you, Gwennie,' he said humbly. 'Thank
you for last night.' He was awkward – he didn't
have a way with words as Caradoc did – but he
was honest and sincere, and Gwenllyn smiled up
at him even as she held the bedclothes modestly
over her breasts.

'I want to be a proper wife to you from now on,
Harry. You've been so good to me.'

He sat down on the bed beside her. 'I know you

don't love me, not in the way I love you, but I'm grateful for what you can give me. You do care a little, don't you, Gwennie?'

'Of course I do, Harry. I know you for a good, kind man.' Tentatively she touched his hand. 'I'll try my best to be a good wife, I really will.'

'Right then.' He stood up. 'I'd better see if I can get my beasts back.' He walked to the door and glanced back at her. 'I love you, Mrs Rees.'

She had tears in her eyes as she heard him clatter down the stairs. He deserved something better than what he offered him, but he chose to love her, to be with her, and she would make the best of the bargain they'd made together.

The baby began to cry and she roused herself from bed. David was sleeping through the night now and life was so much easier. He was a good baby, contented, once he was fed and changed, to lie in his crib and wave his small arms and feet at the world. And in a strange sort of way, Gwenllyn was content too. She had a good hard-working husband and a beautiful child.

Later, Harry returned to the cottage looking cheerful. His face was red from the sun and wind but he was smiling. 'All the beasts are safely gathered in,' he said. 'The big bull soon followed when I led the two females back home.'

'I'm very glad you found them,' Gwenllyn said. 'I felt so silly, letting them run away like that.'

'The bull wanted a mate and one of the heifers

was willing,' Harry said. 'Nature took its course and I hope to get a good calf out of it, so don't feel too bad.'

He smiled at her and Gwenllyn thought again how attractive he was. She should be thankful he wasn't the sort to spend his nights drinking his money away. He went out occasionally to be with the other men down at the inn, but lately he'd spent most evenings sitting with her, studying his reading books or doing endless calculations concerning his proposed new business as a cattle drover.

She liked Harry, she realized, liked him very much. He gave her every consideration and loved her with every inch of his being. How simple life would be for her if she hadn't fallen in love with Caradoc Jones.

She made Harry a meal and then sank into the rocking chair, nursing her baby and marvelling at his glowing cheeks and bright, clear eyes. Harry had advised her to put the baby outdoors in the garden, 'to get fresh air into his lungs,' he explained.

'How do you know so much about children?' she asked, looking up at him. He wiped the back of his hand across his lips and she gave an involuntary shudder. He noticed and bent his head apologetically.

'Sorry. I haven't improved my table manners, but I'll try to.' He paused. 'As to the little ones,

I've had some practice with my own family as well as with the young cattle. It might not seem to be the same thing, but animals are very much like humans in their needs.'

'You're a very wise man, Harry, very wise.'

The redness began at his throat and flushed his cheeks. He frowned as if he was displeased, but she knew he was happy at the compliment. She felt sad: she gave him so little and took so much from him, she should be ashamed of herself.

'I'll try to remember my manners too, Harry,' she said softly. 'I shouldn't make you feel uncomfortable. After all, this is your home as much as it's mine.'

'I can't be like Caradoc Jones,' he said, 'it's no use me trying, but I'm learning something from you every day and I'm grateful.'

His words made her feel even guiltier. 'You don't need to be like anyone else, you are all right as you are.'

'Gwenllyn . . .' He made to speak and she lifted her hand to stop him. He'd been about to declare his love, she just knew it; her soft words had encouraged him to speak out but she wasn't ready to hear it. She still loved Caradoc as deeply as ever and nothing Harry could do would change that.

'It's all right, Harry, I understand what you're trying to say, but let's just take things a day at a time, shall we?'

After a moment he nodded. 'Aye, let's take things a day at a time.'

Non frowned at the figures in her account books. The London shops were not bringing in the money she would have expected, judging by the way the stock had diminished. Was it possible that Carrie had made an error? But no, Carrie was too clever for that, so what exactly was going on?

She sighed. It meant another trip up to London, a trip she would rather have done without now that Caradoc was home again. She glanced at him. He was busy reading the paper but later she would talk to him, ask his advice. She pushed away the books and sat staring through the window, seeing the glitter of the sea far below and the drowsing heat of the garden. It was a beautiful sunny day outside. The last thing she wanted to face was a setback in her business affairs.

Non sighed again and forced her attention back to the books and the seemingly inexplicable discrepancies. She could hardly bear to be suspicious and yet figures never lied.

That night, after dinner, she raised the subject with Caradoc. 'I don't know what it is but there's something wrong with the accounts,' she said.

He met her eyes then. 'What do you mean, "wrong"?'

'The figures apparently add up, but the stock

that's gone out should have brought in twice the income it has.'

'You don't think your girl in London is putting her hand into the till, do you?'

'I wouldn't have believed it possible . . . well, perhaps you'll look over the books for me, see if you can work it out?'

'Of course I'll look over the books. Do you want to fetch them now?'

Non nodded. She felt that she had all her husband's attention for once and her heart lifted. Perhaps now that they were home Gwenllyn would be nothing more than a memory.

Caradoc studied the figures for a long time and then shook his head. 'You're right, the accounts have been meticulously written up. But that makes me suspicious: there isn't a single miscalculation, not even an ink blot.' He closed the books. 'Perhaps you should have a talk to the girl, ask her to explain.'

'It will mean I'll have to go to London,' Non said. 'Would you mind?'

He glanced at her and then looked away. 'Of course I don't mind – I'll have a new drove together soon and I'll be back on the roads.'

He sounded happy to be leaving and suddenly Non felt anger burn in her heart. 'And no doubt you'll find time to visit your woman and her son!'

He held up his hand. 'Please, Non, don't go on about it, not again.'

'We should talk about your affair with that woman, bring it all out into the open. Tell me the truth for once, that you can't forget her.'

He got to his feet and, without looking at her, spoke in a fierce whisper. 'Will you never let that rest, Non? It isn't even possible that I can apologize for my lapse. I didn't know who I was or where I was.'

'But you forgot me very easily, didn't you? You soon slipped into another woman's bed.' She clenched her fists. The pain of imagining him with Gwenllyn, holding her close, kissing her mouth, making love to her, was so intense she could hardly breathe. 'Did you touch her as you touch me? Did you whisper words of love into her ear as you possessed her?'

'Please, Non.' He tried to take her into his arms but she pushed him away angrily.

'Do you know how hurt I am every time you go into a daydream and I know you're thinking of her?'

His arms dropped to his sides. 'I'm sorry, Non. I love you very much, you're my wife, my darling, but I can't help what happened. Gwenllyn and I grew very close and now that she's got the baby . . .' He shrugged. 'Well, I just want to see my son. Is that so very bad?'

Non felt a knife thrust of pain at his words. 'Good thing she's married,' she said, 'otherwise you'd be moving in with her. You'd forget about me and how much I long for us to have children together.'

'Of course I wouldn't, Non. Don't be silly.'

She glared at him. 'I'm not being silly. You love another woman, have a child by her and I'm supposed to be grateful for the little time you spend with me. Well, don't worry, I'll go to London and I may well stay there. I have no peace here with you.'

'I love you, Non.'

'But not enough,' she said dully. 'You rarely make love to me and when you do it's as if your thoughts are somewhere else. I can't stand it any more, Caradoc. I'm going to pack my things and spend a little time with Ruby and Jessie – try to clear my head.'

'Look, I can postpone the drove. Do you want me to come with you?'

Non shook her head. 'And have you gazing longingly towards the cottage above the river Wye? No, thank you!'

She left him standing silently near the window and without turning she lifted her skirts and hurried into the hall and up the stairs. She called her maid to pack her box and sat on the bed, feeling as if the whole world had collapsed around her.

Ruby set the table for her guests and stood back to see if it was done to her satisfaction. The cutlery gleamed in the candlelight and the glasses sparkled like diamonds. Her house was a simple one and she cooked nothing but plain food but she knew she had a reputation to uphold; she was a good landlady and a good cook and now, as usual, she had a full house.

She brought the rabbit pie out of the oven and gestured to the girl who was bringing in the vegetables. 'Hurry up, Dot. The lodgers will be down for their meal in a few minutes.'

Ruby sighed. Young girls today didn't know what a good day's work was all about. When she was a girl, she did everything from cooking to scrubbing the floors, polishing the furniture and making up the fires. She felt herself swell with pride: now she was proprietor of her own lodging house.

At last the supper was served and as her guests chatted and laughed together, enjoying the good food put before them, Ruby took a well-earned rest in the kitchen. She pulled off her cap and rubbed her fingers through her hair.

'Now, Dot, keep an eye on the table. Clear the used dishes away and serve the pudding just as I showed you.'

Suddenly she felt as though she was a hundred years old, not a woman barely into her twenties. But she was born old and destined to be an old maid living out her life alone, instead of having a happy marriage like Non and Jessie.

She was startled from her thoughts by a rapping at the door. With a sigh, she got to her feet. She would have to answer the door herself – Dot would never cope with the extra work.

'Non!' She held out her arms as she saw her friend standing on the doorstep. 'I was just bleedin' thinking about you!' Non dropped her bags in the hall and Ruby saw that her eyes were filled with tears. 'What's wrong, Non? Is anybody sick?'

Non shook her head. 'No, nothing like that but . . .' She hesitated for a moment. 'I've come to stay, if you don't mind.'

Ruby wrapped her arms around her friend. 'Come on in. I'll make you a nice cup of tea and then you can tell me all about your troubles.'

'That won't take long,' Non said wearily. 'I've left Caradoc. I can never go back to him. It's over, Ruby, my marriage is over.'

CHAPTER EIGHTEEN

Gwenllyn stood outside the door of the cottage, breathing in the balmy air. She felt almost at peace with the world. Slowly she was managing to get on with her life and put all thoughts of Caradoc out of her mind. And now that Harry had returned, the village people were at least being polite to her.

She shaded her eyes from the sun and looked down into the valley. Seeing a figure climbing the hill, she smiled: it was Harry, she would know him anywhere – his bearing, the set of his shoulders and the dark matt of hair that refused to stay beneath the cap that he wore.

Harry was proving to be a fine husband – helpful, hard-working and with a keen sense of humour. His reading had improved so much that now he hardly ever needed help with his spelling. Each evening he would sit down at the kitchen table and pore over his notebook, the contents of which he kept well hidden from her. She knew he was writing about their life together, making a diary of events. His expression and the way his arm embraced the paper when he was concentrating told her that.

'Hello, Harry,' she said as he opened the gate. 'I've got a nice shank of lamb cooked for your dinner.'

'That's good, I'm bloody starving. Sorry for the swearing.' He pulled off his cap and followed her into the house. 'David been a good boy today?'

'He's a bit cross, but then he's teething – his little gums are sore.' It was so good to share her feelings with someone who cared, and Harry did care, he'd proved that without doubt. And she knew she could make a good contented marriage with Harry if she really tried.

They ate at the kitchen table and Gwenllyn was pleased to see Harry eat heartily. His table manners had improved. She'd been aware of him watching her handle the silverware and her heart ached as she realized he was doing everything he could to match up to her expectations.

She'd learned from him too. Candlelight shimmering on the polished surface of the dining table, pristine napkins folded alongside the cutlery – all these things, luxuries though they were, didn't make up for the feeling of companionship she shared with Harry while they sat together in the kitchen.

Harry seemed to pick up on her thoughts. 'We haven't eaten in the dining room lately. Is that my fault?'

Gwenllyn shook her head. 'What's the point? We have no servants and anyway we're comfortable here in the kitchen.' She gestured round her. 'Everything is to hand and I don't have to fetch and carry the food down the passageway. No, the dining room is fine for folk who want to have formal dinners, but we've no need to stand on ceremony, have we?'

'Did you have these formal dinners? Before I came along, I mean.'

'You know I didn't. My gran and I were never popular around here. Though now that the villagers know you're home with me again, I'm considered more respectable than I was before.'

'Why is that?' Harry leaned back in his chair. He had a spot of gravy on his chin but she didn't have the heart to remonstrate with him.

'You know the story about my gran being mistress to a rich man. Well, because of that, we were resented. I think now the village people at least can see I'm just like them, in spite of the big house. They see you working and trying to make your way in the world with your cattle and they respect you for it.' She paused. 'So do I, Harry. Never doubt that.'

He looked up at her and dabbed his face with his napkin. He sat up straighter in his chair and

Gwenllyn could see he was pleased. His eyes sparkled and there was a lift to the corners of his mouth.

She felt a sudden surge of warmth towards him. She would never be in love with Harry, but perhaps she could love him just a little?

'Gwen,' he said, 'I know you won't like what I'm going to say, but I've got to say it: I've fallen in love with you.'

She looked at him kindly. 'I know you have, Harry.'

'And do you think you could ever love me back?' His voice held a pleading note and Gwenllyn didn't have the heart to hurt him.

'Maybe, one day, love will come,' she said softly. 'In the meantime, let's make the most of what we have, shall we?' She held out her hand to him and a warm look came into his eyes.

'Gwenllyn, are you offering what I think you're offering?' He was smiling as she nodded.

'Come with me.' She left her meal uneaten and took his hand. 'Let's go upstairs,' she said softly.

In her bedroom, he stood as though in a daze. 'I want you to come to bed with me, Harry,' she said. 'We don't always have to wait for darkness, do we?'

She felt his hands tremble as he undid her gown, felt the hardness of his hands against her skin, and she knew she wanted him to make love to her.

They lay naked on the bed together and she saw how fine his body was, how muscular his shoulders and chest. He was dark-haired, so different from Caradoc, who had fine, light hair. But she must not make comparisons; this was a new life, a life where there was no Caradoc Jones. She must just be thankful for what she had: her baby and a strong man who loved her and who would be at her side for as long as she needed him.

When he entered her she felt herself tense against him, but he seemed to understand; he gentled her and smoothed back her hair and kissed her eyes, her lips and then her breasts. She began to feel aroused as he imprisoned her mouth with his. She touched his shoulders, then put her arms around him and held him close. There was no need to feel fear or guilt; he was her husband and they were not doing anything wrong. Her passion blossomed as he moved more quickly inside her. Passion without love, was it possible?

She moaned softly, clinging to him, lifting her body up to him in complete surrender. Perhaps this was a sort of love she was feeling. In any case, for now, this tumbling feeling of passion was enough.

Caradoc stopped the drove by the riverside and looked up at the cottage standing out against the clear sky. The temptation to see Gwenllyn and the baby was too much for him.

'I'm going to ride up ahead,' he said to one of the men. 'I won't be long.' As he rode up the hill he set his mouth in a firm line. He owed Non nothing: she'd gone off to London, left him with no intention of coming back.

As he neared the cottage, he pulled up his horse and slipped from the saddle. He felt joy bubble inside him. Soon he would be holding his son in his arms. It was only right, he was the boy's father, and Gwenllyn had no right to prevent him from seeing the child.

He heard them as soon as he entered the cottage. Caradoc stood at the foot of the stairs, listening to the sounds of love-making, and his hands clenched into fists. He was struck by the absurd thought that Gwenllyn was his – she had no right to go to bed with any other man.

Anger drove out reason. He wanted to kill Harold Rees, to punch the man senseless. He stood for a long moment with a bitter taste of gall in his mouth. And then he heard a small cry coming from the sitting room. He followed the sound and saw his son, little arms flailing as he cried for his mother. But she wouldn't come – she was too busy upstairs satisfying her own needs.

He took David in his arms, wrapped him in a blanket and, with one last, angry look towards the stairs, left the house, vowing never to return.

'Where's my baby?' Gwenllyn stared in disbelief at the empty crib. 'What's happened to him, Harry?'

'The front door is open. Someone has been inside the house!'

'But who would want to take a little baby and walk off with him?'

Harry took her arm and led her to a chair. 'I'll just look outside. There must be some sign – fresh hoof prints, anything.'

Gwenllyn sat in total disbelief, staring into the empty crib. Her son, her wonderful little David, was gone. She put her hands over her face and felt the tears run between her fingers. This was a nightmare; she would wake soon and find it was all a dream.

Harold came back into the house. 'There's fresh hoof prints, all right, and I've got a fair idea who's taken the boy.'

She looked up at him hopefully. 'Who, Harry? Just tell me who would want to steal my son.'

'Caradoc Jones,' Harold said fiercely. 'I can hear sounds of the drove down in the valley. The bastard has been here. He must have heard us upstairs and for revenge he's taken David.'

Gwenllyn got to her feet and clasped Harold's hands. 'Go after him, please, Harry. Get my baby back.'

'I don't think it will be that easy,' Harold said.

'I'll go after Caradoc Jones and I'll find him – I know these roads as well as he does – but he's the boy's father: he'll have the law on his side.'

'But what can he say? David is well looked after, he's loved and cared for, and no one can take a child from his mother and get away with it.'

She began to feel calmer. The more she thought about it, the more she realized that Harry was right. Caradoc was the only one who'd want to steal David from her.

'I've just thought of something,' Harry said. 'Everyone believes that David is my child – we were married when he was born – so maybe Caradoc Jones would have a bit of trouble proving any rights to David.'

Gwenllyn sighed softly. 'I hope you're right, Harry, but getting him away from Caradoc will still be difficult. Once he has David in his home, surrounded by servants and footmen, what chance will we have?'

'If necessary I'll follow him to Swansea,' Harold said. 'I'll be as cunning as that Jones bastard. I'll go like a thief in the night and steal the baby away just like he did.'

'I want to come with you,' Gwenllyn said. 'I couldn't bear just sitting here not knowing what's happening.'

'All right, but you must stay calm, mind. The drove will be heading for the pass over the river Wye. We'll watch through the night, then I can seize my chance and get David back.' He put his hands on her shoulders. 'Try not to worry, Gwennie. At least the boy is safe.'

Gwenllyn leaned against his shoulder and as he put his arms around her she drew comfort from his nearness. Soon, pray to God, Harry would get her son back for her; and when he did, she would swear to love him for ever.

CHAPTER NINETEEN

'Something funny's going on round 'ere.' Ruby kneaded her fists into her hips as she confronted Carrie. 'I've had a good look at the books and the figures add up all right but the shelves are practically bare of stock. Where's the money gone that should have bought new stocks of bottles and the like?'

'It's all in order.' Carrie spoke in such a dignified manner that for a moment Ruby wondered if she was wrong about the girl. The evidence suggested that Carrie was on the fiddle, but she looked as if butter wouldn't melt in her mouth. 'And if she's so worried, why hasn't Mrs Jones come herself?'

'She's not feeling well enough. Anyway, don't change the bleedin' subject. What's going on round here?'

'I don't know what you're talking about. Everything is in order,' Carrie said sulkily.

Ruby's jaw jutted. 'You'll start telling me the truth, if you don't want a fist in your face. Talk.'

'It's the new shop,' Carrie said at last.

'What new shop?'

'Mrs Jones asked me to look out for new premises and that's just what I've been doing. I've found a fine little building just near the market and I've put most of the stock in there. I'll take you to see it if you like.'

Ruby hesitated. 'Even so,' she said at last, 'it's pointless to open a new shop if the old one ain't doing any business.'

Carrie sighed. 'I know that, Ruby, but I'm on my own, remember? Mrs Jones should be dealing with all this herself.'

'I told you she's not well,' Ruby said quickly. 'Right then, let's go and see this bleedin' shop, shall we?'

It was a fair walk to Smithfield and Ruby felt agitated about the time it was taking. She had her own business to see to and her lodgers would be expecting their dinner.

The market was, as usual, thronged with people and there was the ever pervading reek of flesh and blood; huge sides of beef hung up outside the butchers' shops. Still, anything was an improvement on the stink of the river.

The shop was just at the corner of Giltspur Street. It was, as Carrie had said, quite small, but in a situation where it was bound to be noticed.

'There's no sign over the door.' Ruby stood, hands on hips, surveying the building. 'But the window is large enough and it's a good spot to start a business in.' She turned to Carrie. 'And Mrs Jones told you to arrange all this?'

'She did.' Carrie spoke calmly. 'As for a sign, I've yet to get one painted, but I will, as soon as I can. Give me time, Ruby. I'm just a young woman trying to do my best for my employer, remember.'

After a moment Ruby nodded. 'Right, let's go inside.'

'Is that necessary?' Carrie asked. 'I mean, we both have other things to do. As you pointed out, I've got to get more stock for all Mrs Jones's shops and I know you have your own business to deal with.'

'Just a quick look,' Ruby persisted.

The inside of the shop was larger than it appeared from the outside. The big window cast a lot of light and that had the effect of making the room seem welcoming and fresh. Ruby could see that most of the shelves contained bottles of elixir and jars of ointment. From the low ceiling hung bunches of dried herbs. The place was well stocked and Ruby frowned.

'There's not much bleedin' point in having a lot of stuff in a shop that's not yet opened while letting one that's open look bare and baldy.'

Carrie shrugged. 'I thought Mrs Jones would

have taken charge by now, but seeing as there was a delay I thought I'd best get on with things myself.'

Ruby frowned, still not convinced. 'But even so, the takings on the old shop are down on what they should be.'

'I can't help it, Ruby, I've got too much work for one woman to handle. Perhaps you'd better tell Mrs Jones how badly she's needed round here.'

Ruby sighed and studied Carrie's face. The girl hid her feelings well; there was an expression of meekness about her that was belied by the stiffness of her posture.

'Well, I'd better see Non about all this straight away. I'm not happy with things here and that's telling you the truth. Something is going on, I can feel it in my bones.'

Carrie shrugged. 'What could be going on? We've got the old shop that needs to be stocked and then there's this one. What am I supposed to see to first?'

Ruby nodded. 'All right then, but I'm watching you, madam, and I'm not sure you're telling me the truth.'

Carrie smiled then. 'Watch all you like, Ruby. You won't be able to prove anything against me.'

'Oh, showing your bleedin' true colours now, are you?'

'I work hard and I've made Mrs Jones a lot of

money here in this shop. It's about time I had a bit of luck myself, don't you think?'

'Not if it's going to take money from Mrs Jones, I don't.'

'Well, are you going now? I've got work to do even if you haven't.' Carrie's eyes glinted. 'If that's all, I'll go and collect some herbs and make up some remedies or there'll be no money at all coming in.'

'What a cheek! You're dismissing me as if I'm a naughty child.'

'Not at all, but I have to work, as I keep reminding you.'

Reluctantly Ruby left the shop. She knew in her bones that Carrie was up to no good, but how could she prove it?

She picked up her pace. She would hurry home, see to her lodgers and then sit Non down and tackle her about the state of the shops. Carrie was right about one thing: Non had neglected her business. But she was still distressed about leaving her husband . . . Perhaps she should have a few days' rest before she heard the bad news? Ruby sighed. She'd better get moving, otherwise Non wouldn't be the only one to have a business in trouble.

Jessie sat behind the counter in her servery and watched as Emily dealt sweetly and efficiently with the customers. The young girl had blossomed in the time she'd worked with Albie and Jessie felt a pang of worry. She'd been in the same situation herself and, when she was, she'd imagined herself in love with her boss. Was Emily playing the same games with Albie?

How Jessie wished that the baby was born and she could feel young and slim and desirable again. Part of her didn't even want the baby because as it was growing in her belly it seemed to be driving a wedge between her and her husband.

Albie came into the shop through the back way. 'Hello, my sweet.' He carelessly brushed her cheek with his lips. 'Having a rest, then? Leaving the work to young Emily? Good thing too: you're looking pale. Why not go home and have a little sleep?'

Those were not the sort of words she wanted to hear from her husband. 'I'm all right.' She heard the irritation in her voice but couldn't control it. 'What's taken you so long with the milk round anyway?' she added sharply.

Albie looked at her in surprise. 'I've been finding new customers – that's what you wanted, wasn't it?' He smiled at her, his face lighting up. 'You didn't want me under your feet, so you said – you wanted me to be out on the road, making money. Well,' he patted the bag at his side, 'I've got us some damn fine business. You should be happy, not snarling at me like a hungry dog.'

Jessie held out her arms to him. 'I'm sorry, my lovely boy. Come here and give me a kiss – a real one this time, mind.'

He took her in his arms, pretended to manoeuvre around her belly and kissed her soundly on the lips. There were jeers and catcalls from the queue of people waiting for milk.

'Got you under her thumb,' one of the women called. 'Keeping her eye on you in case you run off with young Emily, that's the top and bottom of it.'

'Now, Mrs Murphy, don't stir up trouble for me.' Albie was still holding Jessie and his eyes were merry. 'In any case, I ain't looking for no one else: I got all I want right here in my arms.'

His words warmed Jessie's heart. She leaned against his shoulder, feeling guilty for doubting him.

'I'll take you home,' he said softly. 'I want you well and strong for when the baby comes.'

He gave some instructions to Emily, warning her to clean out the milk urns and shut up the shop carefully before leaving, and the girl looked up at him with limpid eyes.

'Will you come back and make sure I've done things right?'

After a moment Albie nodded. 'All right then, but I might be some time.'

'There's good of you to come back at all,' Emily said in her singsong Welsh accent.

Once again, fingers of fear clutched at Jessie's

heart. The girl liked Albie, more than liked him, and she was making her feelings plain. 'Surely you can manage a few chores, Emily?' Jessie said. 'I did it all myself before I fell for the baby.'

'Oh, yes, Jessie, of course I can manage. I'm just a little bit worried about seeing to the beasts, that's all.'

'I'll do that,' Albie said. 'You just do as I said and wash out the milk churns and close the shop up. Don't worry about the animals.'

Jessie felt a flare of irritation. Emily had got what she wanted. Albie was going back to her, and there was a bitter taste of jealousy in Jessie's mouth.

Later, as she sat in the warm, comfortable kitchen redolent with the appetizing smell of roast beef, she looked around her. The house she and Albie had set up together was perfect. The kitchen was bright with good curtains at the windows but they couldn't conceal the grime that clung to the outside of the panes of glass.

London was a dirty town and yet Jessie had come to love it. London was where Albie had been born – and if he loved the place, then she would too. Wasn't there a woman in the Bible who said, 'Your home is my home, your people my people?' Well, that's just what she felt about Albie and London.

She glanced at the clock. Where was Albie? He was taking an inordinately long time to see to the animals. She imagined him alone with Emily and the girl making sheep's eyes at him, egging him on to goodness knows what. But she was being foolish: Albie wouldn't betray her, he loved her; at least, that's what he was always telling her.

She bit her lip, imagining them together, Emily tempting Albie with her soulful glances and her young slim body. How could he resist when his wife was as fat as a pig and as grumpy as an old sow?

She heard the sound of the door and her heart lifted. He was home, Albie was home; he wasn't making love to Emily, he had come back to her, and she smiled as Albie came into the kitchen.

'Lovely smell of roasting meat in 'ere.' He kissed her and she made a face at him.

'You're not smelling so good, though. Have a wash and get ready. Your dinner will be on the table, waiting for you.'

'All right, boss; just as you say, boss.' He laughed and his face lit up and Jessie loved him so much that it hurt.

That night as they settled in bed, Jessie curled into Albie's arms and was content. He was here with her, safe and warm in their own house; he was her one true love and she was his. She must stop her nagging or one day he might well turn to Emily for love and affection, and if he did it would be all her fault. She kissed his face so close to hers.

'I love you, Albie. I really, really love you,' she said softly.

'And I love you, my Jess,' he said gently. 'I love you very much and don't you ever doubt it, my sugar.'

Jessie closed her eyes, feeling content and happy, all her silly fancies forgotten. She was in Albie's arms and he was hers for ever more.

CHAPTER TWENTY

Non studied the books again and she knew from what Ruby had told her that Carrie was somehow draining the profits from the business. She rubbed at her forehead. It was hot, but she'd taken some of her camomile infusion and, once she felt better, she would see Carrie herself, have things out with her.

'Not still working on those blasted figures, are you?' Ruby came into the room and rested her hand on Non's shoulder. 'You know as well as I do that the girl is robbing you blind. Do something about it before it's too late.'

Non covered Ruby's hand with her own. 'I will as soon as I feel better.'

'And when are you going to feel better? When you put this silly nonsense about Caradoc out of your head, that's when. You're afraid he loves that woman more than he loves you. Face up to it, girl,

Caradoc is only a man: he took another woman but it's you he really loves and that's all there is to it.'

'Is it? Look, I saw Morgan the blacksmith in town. He told me that Caradoc has taken his son home to my house,' Non said bitterly.

'Well, I don't know anything about that – perhaps it's all just gossip. And if it's true, I'm sure Caradoc didn't realize how much it would hurt you.'

'But he should have known!' Non felt tears in her eyes. 'I'm his wife and he has the audacity to take a bastard child into the home we shared. It's driven the last nail into the coffin of our marriage. I can never go back while that boy is there.' She brushed away her tears and tried to compose herself. 'Anyway, one thing is clear: I've got to sort out my affairs while I'm here in London, otherwise I'll have nothing to hold on to, no husband and no business.'

'You're right on that score at least,' Ruby said. 'I think you should give Carrie her marching orders before she ruins you.'

'I'll go tomorrow,' Non said firmly. 'I'll be feeling a little better then.'

'That's my girl!' Ruby smiled. 'Sort out your business but, remember, there's too much love between you and Caradoc. Don't let it go to waste.'

'I think it's too late for us to make our peace,'

Non said sadly. 'I do love Caradoc but I can never go back to him. Not now.'

Non stood outside the new shop and stared at the large window stocked with herbal remedies. The sign above the door caught her eye and she drew a deep breath. It read: 'Carrie Mayhew, proprietor'.

Non pushed open the door and marched inside, struggling to keep control of her temper. There was little point in attacking Carrie. She must find out what the girl was up to in a peaceable manner.

Carrie looked up as Non came into the room and she didn't flinch as she met Non's eyes. 'Mrs Jones, you are well, I hope? I heard you had caught a fever.'

'I'm perfectly well – just a little puzzled, that's all.' It was an understatement but Non didn't want to antagonize Carrie, she just wanted answers from her. 'I'd like you to explain why you have your name above the door.'

Carrie folded her arms across her stomach. Her head was high and she was not in the least perturbed by the question. 'You weren't taking any interest in the business,' she said briskly. 'The stocks were running low; people were losing patience with your many absences. In the end the custom was so poor, the business couldn't be maintained.' She made a deprecating gesture with her hand. 'I saw an opportunity and I took it.'

'But who has paid for all this stock?' Non asked. 'Where would you have the money for such an enterprise? You must have been creaming away a cut of my business for some time, otherwise where did the money to run a business of your own come from?'

'I haven't touched your money.' Carrie spoke with authority and for a moment Non actually believed her. 'I merely practised the mixing of the herbs myself,' she said airily. 'I gathered the flowers and roots and mixed and infused just as I've seen you do many times.' She smiled. 'There's not a lot to it, is there?'

'But there is!' Non said. 'If you make the wrong mixture, it could kill somebody. Haven't you thought about that?'

'Don't be silly, I have all your notes at hand, why should I make any mistakes?' She took a deep breath. 'If somebody came to me with a pain in their belly I'd tell them you invented the mixture, so, you see, there would be no blame attached to me.'

Non felt chilled by Carrie's words. 'I want to see the books,' she said, and Carrie swept out her hand, indicating that Non should go through into the back room. Non felt rather like a naughty child being patronized by an overzealous teacher.

The books, as Ruby had told her, were in good order. 'Where's the other set?' Non asked. 'Where are you keeping the real accounts that show how much money and time I've put into the shops?'

'Those are the only books,' Carrie said firmly.

'I don't believe you.' Non spoke angrily. 'I think you have cheated me out of my rightful profit and put the money into this shop for yourself.'

'Prove it.' Carrie smiled unpleasantly. 'All the old books you kept are gone. No one will ever see them again. My figures add up and I think you will find you have to close down the other shops. There's not enough business for both of us.'

'What if I speak to the authorities about your little scheme?'

'Speak to whom you wish,' Carrie said. 'I repeat, try to prove I've done wrong and you'll end up looking an incompetent fool.' She touched her hair with slim white fingers. 'The customers trust me now. They see me all the time. On the other hand, they hardly see anything of you, so why do you expect loyalty from them?'

Non stared at Carrie in disbelief. 'How could you cheat and lie and steal my business from me like this?' she asked. 'I helped and guided you; I trusted you to look after my affairs. How could you stoop so low, Carrie?'

Carrie didn't flinch. 'I think it's time you left my premises, Mrs Jones. I don't wish any of my customers to be embarrassed should they come into my shop.'

'Ah, the premises . . .' Non said eagerly. 'Who signed the papers and handed over the money?'

'I did, of course,' Carrie said, 'and I defy you to prove that there was any wrongdoing on my part.'

'You've really thought it all out, haven't you?' Non said. 'You've been cold and calculating and I can't believe you'd be so evil.'

Carrie swept past her and opened the shop door. The little bell tinkled as she indicated that Non should leave.

Non stopped in the doorway. 'I wouldn't have believed such treachery was possible.' She spoke heavily.

'Well, you know something, Mrs Jones? If you weren't so set on your muddled private life you would have put your affairs in order a long time ago. Good day to you.'

The door closed behind her and Non found herself on the pavement. She could think of nothing to do except to go home to Ruby and talk to her, see if she could come up with some answer to the dilemma. Ruby was sensible, she might see some flaw in Carrie's reckoning, but she doubted it. Carrie had played a devious game and been clever enough to cover her tracks, and so it seemed that she had won.

'The brazen hussy!' Ruby looked at Non. The girl's face was chalk-white and there were dark circles beneath her eyes. 'I knew that Carrie was cheating you but I never thought she'd go this far. The cheek of her, putting the shop in her name!

Surely you can take all that to a court of law?'

'On what evidence?' Non asked. 'If she's prescribed the wrong medicine, I might be able to prove she's been incompetent, but she's arranged the books so that she looks innocent of any wrongdoing.'

'Yes,' Ruby pursed her lips, 'maybe the law can't get her but I might know someone who can.' She was aware of Non looking at her in surprise. 'Oh, I have contacts these days,' Ruby said, 'folk who break the law so often they know how to use it to their advantage. Remember there's more than one way to skin a cat.'

'What do you mean?' Non asked warily.

Ruby tapped the side of her nose. 'Just leave it to me, girl, leave it to me.'

Gwenllyn stood outside the high gates of the palatial house where Caradoc lived. Inside those hard stone walls was her baby and she wanted him back. Harry had been against her coming to Swansea, then when he could see she was set on it he offered to go with her, but Gwenllyn had begged him to stay at home.

She'd argued that he would be better off caring for the beasts. In any case, what if Caradoc had a change of mind and brought David home? In the end she'd persuaded him to stay behind and now here she was in Swansea, ready to throw herself on Caradoc's mercy.

She pushed the gate wide and the door of the small lodge opened. 'Can I help you, miss?'

'I need to see Mr Jones,' Gwenllyn said. 'I've important business to talk over with him.'

'Well, you're out of luck, miss.' The man was affable enough but by the set of his shoulders and the way his hands gripped the gate it was clear he had no intention of letting her in.

'What do you mean, I'm out of luck?'

'Mr Jones is not at home, miss. He's an important businessman and he never sees anybody without an appointment.'

'But this is personal,' Gwenllyn said pleadingly. 'Just tell him I'm here. I'm sure he'll see me.'

'Perhaps you could come back tomorrow?'

'No, I have to see Caradoc today.'

'Well, truth to be told, miss, he's not here.'

The man was closing the gate in her face and Gwenllyn panicked. 'He's got my baby,' she said breathlessly. 'He's taken my baby from me and brought him here.'

The man straightened. 'I'm sorry, miss. All this has nothing to do with me. Now, will you leave before you get me into trouble.' She stood her ground and he shrugged and pushed the gate, forcing her to move away. 'Write a letter to Mr Jones,' he suggested kindly. 'I can't do anything to help. It's more than my job's worth to let you in.'

'Can I see Mrs Jones, then?' Gwenllyn asked desperately. 'I'm sure if you tell her who I am she'll want to talk to me. We know each other quite well.'

'You can't know her that well, miss, or you'd be aware Mrs Jones is in London.' He closed the gate with a click of finality and stood, arms folded across his chest, and watched until Gwenllyn walked away.

As soon as she was out of sight, she turned and crept back towards the back of the building. She felt her way along the high wall and her heart sank; she would never get inside the house: the grounds were impregnable.

She sank onto the soft grass and put her head on her knees. She was filled with despair. Somewhere behind those walls was her son, perhaps asleep, perhaps crying for her. How could Caradoc do such a thing to her? Tears ran down her cheeks, hot bitter tears. 'Caradoc Jones,' she sobbed, 'I hate you. I'll never forgive you for taking my son, never.'

CHAPTER TWENTY-ONE

Albie looked down at his wife as she lay in the bed beside him. Her hair curled damply on her forehead and her long lashes threw shadows onto her face. Poor Jess, she wasn't having an easy time of it; carrying their child was taking all her strength. Well, she wouldn't work any more in the servery. He would see to it that she took better care of herself, put up her lovely feet on cushions and rested.

He slipped out of bed, careful not to wake her, and took his clothes out onto the landing, glancing back at Jess before he dressed. He hurried downstairs to light the fire, but it was already blazing in the hearth.

''Morning, Albie.' Emily looked up at him with a wide smile on her face. 'I made a good fire for us this morning.'

'You should have waited till I got up. Look at your hands – black as the coals themselves.'

'I'm just going to have a wash and then I'm going to the shop. I'll see you there later, won't I?'

'Of course you will, and thanks for your help, Emily.'

He crouched beside the fire and added a few more coals just as Jess came into the kitchen, her eyes still full of sleep. 'Why didn't you wake me, Albie?' she said. 'We've got a lot of work on today, mind. There's all those new customers to serve.'

Albie smiled. 'Aye, I know, but Emily's gone in early so there's no need to worry. Anyway, I wanted you to rest. You're looking tired, my lovely sugar, and I don't want you getting sick, do I?' He kissed her warmly. 'You're not going to work any more. I've decided it's time you looked after yourself and that little baby you're carrying.' He put his hand on the swell of her belly and felt excitement rise within him as the baby kicked against his hand. He held Jess as close as he could and nuzzled his mouth against her warm neck. 'Just think of it, Jess: we're going to have a son.'

'Stop it, you daft man!' She held him away from her. 'I could be carrying a girl and I'll love her just as much as I would a son.'

'Of course you will, Jess, whatever it is we'll love it. But for now I want you to rest and build up your strength. I won't have you standing for hours in the shop or bending over milk churns, do you hear me?'

'I should think half the neighbourhood heard

you, Albie. Now, go and wash your hands while I make your breakfast.'

Albie whistled happily as he sluiced the coal dust from his hands. His Jess was a fine woman, a beautiful woman, and he was lucky to have found her. If it hadn't been for the cattle drovers coming from Wales bringing beasts to Smithfield he would never have met her. The thought made him shiver. His Jess was everything to him. He loved her more than anything in the world.

When he arrived at the servery Emily was already busy at the counter. She glanced up at him from under her lashes and a soft smile touched her mouth. 'I've had plenty of customers already, mind,' she said in her singsong Welsh accent. 'I've even managed to get some new folk to buy from us.'

'Good girl, Emily,' Albie said absently. 'I'd better go and see to the animals. Are you all right to carry on serving on your own?'

'Isn't Jessie coming in, then?' Her eyes were wide. 'She's all right, is she?'

'She's just tired. It's only natural really and she shouldn't be working while she's so heavy with child.' He smiled, not really seeing Emily's face, so he was unaware that her eyes had lit up and she had moved nearer to him.

'I'll manage just fine on my own. You go and see to the beasts, boss.' She rested her hand on his arm. 'I'll do everything I can to help, mind. I'll see the customers and wash out the pails and do anything you ask of me.'

He patted her shoulder. 'Good girl, Emily. I'd be bleedin' lost without you, and for gawd's sake call me Albie, will you?' He laughed. 'I'm not some old geezer you got to be polite to.' He turned away just as Emily flashed him a happy smile. 'See you later, then.' He walked away, unaware that Emily was looking longingly after him.

'How can I get my son back?' Gwenllyn stood in the kitchen, rubbing her palms together, her voice quivering as she spoke. 'You know, Harry, I couldn't even get into the grounds. The place is like a fortress.'

'I'll find a way in,' Harry said, his brow furrowed, his mouth stern.

Gwenllyn looked at him. 'No, Harry. I don't want you going anywhere near Caradoc Jones's place – they'd have you taken into jail as soon as you showed your face. No,' she took a deep breath. 'I'll go and see Non Jones, ask her to get my son back. She's a compassionate woman – I knew that when she agreed to nurse me even though she didn't want to be in my house.'

'But Mrs Jones is in London, so you'd have to travel all that way, Gwennie. I can't say I like the idea. Perhaps I should come with you?'

She shook her head. 'You stay here in case

Caradoc comes to his senses and brings David back.' She put her hand on his arm. 'I'll be all right, Harry. I'm not some country bumpkin, I'm an educated woman and I can make my way in any society.'

'I'm not questioning that.' Harry sounded hurt. 'I just wanted to look after you, that's all.'

'I know,' she said more softly. 'You're so kind to me, Harry. I really don't deserve a good man like you.'

He lifted his hands as if to hold her and then dropped them to his side again and Gwenllyn knew what he was thinking. She allowed intimacy in the bedroom but other than that she acted as if he was little more than a brother to her. She sighed. Poor Harry, it was an uneven bargain for him, but he put up with her rules because he cared about her.

'You go and stay with that Ruby woman, then,' Harry said. 'I know from riding with the drove that Ruby is an honest landlady and will look after you well. Come to think of it, Mrs Jones is probably staying at Ruby's lodging house.'

'Thank you, Harry, that's very helpful.' She reached up and kissed his cheek briefly and his face lit up. 'I'll go as soon as possible,' she said, quickly drawing away from him.

He took her hand and held it for a long moment. 'Be careful and promise you'll come back to me.'

'Of course I'll come back. This is my home.'

'I'll be waiting for you,' he said softly.

It took her little more than a day to prepare for the journey. She planned to catch the midweek mail and carry simply an overnight bag. She wouldn't need much by way of clothes: she wouldn't be staying long. She would speak to Non Jones, ask her – beg her on bended knee if necessary – to help her get her baby back. After that there wasn't much she could do but wait.

Gwenllyn had only been to London once in her life. She had travelled up with her grandmother and spent the night in a splendid hotel situated in the west of the city. From memory it was a noisy, smelly place with people milling around in crowded streets and a terrible fog draping every building in a shroud.

Now, as she alighted from the coach, she saw that the sprawling streets were still the same: full of people and thronged with coaches and wagons, with bellowing street sellers advertising their wares adding to the chaos of the place.

'Do you know Ruby's lodging house?' she asked the driver and he pointed the way along a narrow court to where a row of tall houses stood huddled together as if for protection against the spiteful rain that was falling.

Gwenllyn picked up her bag and with her heart beating fast she hurried along the row, praying that Ruby had a spare room. The door of the lodging house was open and Gwenllyn stepped inside, feeling the warmth of the house wrap itself round her.

A woman came out of the kitchen, wiping her hands against her spotless apron. 'Yes?' She looked enquiringly at Gwenllyn.

'I'm looking for a room,' she said, and waited with bated breath until Ruby nodded.

'You're in luck, there's one spare.' She looked at Gwenllyn's bag. 'Just for one night, is it?'

'That's right,' Gwenllyn said. 'I've come to London in the hope of seeing Mrs Caradoc Jones.'

Ruby's eyes narrowed as recognition dawned. 'If your name is Gwenllyn,' she stumbled over the unfamiliar name, 'I don't think she'll want to see you.'

'I'll see her, Ruby. It's all right.' Non came out of the kitchen and stood silently waiting for Gwenllyn to speak.

'I need your help, Mrs Jones.' Gwenllyn's voice shook as she saw that Non was looking at her with a mixture of curiosity and loathing.

'If it's to ask about your baby, then I don't know any more than you do. Apart from that, I have no influence over my husband. If you want to know the truth, I've left him for good, so it's pointless pleading your cause with me.'

Gwenllyn put her hand to her mouth in an

effort to stifle the tears. 'Is there really nothing you can do, Mrs Jones?'

'Nothing at all.'

Gwenllyn leaned against the wall, her knees trembling. Mrs Jones had been her last hope and now that hope had been cruelly taken away from her.

CHAPTER TWENTY-TWO

Gwenllyn's return journey was marred by delays; first a wheel on the coach worked loose and then one of the horses threw a shoe. The nights in the roadside inns were long and Gwenllyn thought she would never get back to Wales. Her journey to London had been fruitless and her only option now was to go back to Swansea, try to see Caradoc and beg him to return her son.

The journey seemed endless, but when at last the coach came to a stop outside the Castle Hotel in Swansea Gwenllyn felt a dart of fear. What if Caradoc's good standing in the town told against her? He could say the baby had been neglected, left alone, that she was an unfit mother. Anyway, who would defy Caradoc to defend her, a stranger in the town?

She took a cab the short distance from the centre of town to the Joneses' residence, prepared to try a gentle approach, relying on Caradoc's sense of fair play, before she did anything drastic such as calling in the law.

As she climbed down the steps from the cab, she saw that the gates of Caradoc's imposing residence were open and ahead of her she could see Caradoc's tall figure moving towards his house. The sunlight glinted on his bright hair and she felt the old sweep of love and anguish at the sight of him.

'Caradoc!' she called. 'Wait, please, Caradoc.'

He turned and saw her and, frowning, retraced his steps. 'Gwenllyn, I suppose I might have expected you.'

He didn't sound pleased to see her and she moved swiftly inside the gates before the man standing anxiously beside Caradoc closed them.

'Come into the house.' Caradoc's voice was heavy. He led the way through the massive hall and into a drawing room. She looked around: the place was palatial. She'd thought her own large cottage was impressive but it paled into insignificance compared with the luxury of Caradoc's home.

'I've seen your wife,' she said breathlessly. 'She's so angry with you for bringing David into your home.'

'What else could I do when I find him alone and you . . . cavorting with a man in your bedroom?'

The realization hit her like a slap across the face: Caradoc was jealous. He didn't want her but he didn't want anyone else to have her either.

'I married Harry to give my son a name, you know that,' she said softly. 'I still love you, Caradoc. I will always love you.'

He turned away from her. 'So you show your love for me by jumping into bed with a man like Harold Rees.'

'What's wrong with Harry?' Gwenllyn knew she sounded defensive but it pained her to hear Caradoc's slighting tone. 'He's been a good husband; he works hard and he takes care of me.'

'I can't bear to think of you in bed with him.' He crossed the floor in a few rapid strides and then he had her in his arms and his lips were on hers, avid for her response.

For one blissful moment she let him kiss her and then, realizing she was falling into an abyss of tears and disaster, she drew away from him.

'All I want is my son back,' she said breathlessly. 'Your wife won't come back to you while you have David in the house.'

He stood for a long moment looking at her and she drew on all her strength to speak to him in calm and even tones.

'Please, Caradoc, let me have my son. He belongs with me and if Non does come back to you she won't want him. David can't thrive in a house where there's friction, can't you see that?'

He thrust his hands into his pockets without speaking but she could see he was giving serious thought to what she said. Then he looked directly at her.

'My wife may never come back to me, in which case my son is all the family I'll have. You can't ask me to give him up.'

'Do you want me to go through life hating you?' Gwenllyn said steadily. 'And how do you expect to get Non back when you have another woman's son under your roof?'

'I don't know.' Caradoc rubbed his hand through his hair. 'I just don't know what to do about the baby, about Non.'

For the first time Gwenllyn felt sorry for Caradoc. He seemed genuinely bewildered by all that was happening to him.

'I'm sorry, Caradoc, but you can't put your marriage together unless the baby and I go home where we belong.' She moved closer to him and saw the beginning of tears in his eyes. 'You do still have feelings for me, don't you, Caradoc?'

'I do, God help me.' He reached out his arms and without thinking Gwenllyn went into them and rested her head against his chest. The rhythm of his heartbeat, the closeness of him, renewed all her longing for him. This was Caradoc, her first, her only, love.

She put up her hands and drew his head down to hers. The kiss lasted a long time and a tumult of sensations rushed through her. At last, she drew away. 'I still have feelings for you too, Caradoc, but we are not free to give in to our desires.'

'I know.' He turned away from her and she felt her heart flutter in fear. Was he still going to deny her wish to have her son back?

She put a hand on his arm. 'I'll come to bed with you, Caradoc, if you'll just give my baby back to me.'

He turned and smiled sadly. 'I know what effort it cost you to say that, Gwenllyn, and I wouldn't take advantage of you like that.' He shook his head. 'Take the baby. I know he belongs with you.' He pointed to the stairs. 'First room on the right. His nurse is with him. Tell her you have my permission to bring David downstairs.'

Gwenllyn lifted her skirts and ran up the stairs, her heart beating so fast she could hardly breathe. She pushed open the door and smelled the soft milky smell of baby and there he was, her David, her darling little boy, nestled in the arms of a woman whose neatly starched apron spoke of her attention to detail. There was no doubt David had been well cared for.

'Caradoc . . . Mr Jones has given me permission to take the baby,' she said breathlessly.

The woman looked her up and down before she moved to the top of the stairs. 'Mr Jones, am I to let this woman take David?' she called.

Caradoc hesitated for a heart-stopping moment

and then nodded his head. 'Yes, give the baby to his mother. His place is with her.'

Gwenllyn wrapped the baby in a pristine white shawl and held him close, kissing his downy hair again and again. David snuggled into her warmth, his eyes closing sleepily, his head heavy against her breast.

'Thank you, Caradoc,' she said, very aware that the nurse was watching with curious eyes. 'I'm going now but I'll always think kindly of you.'

'Wait,' he said as she moved to the door. She stopped, her mouth dry, waiting with bated breath to hear what he had to say. Was he even now going to forbid her to take David home?

'I'll send for my coachman. He'll take you home to the Wye Valley. It's the least I can do.'

'Thank you, Caradoc,' she said simply. She looked down at her sleeping son. 'We'll soon be back home, my darling, and I won't let you out of my sight ever again.'

Jessie felt more rested now. Albie had been right: she shouldn't work now that she was so big with child. She sat in the comfortable sitting room and picked up her knitting. She wasn't very good with the needles, not like the women who walked the trail with the cattle drovers, but she could do well enough to make her child a few clothes.

Albie came into the room and smiled as he saw her sitting calmly in her chair. 'That's a picture to delight any man's soul,' he said: 'a beautiful wife and a baby on the way, not to mention a thriving business. What more could any man want?'

'Are you really content with me, Albie? Even as fat as I am and complaining constantly about my backache?'

'I wouldn't change you for the world.' He knelt on the floor and rested his head in her lap, a smile turning up the corners of his mouth. 'Not much room for me, not with that fine son you got in there, kicking and pushing.'

Jessie put away her knitting and smoothed back his hair. 'You might get a girl, Albie. I can't guarantee it will be a boy, mind.'

'Our child will be handsome, coming from so fine a woman.' He took her hand and kissed it and rested his cheek in her palm. 'I'm so happy, Jess – bloody happy, if the truth be known. I love you, Jess, and I'll love our child whatever it is.' He looked up and smiled mischievously. 'But I hope it's a boy. I'd like a son to follow in my footsteps.' He scrambled to his feet. 'I suppose I'd better get back to the servery, see how young Emily is managing on her own.'

'I thought you were having the whole day off to spend with me?' Jessie was aware she sounded petulant but she felt the old tug of fear at the mention of Emily's name. 'You seem very keen to get back to Emily.'

Albie looked at her in amazement. 'What do you mean?'

'I mean she's a pretty girl who worships the ground you walk on and furthermore she's not as fat as a pig.'

'That's silly talk,' Albie said. 'I see Emily only as a child – and if she bleedin' worships me, she's dafter than she looks.'

Jessie felt her tension ease. 'Are you sure you don't have a fancy for her?' She heard herself asking the question and despised herself for it. She should trust Albie: he was her husband and he loved her.

'Of course I don't.' He kissed her gently. 'I fancy you, Jess, and only you. I love you so much that it hurts. Why would I ever want to look at another woman?'

She took his hand. 'You see, Albie, I'm so lucky to have met you and I'm afraid sometimes that I'll lose you.'

'You won't lose me, Jess, and it's me who's the lucky one. I remember the old days when I dipped into folks' pockets to scratch a living. There wasn't one person in the world who cared if I lived or died. Now I have you to love me and you needn't be afraid you'll lose me. I'll stick to you like glue.'

Jessie breathed a sigh of relief as Albie smiled at her. Of course he loved her and he wouldn't ever hurt her, she knew that, so why did her uneasy suspicions keep torturing her?

* * *

Caradoc looked round the empty house. He hated being alone and now he had no wife, no baby, to care for. He loved two women: how could that be? He wanted Non back. She was an ache in his bones, her presence lit up his life, and now without her he felt lost. And yet, and yet, there was still a longing for Gwenllyn. He had lived with her for a whole summer and now he couldn't get her out of his mind. He walked out into the garden and stared, unseeingly, at the rolling lawns, at the graceful fountains splashing water like diamonds in the sun. He was blessed with riches, he had every material advantage he could want. Even if he never went on a cattle drive again he would still be a rich man. And yet riches were no good without love.

He should be gathering a herd together right now but his heart wasn't in it. He sat on one of the carved wooden benches that graced the wide paths between the flowers and closed his eyes against the sunlight. He should be rushing up to London again to fetch his wife home and yet something held him back – was it pride or was it something deeper? What did he want? Who did he want? He was so confused, he couldn't think straight.

'Damn all women!' His voice carried across the quiet garden and a flock of birds rose up like a cloud against the sky. It was like an omen, but an omen of happiness or of doom? He searched his mind for an answer but none came.

'I've seen to everything.' Emily looked at Albie – he had come back to help her so he must care for her just a little. 'I've scrubbed the urns and the pails and I've even cleaned out the animals' stall.' She was pleased with herself and she hoped Albie would be pleased with her too.

'You're a good girl, Em.' Albie rested his hand on her shoulder. 'I'd be bleedin' lost without you.'

Emily bristled with pride. He was saying he couldn't do without her and that's all she wanted to hear. She went closer to him and looked up into his face. 'I've got to tell you something, Albie.' She felt her heart beginning to pound and her mouth was dry.

'Go on, then. What is it? Have you broke something or been rude to a customer? Whatever it is, there's no need to look so fearful.'

She knew she had to take the lead. Albie was probably afraid she'd reject him if he took her in his arms and kissed her. She plucked up her courage and, standing on tiptoe, pressed her lips against his cheek.

Albie smiled down at her. 'You're like a friendly little kitten, Em, and there's no need to feel grateful to me. You work for your money and you're a damn good worker too. I would need two girls to take your place if you left.'

'There's no fear of me leaving,' Emily said breathlessly. 'I'm in love with you, Albie.' She pressed her palm against his cheek, turning his face towards her, and then she kissed him full on the lips.

Emily was lost for a moment in the magic of feeling his lips against hers, then she was brought back to reality by a small cry coming from the direction of the doorway. She moved quickly away from Albie as Jessie came into the servery.

'Albie, how could you?' Jessie was white-faced; her hands cupped her swollen belly and tears brimmed in her eyes.

'No, Jess, it's not what you think.' Albie went to his wife and took her hands in his. 'It was just that Emily was grateful for her job and I said how good a worker she was and then, well, that's all, she gave me a little kiss.'

'How could you?' Jessie repeated. 'I trusted you, Albie. I trusted you with my life.'

Emily took a deep breath. She needed to fight for Albie: she could see that Jessie wasn't going to let him go easily. 'If you trusted Albie so much, why did you follow him here?' she said, trying to control the trembling of her lips.

Jessie didn't look at her. It was as if she hadn't heard and Emily suddenly felt as though she was invisible.

'My little Jess.' Albie went up to his wife and put his arms around her. 'My dear little Jess, you know I don't love anyone but you. Please listen. It was just a friendly kiss, nothing more. You know that Emily means nothing to me. Not in that way,' he added hastily, with an apologetic glance in Emily's direction.

Emily knew then without a shadow of a doubt that she had lost. What slight chance she might have had of drawing Albie close to her was gone, vanished like smoke in the wind. And the knowledge was so painful she couldn't even find relief in tears.

CHAPTER TWENTY-THREE

Non was awakened in the night by Ruby, who was dressed in her long nightgown with a shawl around her shoulders.

'It's Jessie,' she said, her voice hoarse with tiredness. 'A street boy brought a message from Albie. The baby is coming early and Jessie wants you with her.'

Non was awake at once. Something was wrong, otherwise Jessie would have called one of the midwives who lived close by the servery. She dressed quickly and lastly pulled on her boots.

'I'll come with you.' Ruby hurried from the room as Non began to put the medicines she might require into a basket.

It was strange travelling along the dark London streets, the wheels of the cart hitting every bump in the road. The smell from the river was overpowering but Non had become accustomed to it.

She strained her eyes to see where Ruby was taking her, but at night everything was different, unfamiliar.

Ruby's knowledge of London was profound. She'd been born and bred there and knew the streets as she knew the lines on her hand, and soon she reined in the horse outside Jessie's house.

Non climbed down from the cart, holding her basket away from her so that the contents would be safe. The light from the street lamp threw shuddering shadows across her path and Non had an uneasy feeling that tonight would prove to be a long and difficult one.

'Come on,' she urged as Ruby tethered the horse to the lamppost. 'I've got a feeling this night is not going to bring happiness to anyone.'

The door was flung open and Albie stood there, his hair standing on end, his eyes haunted and shadowed.

'Help her, Non, please help my darlin' Jess.' He was almost in tears and Non touched his arm.

'I'll do everything I can. Now, where is she?' Non injected a cheery note into her voice, but as she followed Albie upstairs her heart was cold. She had an overwhelming fear that she would be powerless to stop a tragedy from unfolding that night.

★   ★   ★

Gwenllyn saw the familiar hills come into sight as the moonlight splashed silver over the crags and crevices of the rock. And there, nestling under the hills, was her home, her cottage, and her heart lit within her.

'Davie, *boy bach*, I'm taking you home and you'll never leave my side again.'

As she climbed from the coach Harry was waiting for her. He looked anxiously at her face and then his gaze moved to the embossed lettering on the coach.

'So he's sent you home in style, has he?' Harry looked unhappy. 'Tell me you didn't . . . well, you know what I mean.'

'I've got my baby back, that's what's important.' She nodded to the coachman. 'You can spend the night if you wish. There's plenty of room in the cottage.'

The man touched his cap. 'No need for that, mam. I'll be back in Swansea by morning, but thank ye kindly.'

Harry led her into the hallway and put his arms around both her and the baby. 'I've missed you so much and I've been so fearful.' His voice was shaking with emotion. 'I thought Caradoc Jones would persuade you to stay with him. I thought . . .' He rubbed his hand through his hair. 'I don't know what I thought.'

'Look, Harry, nothing happened between me and Caradoc. He saw sense when I talked to him.

I said Non would never come back to him while he had the baby in the house and so he let us go.'

'Thank God for that.' Harry kissed her hair. 'It's so good to have you here with me, my lovely girl. Since you went, it's like I've had an arm or a leg missing.' He led her into the kitchen. 'I've kept the fire alight and the kettle's on the boil. What if I make you a lovely cup of tea?' He rubbed her shoulder as though reassuring himself that she was really there.

Gwenllyn warmed to him. He loved her and cared about her and she should count herself lucky that she was married to such a good man. She touched his cheek. 'Thank you for being so kind, Harry.' She sank gratefully into a chair and moved the shawl away from David's face. 'Look at the little darling. He slept all the way home.'

Harry brewed the tea and put out the cups. His eyes were alight and his movements quick. 'I can't tell you how good it is to have you back,' he said. 'I've been so lost and alone without you.'

Gwenllyn smiled. 'I know.' She looked up at him and made an effort to lighten the mood. 'Your vocabulary has improved, Harry. You talk like a gentleman now.'

'I don't want to be a gentleman, I just want what I've got, Gwenllyn: a beautiful wife, a woman I love more than life itself. I only wish you could love me back, even if it is just a little.'

'But I do, Harry!' Gwenllyn said. 'You're my

husband. I respect you and honour you and there is love, but perhaps a different sort of love.'

'Different from what you feel for Caradoc Jones, is that what you mean?'

'I suppose so, Harry, but I love David in a different way too. There are many ways of loving, every one of them precious. Let's just be happy with what we've got, Harry. Now, where's that cup of tea?'

Later, as morning was creeping in through the bedroom curtains, Gwenllyn sent up a prayer of thanks that she was home and her baby was safely at her side. And there on the other side of her was Harry – faithful, loving Harry. She reached out and touched his hand and immediately he was awake.

'Gwenllyn, is everything all right?' He leaned on one elbow and looked down at her. Suddenly she began to cry. 'What is it, my darling?' Harry smoothed her cheek. 'Are you worried Caradoc will come and take the baby again?'

She shook her head, unable to stop the tears from rolling down her cheeks. 'It's not that,' she gulped back the sobs, 'it's just that I'm so lucky – lucky to have David and to have you.'

He held her in his arms then, his heart beating against hers, and Gwenllyn clung to his broad shoulders. 'Look,' he said, 'the sun is rising. It's a new morning and a new start for us, don't you see that, Gwen?'

'Yes, Harry, I see that more clearly than I've ever seen it.' And she meant it: she would put Caradoc right out of her mind; he wasn't hers, he was married to another woman, and all the sunny days they had spent together amounted to nothing more than a pleasant dream. Harry was right, she had a new start to look forward to, and he was a big part of that; she didn't know how she'd ever managed without him. 'Thank you, Harry,' she said simply.

'For what?'

'For being so wise and standing by me when I needed you most.'

He bent and kissed away her tears and Gwenllyn felt closer to her husband than she had ever been before. 'I do love you, Harry,' she said softly, and in that moment she meant every word.

Jessie was thrashing on the bed and Non knew she was in real trouble. She ran her hands over Jessie's swollen, straining belly and felt that the child was the wrong way up. It was going to be a breach birth.

'Take a little laudanum to ease the pain.'

Jessie shook her head. 'No. It might hurt the baby.'

'The baby is coming now and you are going to need all the help you can to bring him out into the world.'

'I'm all right.' Jessie's face was beaded with

sweat and her eyes were wide with fear, but she was a brave little thing and determined to hide her pain.

'Take the bleedin' medicine if it will help you,' Albie said, leaning over Jessie and taking her hand. 'You're having a rough time, I can see that.' He was almost in tears. 'If only I could 'elp you I'd give my right arm.'

Ruby came into the room with a bowl of steaming water and a pile of clean cloths over her arm. 'You *can* help,' she said briskly. 'You can go and make us each a cup of tea.'

Albie looked down at his wife. 'Do you want a cuppa, darlin'?'

Jessie winced as another pain crawled around her belly. Her face became pinched and white and Non knew that if she wanted to save Jessie's life she would have to take drastic measures.

'I can't go and leave her like this,' Albie said.

'Go on. This might take a long time.' Non spoke as calmly as she could but she knew that she would be changed forever by the ordeal Jessie was suffering.

She followed Albie down to the kitchen. 'I'll tell you straight, Albie: Jessie will die unless I do something.'

He looked at her, the kettle in his hand, and his eyes were shadowed. 'I know what you're going to say: the baby will have to be got rid of.'

Non took a deep breath. 'Put some laudanum

into Jessie's tea and try to make her drink it.' She hesitated. 'I need the sharpest knife you've got, Albie.'

'What for?'

'Don't think about that, not now.'

'You'll have to use the knife to get the baby out – is that what you mean?'

'It's that or let Jessie die. I'm sorry, Albie, I've never had to do this before and I'm dreading it, to tell you the truth.'

After a moment Albie nodded. 'Save my Jess. I can't live without her, so do what you 'ave to do.'

Non's legs were trembling as she followed Albie up the stairs. He was carrying teacups on a tray and she had a knife hidden in her skirts. She would have to wait until Jessie was sleepy before she could start the delicate, dreadful operation that would destroy Jessie's child.

She bit her lip. Was she doing right? Should she let nature take its course and see what happened? Jessie might live even if Non did nothing. But in her heart she knew Jessie could never bring the baby out. To let nature take its course would be to let both mother and child die.

To her relief, Jessie took the drink of tea. 'It's so hard,' she murmured. 'It hurts so much. Is this the way all babies come into the world?'

Ruby fussed gently around Jessie. 'You just try to relax. It will help if you can rest a little.'

Jessie finished her tea and her eyes grew heavy.

She lifted her hand to Albie. 'If I don't live through this, you find another little woman to help you with the milk.' She sighed. 'Emily will stay by your side – she's in love with you.'

Albie knelt beside the bed and smoothed back Jessie's hair. 'I don't want Emily,' he said. 'What you saw was just a silly girl trying to kiss her boss. It meant nothing to me, Jess, believe me.'

She touched his hair. 'I know, my lovely, I know.'

She closed her eyes and Non knew she was asleep. She hesitated for a long moment, not wanting to insert the blade, not wanting to destroy the child, but she knew she had no choice.

Even as she hesitated, Jessie began to haemorrhage. The blood pumped out thick and red and Non let the knife slip from her fingers onto the floor. She was too late: she could not save mother or baby now. Nature had taken its own course and all she could do was to wait helplessly as Jessie's life-blood drained away. She stood aside as Albie, white-faced, took his wife's hands in his own.

'I love you, my Jess,' he said thickly. 'I'll always love you, my darlin' girl, and wherever you're going I'll follow you one day and we'll be together for ever more.'

Non sank onto the floor, her head in her hands, and hot tears gathered in her eyes and ran down her face.

'I'm sorry, Jessie, I couldn't save you,' she whispered. 'I'm so very sorry.' She put her hands over her eyes but she could not block out the vision of Jessie's bloodless face. It was a sight that would haunt her for ever.

CHAPTER TWENTY-FOUR

Albie took Jessie's body home to her beloved Wales and there he buried her with all the dignity he could muster. He stared at the fresh earth in disbelief. His Jess couldn't be dead. Now, looking at the grave, the stark reality of the situation flooded over him; he realized his beloved girl was gone from him for ever.

He felt Non's hand on his arm and he turned to her gratefully. 'Thank you for coming with me. I don't know how I'd have managed without you.'

'I had to come,' Non said. 'Jessie was a good friend.'

'She did know I wasn't unfaithful with Emily; she did know, didn't she, Non? I couldn't bear it if Jess went out of this world thinking ill of me.'

'She believed you, Albie. Her face was content when you told her Emily was just being a silly young girl.'

Albie turned away from Non. 'You and Ruby have both been so good to me. I know you've always loved my Jess.'

Ruby rubbed away her tears with a small lace handkerchief. 'I loved her like she was my own sister.'

He felt Non's hand tighten on his arm. 'Come on back to the house. I've got a little tea prepared.'

Albie nodded. 'You go on. I'll just say my own goodbyes to Jess by myself, if you don't mind.'

He watched as the small knot of mourners turned away and trod uphill towards the gates of the cemetery. And then he was alone with only the black crows flying overhead, as black as midnight, as black as his thoughts.

Non watched from the doorway as the mourners partook of the small sandwiches of egg and chives and the good hot, strong tea. Tea was panacea for all pains: the very act of drinking it seemed to steady the nerves. She caught sight of Albie, his tall frame stooped, a look of shock and hopelessness on his face. He would spend a long time grieving and there was little anyone could do to help him.

Caradoc came up behind her and rested his hand for a moment on her shoulder.

She stiffened against his touch. 'I'm only here because of the funeral,' she said. 'Don't read anything else into my visit.'

'Non, can't we talk? I want to say how sorry I am for bringing the baby home. I didn't realize how much hurt I was causing both you and Gwenllyn.'

Non turned her head sharply. 'Do you always have to bring that woman into our conversations? Have you no sense of decency?'

'I'm sorry.' Caradoc's hand dropped from her shoulders and suddenly Non felt cold, unloved.

'I'll be travelling back to London tomorrow with Ruby and Albie. I've important business to attend to, as you would know if you took a real interest in my affairs.'

'I know your concerns about the business. I realize there must be grave problems with your staff, and all I want to do is help. Look, I'll come with you to London, if you want me to.'

'No. Just leave me alone, Caradoc. This is not the time to have a quarrel.'

He moved away from her and she watched as he gripped Albie's hand and offered condolences. Albie was a good man, he loved only one woman, and she had been taken away from him. Life was so unfair.

Caradoc turned and caught her eye and she looked away quickly, an unexpected surge of love for her husband coursing through her. How could she still love him, want him, now that she knew that what he most desired in his life was his son and most probably his son's mother? She, his wife, was a broken-off corner of the twisted triangle that their life had become.

The next morning, Non joined the mail coach to London along with Albie and Ruby. She tried not to look back as Caradoc stood, holding the reins of his horse, staring after her, a wistful look on his face.

'All right, Albie?' Non put her hand over his and he looked at her through a blur of tears.

'I feel I'm bleedin' deserting her,' he said in a whisper. 'I know Jess wanted to lay to rest in her own home territory, but it's hard leaving her behind.'

Ruby was tight-lipped, her face white as she struggled for composure. 'You were right to bring her to Wales,' she said, her voice hoarse. 'We all know it's what she wanted when she died. But did it have to happen so soon?'

Non was silent. She still held onto Albie's hand as the coach creaked into movement. She didn't want to leave home; she wanted everything to be all right again, for Caradoc to love her and only her. But that was an impossible dream. She had to deal with the matter of her shops, and of Carrie's dishonesty, and it was a job she had little heart for.

She gazed from the window of the coach, watching the softly moving waves that laved the shores of her home town. As the coach moved out of Swansea, leaving its bustling streets behind, she felt desolate.

At the next stage, a couple with a small baby entered the coach and Ruby moved to the corner of the seat to accommodate the little family. Albie remained silent, slumped in his seat, his eyes dull, as undoubtedly he thought of the wife and unborn child he had just buried.

Non watched the couple, so in love, so proud of the baby, cooing over the infant and looking up from time to time, expecting the approval of the other passengers. It reminded her of Caradoc with his son, his illegitimate son, she reminded herself, and yet the thought brought no comfort. Caradoc loved the boy, wanted a say in his future, and that meant staying in touch with Gwenllyn.

She shivered. She told herself again that she would be better off in London, sorting out her business affairs. Closing her eyes, she sank back in her seat. She didn't want to talk: she had too much emotion running through her to engage in polite conversation. Perhaps if she remained silent, it would appear as if she was asleep. She drank in the quietness of the coach and then, suddenly and stridently, the infant began to cry. Non sighed: life would intrude whatever she did.

Carrie was almost ready; her plans were complete. She sat in her small upstairs chambers and looked for the last time at the accounts books. She had successfully taken away most of Non Jones's trade. The local people no longer trusted Non, they believed in Carrie, who was a Londoner born and bred. Non was just an incomer – she would never be a real part of the town of London.

Carrie yawned and put away her money; it was time to go to bed. She had one more task to accomplish and that was to burn the evidence of her misappropriation of funds: the double set of records. But that would have to wait, as Carrie, mean with the coals, had allowed the fire to go out. She warmed herself with the thought that Non would be finished – no one would want to trade with a woman who couldn't be trusted.

Carrie smiled – her own manoeuvring had been masterly. She had given the wrong medicine to several of the regular customers, letting them believe it was all Non's doing. What with the burning of the books, it would be the last nail in Non's coffin. Without records, no one could prove that Carrie had taken the money for herself.

The journey to London proved difficult. The rain poured down, obscuring the hills and making the rivers impassable. The baby continued to wail and cry for the duration. Even the proud parents became fractious, blaming the weather for the child's restlessness. And all the time Albie sat slumped in his seat, blind and deaf to everything but the vibrations of his own grief.

Overnight stops were a nightmare. Many of the coaching inns were full and on one occasion Non and Ruby had to share a tiny room that was bare of curtains and in the way of furniture had only a small bed and a lumpy mattress on the floor. It was a great relief when at last the coach pulled to a halt in London.

As Non alighted, she breathed in the smell of the river and wrinkled her nose against it. A spiteful dart of rain caught her face and ran down her cheeks like tears. Could she spend her life living here, alone without a husband, without a business?

'Come in with me,' Ruby said, 'and you, Albie. I'll give you both a good feed and a bleedin' good night's rest.'

'I'll accept your offer, Ruby,' said Non, rubbing her eyes. 'I'm so tired I could sleep all day and all night.'

'Well, you'll need your wits about you if you're to put one over on that Carrie girl. You'll have to be sharp to win the day over her.'

Non sighed. 'Right now I don't know how I'll get the better of Carrie. She's very intelligent and very strong and I feel as weak as a kitten.'

'Let's not stand in the court nattering about it, let's get inside, out of this awful drizzle.'

'I'll get back to my place.' Albie stood beside Non, his face long with grief. 'I'll have to see to . . . well, everything.'

'No, you bleedin' won't,' Ruby said. 'You need some hot food inside your belly and then to get your head down and sleep. You look like death warmed up.' She slapped her hand over her mouth, realizing what she said, and Non took a sharp breath, watching Albie with fearful eyes.

His face seemed to pale. His back was against the light but Non could see how his shoulders sagged and how his arms dangled beside his body as if he had no use for them. She took his cold hand and warmed it with her own.

'Come on in, Albie, love. You can't do much at home at this time of day, can you?'

'I'm going home.' He released himself. 'I have to go home, Non, but thank you for helping me say goodbye to Jess the way she would have wanted.' He hesitated for a moment and then he set off down the court, his shoulders hunched, his gait like an old man's.

Non stared after him, wondering why the world had turned upside down for the both of them, robbing them of the ones they loved most. Then she turned to the lamplight streaming from Ruby's porch and went inside and closed the door.

'I'm sorry, Albie, so sorry about Jessie.'

Albie looked at Emily with red-rimmed eyes. He could think of nothing to say to her. She reached out to touch his arm and he drew away as if scalded. He didn't want her touch or her sympathy, he just wanted to be left alone.

'I think it best if you find your brother and ask him to take you home to Wales,' Albie said heavily. 'There's nothing for you here, not any more.'

She took a sharp breath. 'But, Albie, I love the job. I love serving the milk and even milking the beasts isn't so bad. Most of all I love being with you.'

He stared at her long and hard. 'I don't want to be with you, Emily, can't you understand that? The only woman I ever wanted or ever will want is my Jess, my lovely Jess.'

He sat on a barrel and the tears flowed from his eyes. 'Oh, Jess, my darling Jess, why did you have to leave me?' The sobs racked his body and he made no attempt to stop crying; he was desolate, lost in a fog of misery without his dear wife.

He felt soft arms around him, holding him close, and for a moment he allowed the embrace to warm him. Then, angrily, he pushed Emily away. 'Leave me, just go, Emily. I want to be left alone – can't you understand that?'

He heard her begin to cry then, as she continued to hold him, his head resting on her soft young breasts.

'I love you, Albie. Don't send me away, please. I can't live without you.'

They clung together like drowning souls and

Albie relented. It really wasn't the girl's fault; she was young and vulnerable like a delicate flower, and he didn't want to crush her.

He held her away. 'Go to see Josh for a week or two and then, when you come back, I'll see if we can work together.'

Emily fell onto her knees and took both his hands in hers. 'Thank you, Albie, thank you from the bottom of my heart.'

He looked into her sweet face. 'Go on, now, Emily. I need to be on my own for a bit.'

She left him then and he felt suffocated by the lonely silence. It wrapped around him like a London Particular – heavy, robbing him of breath. He cried for a long time, until he was too weary to cry any more, and then he got up and went to his lonely bed.

CHAPTER TWENTY-FIVE

Gwenllyn sat at the table opposite Harry and watched him covertly while he ate his evening meal. He had washed before coming into the house but there was still a faint odour of cattle about him.

'How are the beasts behaving? Are the cows in calf again?' She was making conversation as if talking to a stranger. No one would ever think she spent her nights in Harry's embrace. She'd tried to love him, she even felt she did love him just a little, but Caradoc Jones was still in her blood, would always be: he was her first, her only love.

Harry smiled. 'Aye, my little herd is growing. The bull is going to make me more money today – one of the farmers is bringing two cows to be serviced.'

She was pleased for him. Harry seemed to have grown in confidence and stature since he had had his own animals to tend. He was a man come into his own, with a wife and a business at which he was becoming very successful.

She tried to see him objectively. He was a good-looking man, in a big and rugged way; his hair often stood on end, shaped into unruly curls by the wind, and his complexion was that of an out-doors man.

'What are you staring at?' Harry was smiling. 'Have I got a spot on my nose or something?'

Taken unaware, she felt herself blushing. 'No. Sorry. I was thinking how well you look.'

His smile was wide. Any little bit of praise from her and he lit up. He loved her; she had no doubt about that.

'It's nice, isn't it, Gwennie, us two sitting here eating our meal like an old married couple?'

She felt uncomfortable as she always did when he seemed to draw close to her. 'Well, I suppose we are an old married couple,' she said lightly.

'I know, but, Gwennie, I never feel I have you. One day you are kind and, well, almost loving and then you slip away from me again; you go inside yourself to where I can't reach you.'

He was very good at expressing himself these days and she knew exactly what he meant. Some days she was off with the fairies, thinking of Caradoc coming to fetch her and the baby, riding in like a knight of old to save her from a sham marriage.

'I'm sorry if I seem odd at times,' she said. 'The baby takes up a great deal of my time and my attention.'

They both knew it was an excuse but Harry chose not to pursue the matter further.

Gwenllyn smiled gratefully at him. 'Have some more pie, Harry?'

He shook his head. 'I've had more than enough. You're a very good cook, Gwennie.'

She was pleased. 'I've had to learn to cook,' she said. 'Since the last maids left, I can't seem to get any servants, and though the village women are more kindly disposed towards me these days they don't entirely accept me. Still, I'm glad that I can at least get a woman to do the washing and ironing. I don't think I could cope with all that *and* cooking for a husband and child.'

'Well, so long as the local farmers keep me in business I'm happy, though I do think you need servants to help you with a big place like this.' He looked round. 'Your cottage is a fitting place to live for a lady such as you.'

Gwenllyn laughed. 'Harry, I do believe you're becoming a snob!'

He laughed with her, a rueful look on his face. 'Not exactly, but I do like the peace and quiet of sharing the place just with you' – he paused – 'and little David, of course.'

She sobered instantly. It must be difficult for Harry, seeing the baby grow, knowing he was the son of another man. But then Harry had known the truth from the beginning: he hadn't been under any illusions about why she'd married him.

And yet things had changed. The balance of their marriage was now equal; with Harry earning his own keep, he'd become a strong, fair-minded man, and Gwenllyn knew she'd had a hand in the change in him.

'It works well between us, doesn't it, Gwennie?' He seemed to pick up on her thoughts. 'I mean, this marriage, it's not so bad, is it?'

She put down her napkin. 'I'd better get the dishes cleared and washed.'

'I'll help you,' Harry said dully, aware that she was dodging the issue. 'You look a bit tired tonight. Has the baby been playing you up?'

'Not more than usual,' Gwenllyn said, 'but you're right, I do feel a bit tired. Perhaps I'll go to bed early.'

It was a signal to Harry that there would be no intimacy between them. He nodded. 'Aye, it might do you good. You're up at dawn these days, and there's always a lot for you to do.'

She smiled. 'Thank you for being so understanding, Harry. You are a good man, do you know that?'

His face brightened. 'I've changed so much since you came into my life,' he said. 'It makes me ashamed now when I remember my reason for marrying you. It was greed, I was drawn by the money you offered me, but, Gwennie, I've come to realize how lucky I am to be in your life at all. I'll pay you back every penny of the money you gave me one day soon.'

Gwenllyn waved her hand in dismissal. 'Don't worry about that, Harry. The work you do for me in the house and in the garden has more than repaid me.'

'No, I'll pay you back. I'll feel more of a man when I'm not indebted to you.'

'All right, but let's get these dishes washed and put away and then I'll check on David, make sure he's still asleep.'

Since Caradoc had taken the baby away Gwenllyn had been afraid of losing him again. She knew in her heart that the baby was safe with her but she couldn't help being anxious and she'd left him alone far too long this evening.

When she climbed the stairs, the lamp in her hand, she was so tired she could hardly put one foot in front of the other. In her son's room everything was quiet and peaceful except for the soft sound of David breathing. She leaned over his bed and smoothed back his bright curls. He was so like Caradoc that it broke her heart.

At last, weary to the bone, she climbed into bed and relaxed against the pillows. A little later she heard Harry come upstairs. He came quietly into the room and she could hear the rustle of his clothes as he undressed. When he slipped into bed beside her she felt him turn instinctively towards her. He waited a moment and then, when there was no response, he turned his back and Gwenllyn breathed an inward sigh of relief. Tomorrow she would lie with him, she told herself – tomorrow, when she didn't feel so tired.

Albie looked at Emily with approval. She had made a good job of milking the animals. She looked up at him, her face flushed and happy, and he felt a pang of real pain. His lovely Jess had looked at him in that way when she'd first learned to milk the beasts.

'Right,' he spoke more tersely than he'd intended, 'you can wash your hands and then go to the servery and see to the customers. We won't make any money standing around all day.'

'All right, Albie.' Emily spoke humbly and he felt a tug of pity towards her.

'You did well, Emily,' he said, 'and I'm bleedin' lucky to have you helping me.'

She lingered, looking at him hopefully.

Albie felt himself close up, as though to protect himself from her very obvious feelings for him. 'Go on, then, get into the shop. Don't stand there rooted to the spot.'

He turned away so as not to see the hurt in her eyes, and when she'd gone he sank onto the milking stool and put his face against the animal's soft flank. 'Oh, Gawd 'elp me,' he whispered, 'will I ever get over the pain of losing my Jess?' Tears came to his eyes and he made no attempt to wipe them away. His grief was like a stone inside him. He wanted to rail at heaven for taking Jess, but then crying did no good, it didn't take away the pain.

After a while he washed his face and straightened his shoulders. He was needed to make the deliveries; he had his regular customers to see to and he didn't want to let them down.

He left the shed and made his way to the stable, where the pony was waiting patiently, head down and docile as a lamb. He loaded the churns onto the cart and clucked his tongue to the mare. She lifted her head as though scenting the air and then ambled her way out of the yard into the narrow street beyond.

At least when he was working his mind was occupied with the everyday business of serving customers, but always hanging in the back of his thoughts like a heavy cloud was the knowledge that Jess wasn't waiting for him to get home: she would never be there again.

Emily was tired by the time the queue at the servery had dwindled. Evening was closing in but folk still came straggling in – ragged urchins with chipped enamel dishes and the better-off folk from the Jewish quarter – but it was nothing like the big morning rush, so Emily could relax a little.

'Hello there, sis!'

Emily looked over the counter and her face brightened. 'Josh! There's lovely to see you. Come on in, boy. Have a nice cup of milk.' She hugged him and after a moment he held her away from him.

'I came to see if you wanted to come home with me, Em.'

She shook back her curls. 'No!' She took a deep breath. 'Thanks for the offer, Josh, but Albie's realized that he needs me here, helping him, otherwise he couldn't manage.'

'Well, I'll be back and fore to London with the droves and you can always change your mind.'

He took a cup brimming with milk so fresh that threads of green grass floated on the surface. 'Damn me, this is good!' He wiped his mouth with the back of his hand. 'Now, my little sister, why are you looking so pale and pinched? Has Albie been working you too hard?'

She shook her head. 'No, it's not that, but . . .'

'But what, little Em? You can tell me.'

'I'm very fond of Albie and I'm so sorry for him – he's still in a state after Jessie's death.'

'That's natural enough, mind.' He paused. 'You've fallen for him, haven't you?' He touched her cheek. 'See those blushes: they tell tales on you, my girl.'

Emily didn't know what to say so she remained silent.

'Well, there's nothing wrong with that, but give the man a bit of time, Em. He wouldn't be much of a man if he forgot his wife so soon, would he?'

'I know.' Emily smiled at her brother. 'Come on, I don't think there'll be any more customers today. I'll shut up shop and we can go out. What if we went to Covent Garden? That would be nice.'

'I've got to get over to Smithfield,' Josh said, 'but you can come with me if you like.'

'All right, then, you're on,' Emily said. 'Anything to get me out of the shop. I'm fed up with standing here doling out milk all day.' She closed the servery and then took her brother's hand. 'Come on then, Josh, what are you waiting for? Let's go out. I feel like a bit of fun for a change.'

Her brother smiled. 'All right, then – when I've seen to my business, I'll treat you to a bit of supper. How would that do you?'

'Lovely!' Emily's heart lifted. It would do her good to be away from Albie for a little while, and by the time she went home he might realize just how much he needed her.

It was time that Non paid attention to her work. Her business was suffering because she had neglected it over the past months. But she felt as though part of her was missing. She longed for Caradoc so much it was like a pain inside her. How could she live without him?

Even though Gwenllyn was married it was obvious she still loved Caradoc and she held all the cards: she had his son while Non had nothing. However, now she really had to give her full attention to her shops, otherwise she would lose all her customers. The first priority was to see Carrie.

The sun was shining when Non took a cab to Cutler Street. The journey didn't take long and as the wheels jerked over the cobbles she tried to steel herself to be strong, not to let Carrie get the better of her. The girl was as bold as brass, so confident in her own abilities that she didn't even hide her spite from Non.

Carrie was just about to open the door of the shop when Non alighted from the cab. She was smartly dressed in outdoor clothes and she didn't turn a hair when she saw Non standing on the pavement.

'Been out?' Non asked guardedly.

Carrie looked at her as if she was nothing more than a minor irritant. 'I've been to see my solicitor,' Carrie said. She pushed open the door and Non followed her into the shuttered darkness of the shop.

'Well, you may see who the devil you like but this is still my business. I am the founder of the herbal shops and there's nothing you can do about it.'

'I think you'll find there's nothing *you* can do

about it.' Carrie smiled and her eyes gleamed through the gloom. She flung open the shutters. 'My solicitor has taken care of everything. You were filed as a bankrupt by the bank, didn't you know?'

Non took a sharp breath. 'What do you mean?'

'I mean what I say. You are a bankrupt. You no longer own anything. The auditors have been through your books and the matter was taken up by the court more than a week ago. There's nothing left for you in London – no shops, no credibility; even your most valued customers have turned to me for help.'

Non stared at her, trying to take in what Carrie was telling her. 'No, it can't be true,' she said at last.

'Of course it can. I have all the proof upstairs. As I told you, my solicitor has seen to everything.'

Non followed Carrie up the rickety stairs and tried to calm the pounding of her heart. It couldn't be true: Carrie couldn't have been so devious, so clever.

The upstairs rooms were just as Non had left them; nothing had been changed. It looked as if Carrie meant to live there.

Non sank into a chair as Carrie handed her the papers and there it was in black and white. The business owned by Manon Jones had ceased to exist and the shops had gone to the one and only bidder.

'How did you manage this?' Non asked, her voice heavy. 'How did you keep all this secret?'

'As I said, my solicitor handled everything very well. There was no opposition to the bankruptcy order, no last-minute attempt to pay off the deficit, and so I stepped in and bought everything on the cheap. Clever plan, wasn't it?'

'How could you do this to me, Carrie? I taught you everything you know about the herbal remedies. I even showed you how to keep the books.'

'It seems you taught me too well then, doesn't it? Go back to your little Welsh village. There's no place for you in London any more.'

Non looked down at the papers in her hands and in a moment of anger tore them into shreds.

Carrie simply laughed. 'They are mere copies: the originals are lodged with the court. You're beaten, Non, and there's nothing you can do about it.'

'I'll get my own solicitor to look into this,' Non said. 'I don't see how you've got away with such an underhand trick.'

'Well, talk to the solicitors all you like, it's far too late to turn back the clock. Face it: it's over, you're finished, done with.' There was a smile of triumph on Carrie's face and Non felt the urge to slap the smile away.

'Don't be too complacent,' Non said. 'There

must be a way I can defeat you and, believe me, if there is one I'll find it.'

She left the room and made her way down the gloomy staircase. Once out on the street, she took a deep breath. She must be calm; losing her head at such a time would get her nowhere.

But she would fight Carrie every inch of the way, and, what's more, she would win. Too angry to catch a cab, Non walked back through the familiar streets, her heart aching. She had lost everything, but one day, one day soon, she would get it all back, she was determined on it.

CHAPTER TWENTY-SIX

It was market day and Gwenllyn found she was enjoying herself. The sun was shining, the breeze coming in from the river was warm, and Gwenllyn's spirits were light. Harry was at home, taking care of David. The baby had been asleep when she left him and she was sure that Harry wouldn't let him out of his sight.

Harry's business was improving – he'd employed a labourer to help him with the beasts, a mark of the success he was making of the cattle industry. Harry was a good and fair man and she should learn to appreciate him more. She sighed in satisfaction and stopped at one of the stalls to choose some coloured ribbons. She was feeling content with her lot. And then she saw Caradoc.

She dropped the ribbons and attempted to turn away, but he had seen her. He was already making his way through the crowd towards her.

'Gwenllyn, I was coming to see you. How are you?' He stood very close to her.

She could smell the scent of him and her heart and body responded at once. She took a deep breath, hoping her feelings didn't show on her face. 'I'm very well,' she said politely; 'and how are you?'

'Gwenllyn.' He lifted his hand as though he would touch her cheek and she made an instinctive move towards him. 'Gwenllyn, I can't forget you. I've tried to get you out of my mind but it just won't happen.' He paused. 'I suppose you've heard that Non is no longer with me? She's living in London now.' He took her arm and led her away from the market. 'I've got to talk to you.' His voice was hoarse. 'I love you, Gwenllyn, God help me, I love you.'

'It's no good, Caradoc.' Her voice was shaking. 'Your wife may be gone but I'm still with Harry. He needs me.'

'I need you.' In the shade of the trees he took her in his arms and she let him. Emboldened, his lips came down on hers and she felt the old magic rush through her. She wanted to be in his arms, in his life, but was that an impossible dream? And then he was saying the unthinkable. 'I want to be with you for always, Gwenllyn. I don't know how I could have left you in the first place.'

She tried to untangle herself from his arms but he held her close. 'Please, Caradoc . . . I'm content with my life. Don't spoil everything now.'

'You don't love Harold,' he said, 'you love me. Can you deny it?' He drew her down onto the soft grass, his arms around her, holding her close.

She rested her head on his shoulder. 'Please, Caradoc, don't do this. I can't betray Harry – I owe him so much.'

'But do you love him? Tell me you do and I'll leave you alone.'

'I love you, Caradoc, you know that. I think I always will love you, but we've made our choices in life: you have your marriage and I have mine – nothing can change that.'

'Just let me hold you and love you, Gwenllyn. It's enough for us to be together, isn't it?'

She relaxed against him and he kissed her again, parting her lips with his own. She surrendered, yielding to him, not resisting when he touched her breasts. The sensation of being close to him was heady. She couldn't fight her feelings: this was the man she loved, the man she craved, so how could she turn down this God-given opportunity to taste his love just once more?

'Oh, Caradoc, I love you, my darling.'

The sun filtered through the overhanging branches of the trees, sending patterns of light against Gwenllyn's face. She closed her eyes; this was a dream . . . it was difficult to think clearly with Caradoc's lips on hers. All she knew was that this wonderful moment together would have to last her for the rest of her life because nothing had changed or could change. He was married to Non and she was married to Harry, but for now, just for now, she would forget all her responsibilities and let Caradoc love her one more time.

Non sat in Ruby's kitchen, her head in her hands. 'How could I let this happen?' she said as Ruby poured the tea into the waiting cups. 'I've spent days trying to get out of all the mess I've created, but it's no use: Carrie has beaten me, Ruby, she's won.'

'Don't think like that. There must be something you can do to get your shops back.'

Non shook her head. 'No, I've gone over it a thousand times in my head. I'm ruined. How can I even begin to start again?'

Ruby sat opposite her and pushed a cup towards her. 'Drink your tea and let's think this through.'

Obediently Non took up her cup and sipped the hot tea. 'I've never been so tired, so defeated, ever, in my life. I have no business and no husband. Everything is gone.'

'Take it one step at a time,' Ruby said. 'About your business: do you really think the people of London will even know you're bankrupt? And you're not really, are you?'

Non looked up at her. 'What do you mean, Ruby? I have no money, no shop – nothing at all.'

'Are the herbs still growing in the fields and hedgerows? Do you own a basket and have you a pair of bleedin' good legs?' Ruby paused to draw breath. 'Start again, Non – go round the houses like you used to, go to the markets, go back to Swansea if need be.'

'I don't know if I can start again, if I've the energy.'

'Where's your spirit? Don't let life get you down. You've lived through worse than this.'

'You're right, Ruby, I *can* start again, even if it is on the bottom rung of the ladder.' She smiled ruefully at Ruby. 'Now, can you tell me how to save my marriage?'

'Ah,' Ruby said, 'I ain't got the answer to that. You and Caradoc got to figure it all out for yourselves. You got to forgive him, Non, you know that.'

'I do forgive him for what happened when he lost his memory, but how can I live with the knowledge that he still has feelings for Gwenllyn?'

'Men are funny creatures,' Ruby said. 'They always wants what they can't have and right now he can't have you.'

Non felt stirrings of hope. 'You're right, Ruby – at least about my business. I started from scratch in the beginning and I can try to make a fresh start again now.' She got up from the table. 'I'm going to see what I've still got of my stock,' she said. 'I know I've got plenty of camomile tea and I still have a store of dried herbs.' She smiled at Ruby. 'You've given me hope, Ruby. I'll go out this very afternoon and see what I can do to mend relationships with my customers.'

'What about Caradoc?' Ruby asked cautiously.

'I don't know . . . I'll have to regain my self-respect before I see him. I'll go back to him as a successful businesswoman, not as a millstone around his neck.'

'That's the spirit!' Ruby said. 'Now, sit down again, have another cup of tea and then you can go out around the squares of London and hold your head high. You're a businesswoman, Non, and a bloody good healer into the bargain. Have faith in yourself and you can reach the stars.'

Non smiled. 'That's very poetic, Ruby. You're turning into a real wise woman.' She blinked back a tear. 'And I for one don't know what I'd do without your friendship.'

Ruby waved a tea cloth at her. 'Don't talk so bleedin' daft – that's what friends are for. Now, come on and give me a hug and then we can get back to talking business.'

Later, as Non walked the elegant squares of London, calling on her regular customers, it began to dawn on her that her services were no longer required. She was turned away from every door, not even getting the chance to see her customers in person. She'd been given a bad name and the news of it had spread to many of the people who had once been her faithful followers.

Not to be defeated, she retraced her steps and began a round of the poorer streets of London. Surely there, as Ruby had predicted, folk would neither know nor care that she was no longer the owner of respectable shops. She had the remedies to sell and that was the important thing.

But she grew tired of being turned away from even the poorest doors. Carrie had done her work well and no one wanted Non's services.

At last she arrived at the servery, where she was sure Albie would welcome her. He was sitting behind the counter, his head in his hands, and Non immediately felt guilty. Here was she worrying about her business affairs when Albie had suffered a real loss, the death of his wife and baby.

'Albie, I hope I'm not intruding.' Non stood at the counter and looked at Albie with concern. His face was pale, his eyes shadowed, and, young as he was, hints of grey had appeared in his hair.

'Non, good to see you. I've seen to the beasts and I was just about to go home. Come to the house for a cup of tea – you look beat.'

'I *am* tired,' Non said. 'But I don't want to put you to any trouble.' She looked around. 'Where's Emily?'

'She's gone out.' Albie unwound his long body from the stool. 'She's a good help and she ain't much more than a child. I don't know what I'd do without her, truth to tell.'

Non could see her own loneliness reflected in Albie's eyes, but he had lost Jessie for ever. At least she had the chance to make things right with Caradoc. She took a deep breath. She would have to swallow her pride and ask him, beg him if necessary, to take her back.

When she entered the house Non could see at once that Albie had been neglecting the place. Dust had settled on the furniture that Jessie had been so proud of and the floor needed a good scrubbing. But at least the fire was still alight and Non sat on one of the kitchen chairs, watching as Albie pushed the kettle onto the coals.

Emily arrived as Albie was making the tea and she almost crept into her chair, as though afraid she would disturb Albie by her presence.

He gave her a quick glance and fetched another cup. 'I've had to get the animals bedded down for the night,' he said. 'I thought that was supposed to be your job. Instead you go off without a word, the Lord knows where.' His tone was almost brusque and Emily swallowed hard before replying.

'I've just been out with my brother.' She took her drink of tea and cupped it in her hands. 'I didn't think you'd mind.' She shivered a little and Non felt sorry for the girl. She seemed afraid to breathe in case it upset Albie.

'Are you cold, Emily?' she asked kindly.

'I am a bit. It's getting colder in the nights now. Before long, the droves will finish for the winter. There'll be no chance of me going home then.' She looked hopefully at Albie. 'But I can stay with you, can't I? You'll still need me to milk the cows and serve the milk. London folks still want fresh milk in the mornings, don't they?'

'Aye, I suppose I'll need you.' Albie spoke grudgingly and Non decided she'd have to speak to him about his manner. Either he kept Emily on and treated her with respect or he let her go home.

'Anyway, Non,' Albie said, 'how's business? Still as brisk as ever?'

'I wanted to talk to you about that,' Non replied. 'I'm in a bit of a mess. The girl I employed, Carrie, she's taken all my trade from me. Set up in her own right. She fiddled my books and now it seems I've been declared a bankrupt.'

Albie appeared alert for the first time. He drew his chair closer to her and gave her his full attention. 'She can't do that to you, can she?'

'She's done it.'

'I don't believe it! Perhaps the girl is a bleedin' liar. 'Ave you thought about that, Non?'

Non shook her head. 'I've been traipsing round London most of the day and all I've got is doors closed in my face. No one trusts me any more, Albie. I haven't sold one solitary remedy.' She lifted her hand in a gesture of despair. 'It looks like my days in London are finished. I might have to go back to Swansea and start again.'

'That's bleedin' awful!' Albie took her hand. 'But come on, don't let a few obstacles get you down.'

'I don't know what I can do, Albie, and that's the truth.'

'Can't you write to your customers, tell them it's all a bit of trickery – tell them . . . Well, you're better at the words than I am.'

'That's an idea,' Non said as hope began to lighten her heart, 'but do you think it will work?'

'It's worth a try,' he said. 'Most folk will read their own letters rather than leave it to the servants, won't they? At least that way you'll reach your customers personally.'

'You're right, it's worth a try. Thank you, Albie.' She forced a smile. 'Now, how about we have another cup of that delicious tea before I get back to Ruby's and pick up my pen?'

Gwenllyn wrapped her arms around Caradoc, warm in the afterglow of their love-making. She kissed his cheek, touched the hair at the back of his neck with caressing fingers. How she loved this man, how she'd dreamed of being close to him, and now here she was lying in the grass enfolded in his arms. She wanted the moment to go on for ever. She closed her eyes, feeling the sweet weight of Caradoc against her.

'You are so wonderful, my darling,' she said softly.

Beyond her, away to the left, she heard the sudden crashing sound of someone pushing through the trees. She sat up quickly and stared in horror at the angry face of her husband.

'Harry!' She screamed his name as she wrenched Caradoc away from her. He paused for a moment and took aim and then he hit Caradoc square on the jaw. Taken unawares, Caradoc was felled as if he was a tree. He shook his head, trying to clear it, and then Harry was on him, hitting, punching, kicking him.

'Stop, Harry!' Gwenllyn screamed. 'Stop before you kill him.'

Her words penetrated Harry's rage and he moved away from Caradoc, staring at him with naked hatred.

'Stay away from my wife.' His voice was deadly calm. 'If I catch you anywhere near her again I swear to God I'll kill you.'

He took Gwenllyn's arm and propelled her through the woods and onto the road that led back to the house.

She looked up at him fearfully. He was like a stranger, his face set and white, and the realization of what she'd done swept over her.

'I'm sorry, Harry. I must have been mad. I didn't mean any of it to happen – I was content as we were.'

He didn't reply but his grip on her arm tightened.

'Where's the baby?' Gwenllyn's throat was tight with fear. 'You haven't left him alone, have you?'

'Your baby is safe with the washerwoman.' Harry ground out the words. 'We're not all as feckless as you.' He looked down at her without meeting her eyes. 'I've a mind to walk out on you and your bastard son for good.'

Gwenllyn had no answer. What she'd done was unforgivable, she knew it, and there was nothing she could say to put things right. She'd betrayed Harry in the worst way possible and now their marriage, tenuous as it was, might be over.

Suddenly the thought of life without Harry was intolerable. How would she manage alone in the cottage with a baby to care for and no one to help her? She began to cry.

'How can I say sorry to you, Harry? The last thing I wanted was to hurt you. I beg you to forgive me; I'm so very sorry.'

He stopped walking and spun her round to face him. 'You're sorry!' His tone was scathing. 'Sorry?'

'I know it's a bit late to tell you, Harry, but I need you in my life, I really need you. Please don't go away and leave me.'

'I find you lying in the grass with your lover like a common street girl and you think saying sorry will put things right? If you believe that, you are more stupid than I thought.'

He pulled her along by her arm and when they reached the cottage he thrust her inside. She watched as he gave the washerwoman some money and when they were alone she waited with bated breath to hear what he would say. She trembled. She knew by the look in his eyes that he was not going to forgive her.

'I'm going,' he said. 'I'm leaving first thing in the morning. I've had enough humiliation heaped on me and I wouldn't be a man if I took any more.'

'Please, Harry.' She made an attempt to catch his hand but he drew quickly away. 'Oh, Harry, if only I could turn back the clock I would. I know I've hurt you, I've betrayed you, and I didn't mean to do it, believe me.'

'So you didn't know that low-down scum was in the village, is that what you expect me to believe? No wonder you were so long coming home – and there was I worried you were sick or something.'

'I didn't know Caradoc was here, I promise I didn't.'

'So, out of the blue you saw him and fell into his arms and let him take you like the harlot you are. Well, I've had enough, Gwenllyn. I can't take any more. Now get out of my sight before I take my belt to you as a real man would.'

Gwenllyn hurried up the stairs, her heart thumping. She'd never seen Harry like this before.

His anger was ice cold and she was the cause of all his pain. She fell onto the bed and closed her eyes. She was a stupid fool: she'd played with the feelings of two men and now she had lost both of them. She closed her eyes. She was too sickened with herself and too weary even to cry any more. She turned her face into the pillow and tried to blot out her misery, but it was there like a torment inside her and it would not let her go.

CHAPTER TWENTY-SEVEN

Gwenllyn walked to the window and stared out into the coppery light of early autumn. The leaves were rusty red and still: there was scarcely a wind to move them. The house was silent. David was asleep and Gwenllyn had time to realize just how empty her life had become since that awful scene with Harry. It was like a slap in the face when he sent a couple of drovers to fetch his herd home to Swansea, but even then he had cared enough to leave her the milking cow. She swallowed the lump in her throat. He was miles away from her now in every way.

Since the awful day when Harry had caught her with Caradoc, she'd had a great deal of time to think things over. She loved Caradoc, perhaps she would always love him, but it was in the swooning, magical way an untried girl experiences with her first lover. For Harry there had grown in her an enduring feeling of belonging; he was her husband, her man. She'd realized the truth too late and she had driven him away.

She was startled by a knock on the door. She hesitated. No one came to her door any more – no farmers, no cattle drovers, not even the wise woman from the village came to call on her now. Her husband had gone, for good this time, and her reputation was in tatters once again.

The knocking became more insistent and, fearing it would wake David, she went into the hall and opened the door to look out. 'Caradoc! What are you doing here?'

He stood on the threshold, staring at her, his eyes shadowed. His bruises had faded but she knew he would bear the scars of the humiliation he'd suffered at Harry's hands for ever.

'I wanted to see you, to find out if you were all right or if that clod of a husband had hurt you in any way.'

'Harry is not a clod. Don't talk about him like that. He's a real man and it was only natural he would attack you when you were lying with his wife. I'm no better: I was acting like a silly whore!'

'It wasn't like that, Gwenllyn.' Caradoc edged his way into the hall.

She shrugged in resignation and led the way into the sitting room. The mellow sunlight spilled onto the wooden floor like pools of honey and Gwenllyn tried to concentrate on them – anything so that she wouldn't look up and meet the pain in Caradoc's eyes.

'I've caused you nothing but trouble,' she whispered. 'Your wife has left you and I've lost Harry. I suppose we deserve it: we've both behaved like animals of the field.'

'It was natural that we would want to lie together, Gwenllyn. We lived as husband and wife for an entire summer. That sort of closeness can't be lost overnight.'

She faced him then. 'But you were quick enough to leave me and go back to your real wife, weren't you?'

'I know.' He ran his fingers through his hair. 'I'm so mixed-up, I just don't know what to think or even what to do any more.' He sank into a chair and covered his face with his hands. 'I've no joy in my work, my house is empty like a mausoleum and I feel I'm not living my life as I should. My place is with you and my son. Why don't we give it a go, Gwenllyn? What have we to lose?' He looked up at her earnestly. 'The winter is coming, the nights will be growing dark and cold. If I stay with you I can help you through it.'

'I don't think so, Caradoc,' Gwenllyn said softly. 'We can't turn back the clock and forget our marriages ever existed.'

'Just think about it,' Caradoc persisted. 'Remember the joy we found in each other's arms, how companionable we were, me cutting the trees for the fire, you in the kitchen, cooking a meal? We were content: that was the way our life was then and could be again.'

Gwenllyn sat down, feeling her legs were not going to support her. 'Look, Caradoc, since Harry left I've realized how much I miss him.'

'Yes, you miss having a man about the place, but you don't love him. You love me, don't you?'

'I don't know anything any more,' Gwenllyn said quietly.

Caradoc moved swiftly and knelt on the floor beside her. He cast a long shadow in the pale sunlight. He was here and Harry wasn't and suddenly Gwenllyn felt afraid of living out the rest of her life alone.

'Just let me think about it,' she said. 'I must have time to think this through.'

He took her hands in his. 'At least let me stay tonight. I won't come near you, if that's what you want.'

'I don't know.' Gwenllyn's throat was dry. Could she and Caradoc make some sense out of the mess of their lives and live together? 'What about your wife?'

'You know as well as I do that Non has left me for good. She's still in London and Ruby keeps me informed. It appears that my wife is well and happy; she doesn't need me, not for anything.'

'And I do?'

'I believe you do, Gwenllyn.' He moved back

into his chair. 'Please let me stay. It's a long way to Swansea from the Wye Valley. Just say I can spend the night and then we can think about our future in the morning.'

Gwenllyn relented. It was getting late – how could she turn Caradoc away from her door, not knowing where he would lay his head for the night?

'You can stay for tonight, but just while I think things through. Is that clear?'

Caradoc was humble in his gratitude and Gwenllyn saw him in a new light. He'd once been her close companion, her lover. And then he'd returned to the life he was born to, the son of an old respected family, rich, privileged, a man who had everything he could want in life. Now he was different: he'd lost his confident air, and she wasn't sure she knew him any longer.

For now he could stay under her roof. They could talk things through, decide what was to be done about their future – would it be together or apart? For now she didn't have an answer. All she knew was that the warm glow of excitement she usually felt around Caradoc just wasn't there any more.

Non felt a tremble of delight. Mrs Forster was actually seeking her advice again. Mrs Forster was the leading figure in the social whirl of the elegant squares in London and as Non knocked on the door of the big terraced house she was confident now that she would be welcome.

And so she was. When she was shown into the beautifully proportioned sitting room, Mrs Forster even rose to greet her.

'Mrs Jones, it's so good to see you.' Mrs Forster took her hands. 'I do hope you can help me. It's my eldest son, he's come down with some sort of sickness. I've consulted so many people about his problem but no one has the remedy.'

'I'll be happy to help in any way I can,' Non said.

Mrs Forster sent for the maid to take Non upstairs and as she mounted the elegant staircase Non wondered what was before her.

The young man lay on his sick bed, a pale wraith against the elegance of the huge bedroom. He looked up at her but didn't meet her eye. 'Can you cure me, Mrs Jones?' His voice was cultured and he had the arrogance of the very rich, but now he was discomfited, not knowing how to talk to her about his illness.

'I'll do my best,' Non said. 'Can you tell me what ails you?'

He waved his hand at the maid and she bobbed a curtsy and disappeared discreetly through the door.

'It's an affliction of my . . . my private parts,' he said bluntly. 'I'm afraid I might have caught some nasty sickness.' He coughed to hide his embarrassment. 'I was foolish enough to take up with a woman of easy virtue.' Suddenly his arrogant manner vanished and a pleading look came into his eyes. 'Can you help me, please?'

'Let me see.' Non bent over him as he uncovered his lower body.

'You are red and swollen there,' Non said gently, 'and you have a rash, but I assure you it is not what you think.'

He brightened. 'So I've not gone down with the pox! Thank God for that. You can cure me then? How will you do it?'

'I will bring some roots of the madder and apply them to the affected parts. The ointment works well and you should be clear of any trouble in a few days.'

'See to it at once.' The young man seemed to have recovered his arrogance. 'My mother will pay you what's due. And not a word to anyone about this – I don't want to be the laughing stock of the town.'

'Discretion is my middle name.' Non controlled her irritation. 'It's not in my interests to give away my clients' secrets.' She left the room and, outside, took a deep breath. Sometimes she needed all her patience to deal with the problems of the rich.

Downstairs, she spoke to Mrs Forster. 'I shall be back this afternoon with a remedy for your son, but I can assure you there's nothing to worry about.'

'You can cure the silly boy, then?' Mrs Forster was clearly relieved. 'That other woman who took your place was useless. She had no notion of what was wrong with my son, let alone the means to cure him.'

She handed Non a bag of money. 'I can rely on you to keep this quiet, can I?' She smiled warmly. 'And in return I shall sing your praises to my friends. From now on I think you'll find that clients will be clamouring for your services.'

Non sighed with relief as she left the house, pleased that the matter could be resolved very easily. And now, she hoped, she could resume her business without the threat of Carrie hanging over her.

By the end of the day, Non had a sheaf of requests to call and minister to a variety of patients; she was back in business, there was no doubt about that. Now she must find a small room where people could call on her in confidence. This time she would not be able to afford a light and airy shop; she would start in a small way, slowly building up her business again. She would be a success, she was bent on it. She would show Caradoc that she was capable of fending for herself, that she didn't need his money or his name. And yet inside her was an emptiness, a feeling that nothing would ever be the same without Caradoc at her side.

* * *

Harry stood at the gate, looking into the field where his animals grazed peaceably. The summer was almost done, the colours of autumn were everywhere; it was a season of change, when the beasts would rest and feed and grow fat. Some of them would yield milk; some would go for breeding stock; a few of the older ones would be slaughtered. There was enough work to keep him busy in the winter months. Long winter months when he would be separated from Gwennie.

How could she have betrayed him? He'd been loyal to her, a support. He'd enjoyed his life with the woman he loved and he'd even accepted the presence of Caradoc Jones's son. He longed to be with her. He missed her breathing close to him in bed, the softness of her limbs, the passion with which she responded to his love-making. She was his wife in every sense of the word and yet she had thrown it all away for a tumble with another man.

His life was empty now. He had his business, small though it was, and he had his self-respect, but what use was all that without the woman he loved? He took a deep breath. That was enough brooding: he would do no good standing around like a lovesick youth, he had work to do.

Later, he went to the market in Swansea. Mingling with other people would do him good. He would talk with the cattle drovers, drink a beer with them, feel like a man again. He had beaten the daylights out of Caradoc Jones and that at least brought him some satisfaction.

At the market, he kept his eye out for Caradoc. Perhaps the man would face up to him, claim he was the one Gwennie wanted all along. If so, he would have another thrashing to go with the first one.

In the taproom of the Old Castle inn, the drovers had gathered for a drink before embarking on the final drove of the season. Harry kept his eye on the crowd but there was no sign of Caradoc Jones.

'Hello there, Harry.' Josh smiled up at him. 'How's things going, then? I hear you're a businessman now.'

'Aye, that's right.' Harry had little time for Josh. The boy was out to line his own pockets; he had no thought for anyone else, not even his own kin, if the drovers' tales were correct. 'How's that little sister of yours?' Harry asked pointedly.

Josh seemed at a loss for words and then he gathered his wits. 'I'm going up to London with the drove – we're setting off first thing in the morning,' Josh said. 'I'll want to see Emily, of course. As it happens, I've got plans for her.'

'Very brotherly.' Harry didn't like the sly look on the other man's face but he was here to circulate with the men of the drove. He badly needed to know the whereabouts of Caradoc Jones. 'Are you worried about her, then?'

'I'm not worried exactly,' Josh was saying, 'but she's working for that Londoner Albie something-or-other. I just want to know if he's treating her fair, like, and not putting too much weight on her shoulders. She's just a girl really.' Josh supped his beer and then looked up at Harry with a spiteful gleam in his eyes. 'Don't know when the boss will join us, mind,' he said.

Harry was suddenly alert. It looked as if he might find out just what he wanted to know. 'Why, is Caradoc Jones sick?' He tried to hide his anxiety by speaking casually.

Josh wasn't fooled for an instant. 'Oh, didn't you know he's staying up in the Wye Valley for the time being? I doubt he'll even show his face to the drove. I hear he's bedded himself in, made himself at home, that sort of thing.'

'With my wife, you mean?' Harry took Josh by the collar and shook him. 'Is that what you mean, you little worm?'

'Let me go, man, I didn't mean any harm. I thought you ought to know what's going on, that's all.'

Harry pushed him away. 'And you took great pleasure in telling me, didn't you, you bastard!'

Breathing deeply, he went outside into the crisp autumn air and stood for a moment, unseeing, blind with anger and jealousy. The last thing he'd expected was to learn Caradoc Jones was living with Gwennie. The pain twisted in his gut, making him want to vomit. He leaned against the wall of the inn and tried to steady the beat of his heart, but the thought of Caradoc Jones living with Gwennie, sharing her bed, was too much to bear.

He began to run. He'd get a horse, ride up to the Wye Valley and throw Jones out on his ear. Then he would move back in, claim what was rightfully his. His wife would not welcome him, but then he'd lived in sufferance with her before and it had worked quite well. Since then, they'd built something together. It had been a good marriage and Caradoc Jones had ruined it. Well, he would soon learn he couldn't take another man's wife and get away with it.

He calmed down and slowed to a walk. He'd been a fool to leave the coast clear for Jones to step into his boots, but he would be a fool no longer. He smacked his fist into the palm of his hand. Caradoc Jones, it seemed, needed teaching another lesson and Harry would not be slow in giving it to him.

CHAPTER TWENTY-EIGHT

As the days passed, slowly but surely Non found her customers coming back to her. Carrie, it appeared, had not handled the business as well as she should have done. Non found she was working harder than ever, but she was making a living, albeit a modest one, and at least she wasn't weighed down with debt. She had that much to be thankful for.

She'd managed to rent a shop. It was a tiny room in a house right on the river banks, and it was smelly and damp, but at least it was a beginning. She was busy making a plaster of mustard for one of Mrs Forster's younger children when the door opened and Ruby hurried into the shop. By the look on her face, Non knew there was something badly wrong.

She put down her pestle and mortar and wiped her hands on her apron. 'What's happened, Ruby?

Is it Caradoc? Has he had an accident? Is he sick?'

Ruby shook her head. 'He's not hurt, so don't worry about that, but there is news of him and it ain't good news.' She paused to take a deep breath. 'I've just come from the market – there's a new drove arrived.' She shook her head at the question in Non's eyes. 'It ain't the Jones drove, they 'aven't come yet, but from all the gossip it seems they're on the road.' She took Non's hand and fell silent for a moment.

'And?' Non knew the drovers brought all the gossip from home and her mouth was dry as she waited for Ruby to go on. Perhaps Caradoc had sent a message for her? Perhaps he wanted her back? She gripped Ruby's hand. 'Well, Ruby, what is it? Tell me before I faint with worry.'

Ruby squared her shoulders. 'He's only gone to live with that bleedin' woman, hasn't he? Moved into the cottage in the Wye Valley like he owned the place.'

'That can't be true,' Non said, stepping back a pace as though she'd been struck. 'Gwenllyn has a husband. What about him?'

'Seems he's given up on the girl, moved out, left her. He caught 'em both rutting like the animals and he don't want anything more to do with her.'

Non tried to speak but her throat was dry. She sat down on her stool and made an effort to compose herself.

'You should never have left the man alone,'

Ruby said gently. 'They gets up to all sorts of trouble without a woman's hand to guide them.'

'But he loves me!' The words came from her mouth like a wail. 'He's always told me he loves me.'

'Well, perhaps you should have forgiven the man for the past, then. He couldn't 'elp it if he lost his mind. Soon as he knew the truth he came home to you, didn't he? That's enough to tell you where 'is loyalties lie.'

'But he still had feelings for Gwenllyn, he admitted it.' Non bit her lip. It was all too painful to bear. She'd believed Caradoc would come home to her, that he would realize which one of them he really loved. Well, he had chosen Gwenllyn. 'I can't do anything about it, can I?' Non said. 'If he's made his home with her, it's Gwenllyn he really wants.'

''Course you can do something about it,' Ruby said: 'go get him, sort things out.'

'It's too late, Ruby. He's made his choice. Gwenllyn has his son and that's everything to Caradoc.'

'You're a young woman,' Ruby said. 'You can have sons, lots of them, but not if you don't get back to that husband of yours.' Her tone softened. 'Go home, Non – see to your private affairs. The business can wait.'

'You're right, I shouldn't have given up on my marriage so soon,' Non said, 'but I really thought

Caradoc would come to his senses, come to find me and take me back to Swansea. The last thing I expected was for him to move in with Gwenllyn.'

'Well, he has moved in and it's about time you showed a bit of spirit, girl. That Gwenllyn is no bleedin' match for you. Come on, shut up shop, come back with me and get ready to travel.'

Non nodded. She pushed aside her pestle and mortar and as she took up her shawl from the hook on the door it swung open.

'Oh, there you are, Miss Clever Clogs.' Carrie was standing on the threshold, her face red with anger. 'You think you've taken all my trade from me, don't you, but I'm not going to give up. I'll beat you yet.'

'Get out of my way,' Non said. 'I've got no time for all this. Just leave me alone.'

Ruby squared up to Carrie. 'If you don't get out of the way you'll have to deal with me, you witch!' she said. 'Now shift before I take my boot to you.'

Carrie slipped past her and went over to the counter. 'You're making up something for Mrs Forster, then.' She took up the scribbled note. 'I can do this. Even a child could make a plaster. I'll get my customers back, you'll see.'

'Do your worst,' Non was eager to get out of the shop, 'but I don't think anyone will want to bother with you any more. You've made too many mistakes.'

She caught Ruby's arm. 'Come on, leave her. There's nothing here for her to steal. I've got more important matters to deal with.'

'Your errant husband being one, is that it?' Carrie had a spiteful look on her face. 'Oh, I've heard the stories too. He's had enough of his wife so he's moved on to someone else's.'

'You shut your evil mouth, you!' Ruby said angrily.

Non edged her way with Ruby through the door just as Carrie sent her parting shot.

'You won't keep the customers, just as you couldn't keep your husband. You'll see, I'll be the winner.'

Non and Ruby left the shop and closed the door on Carrie's hateful taunts.

'I'll win in the end, you'll see.' Carrie's voice ended on a screech. 'I'm better than you any day and I'll prove it.'

Non pressed Ruby's arm. 'Come on, let's leave her to it. There's not much harm she can do – the shop is practically empty. Anyway, I want to get back to the Wye Valley and see if I can save my marriage. That's more important to me than all the businesses in the world.'

As the two hurried through the narrow courts, Non tried to clear her head. She would go to Caradoc, plead with him to come back to her, and if that failed at least she would know she'd done her best.

'I'll book the next mail coach,' she said. 'I won't let Gwenllyn take my husband.'

'That's my girl,' Ruby said approvingly. 'I've packed your bag ready and I've booked you a seat on the coach.' She smiled wickedly. 'I knew you'd put up a fight. I was banking on it.'

Non squeezed her arm. 'You're a good friend, Ruby.' Non's voice was thick with emotion.

'Oh, go on with you,' Ruby said impatiently. 'I'm only doing what any friend would do. Come on, don't dawdle, you got a coach to catch.'

Carrie had left the poky shop in a foul humour but at least she had Non's sheaf of notes in her possession. She hurried back to her rooms on the top floor of the building where she'd lived since she'd taken up the business. All the books were there, the real books. They would need to be destroyed before she left. And she would have to leave: there wasn't enough money coming in now to pay the rent.

She climbed the rickety stairs and looked round the room, her eyes wild like those of a savage animal. How she hated Non Jones, hated her learning, hated her clever way with the herbs.

She sank down into the one comfortable chair in the room and looked around her. This was a slum; it was a small, cramped room, not the place a respectable businesswoman should work in.

In a sudden rage, she pushed back her chair and

began emptying the drawers where she kept all her papers, throwing them onto the fire. But the fire was low, almost out, and Carrie looked round for something to fan the flames. There was a newspaper on the counter and with a sick feeling Carrie looked at the facing page, where she read an advertisement for Non Jones's remedies. She saw an endorsement from none other than Mrs Forster claiming Non had cured her youngest child in two days. With a cry of rage, Carrie snatched up the paper and held it across the hearth, fanning the blaze in the grate into life. She was hot, sweating, but she was determined to destroy everything. Without the books no one could prove any wrongdoing on her part.

The flames flared upwards swiftly and caught the newspaper. With a cry of terror, Carrie threw it away from her. It fell to the floor and set the rag rug alight. Carrie heard the sudden roar as the flames shot out across the room and leaped up the curtains towards the ceiling. Suddenly fearful, Carrie looked towards the door which was barely visible through the thick smoke that was filling the room.

She crossed quickly to the door, gathering her skirts to avoid the licking, jumping flames. She reached for the door handle and pulled at it, desperate now to get outside. The smoke seemed to envelop her. She began to cough and her eyes were streaming. Behind her the fire was taking hold, roaring like a beast. The heat was intolerable and Carrie pulled the door open in a panic.

The smoke weaved like ghostly arms behind her as she attempted to run down the rickety stairs. It blinded her vision so she couldn't see any more. She fell against the wall, struggling to get her breath back, but was struck by another fit of coughing. Her eyes were stinging; she felt helpless against the relentless heat and smoke. She made one more feeble effort to hurry down the stairs, but the fire leapt all around her, burning the wooden banisters.

One of the stairs cracked like a pistol shot and Carrie plunged downward and fell in a heap at the bottom. The smoke was thicker now, black and menacing, taking all the air from the building. The flames were intense but Carrie didn't see or feel them. She lay on the floor, unable to move, as the darkness closed in on her. She knew she was doomed to die, but her last thought as the smoke choked her was that she would be taking all Non Jones's remedies with her and she felt a fleeting but overwhelming sense of triumph.

CHAPTER TWENTY-NINE

Emily was tired. She'd done a full day's work at the servery and now she was busy washing out the milk churns. She hadn't seen Albie all day. He seemed to spend most of the day in the house, grieving for his dead wife. Emily's heart twisted in pain. How she felt for him: Albie was so pale and listless these days it was as though all the spirit had been knocked out of him.

With a sigh of relief, she dried the last of the churns and put a cloth over the top. Now she would have to see to the cows. They would need feeding. The grass had grown thin round the sheds and with winter not far away the beasts would need extra food so that the milk kept flowing.

She was pulling out the bales of fodder for the animals when she heard her name being called. A delighted smile crossed her face. 'Josh!' She hurried round the house to the servery and saw her brother, hands in his pockets, his hat askew. 'Josh, there's lovely it is to see you! Give me a hug, my *boy bach*.'

'Hey!' Josh caught her and swung her round. 'Less of the little boy – I'm your big brother and don't you forget it.'

'Are you with the Jones herd, Josh?'

'No, the Joneses seem to be in a bit of a mess. Caradoc Jones don't seem to care about his business; he's in the Wye Valley, living with Harry's wife. I made a point of telling Harry so – he didn't even know, poor sod.'

'Perhaps you shouldn't have done that, Josh.' Emily spoke doubtfully. 'It never does to meddle in other folk's lives.'

He hugged and kissed her and put her down again. 'Well, it's my responsibility to meddle in yours, little sis. Where's that awful London boss keeping himself? I can't see him about. Is he leaving everything to you?'

'Albie is back at the house,' Emily said, her smile fading. 'He can't get over losing his wife, see, poor man.'

'And you're living with him? In the house, I mean,' Josh said.

'Well, yes, I'm still there. Is there anything wrong with that?'

'Don't be dafter than you look, girl. You know what folks are like: they'll add two and two and make five. You're a young girl living with a man who has no wife – what do you think it looks like?'

'I don't care what it looks like,' Emily said quickly. 'We're not doing anything wrong, mind.'

'I know that but the point is other folk will talk, call you a hussy. Haven't you got the wit to realize that?'

Emily shook her head dumbly, fearing that Josh intended to take her home to Wales with him. 'Come over to the house,' she said at last. 'Talk to Albie: you'll see he's a good and decent man and got no bad thoughts about me.'

Josh ruffled her hair. 'Aye, might as well see if he'll put me up for a night or two. I don't feel like staying in some stinking lodgings near the river.'

Albie greeted Josh with a shake of the hand. 'Come inside, Josh; take some supper with us.' He turned to Emily. 'I put a bit of pork in the pot and some potatoes and vegetables. It's the best I could do.'

'That's good of you, Albie. You know I'd have cooked the supper once I got back from seeing to the beasts.'

Josh frowned. 'Seems like you're putting an awful lot of responsibility on my young sister's shoulders, Albie.' Josh spoke mildly and Emily knew he was being careful because he wanted a bed for the night.

'Am I?' Albie seemed genuinely shocked.

'Aye, she's only a slip of a girl. She can't be

334

seeing to the shop and the cows and then coming home to cook and clean for you.'

'I hadn't thought about it like that,' Albie said, 'but you're right, Josh.'

'I'm all right really,' Emily said quickly. 'I love working for Albie and I've grown to love London, so I'm more than willing to do my share.'

'And everyone else's shares as well, by the look of it.'

Emily wished her brother would shut up. The way he was going on he'd make Albie give her the sack and then what would she do? 'That pork smells lovely, Albie. Shall I put the bowls out?'

'You go and wash. I'll see to the food,' Albie said. He turned to Josh. 'Sit down by the fire. The days are getting chilly now with winter not far away.'

Emily hovered in the doorway as Josh sat down with alacrity. 'Aye, I've come into town with the last drove of the year,' he said. 'I'm expecting to join the Jones herds again next year if Caradoc pulls his finger out. I suppose it'll be up to me to run everything for him as usual. I don't get no more pay than a cattle hand, mind, so Jones will have to buck up his ideas a bit.'

Emily sighed with relief. At least Josh had changed the subject. The two men would talk about cattle and droves and perhaps Josh would shut up about the work she was taking on.

She washed as quickly as she could and

changed her clothes before running down the stairs to the kitchen. Albie was cutting great chunks of bread and Josh was watching him with a strange glint in his eyes.

They gathered round the kitchen table for the meal and Emily picked at her food, worried about Josh's questioning looks. She was suspicious of him. If he thought there was something to be made out of the situation, he'd be busy figuring out what might be in it for him.

'You got any thoughts of marrying again?' he asked at last and Emily drew a sharp breath.

'Josh!' she said. 'Albie's only recently been made a widower. He's still grieving for his wife.'

'Well, I'm sorry about that, but it's your good name I'm thinking of.'

'Don't go on about that, Josh,' she said quickly. 'Everything is working out fine and dandy. There's no fear of me losing my good name.'

Albie looked up, suddenly intent. 'But Josh is right,' he said. 'Folk will talk about you living here with me. I should have bleedin' thought of that myself.' He looked at her steadily. 'I don't know what I'd do without you, Em, but I got to admit it's not right, you living here with me. As for marrying again, well, I can't think that far ahead.' He met Josh's eyes. 'If I was thinking of taking another wife, it would be Emily, no doubt about that.' He shrugged. 'But, no, I can't even begin to think of another woman in my life, not now.'

'Well, I can't let my sister live with you like this, you must see that,' Josh said. 'Of course, I could stay for a little while: that would help, wouldn't it?'

'You're needed back in Wales,' Emily said quickly. 'You'll have to be on the spot in spring so you can run the herd again.' She glared at her brother but he took no notice of her.

'I'll go back to Wales when the time is right, don't you worry.' There was a cunning smile on his face. 'For the time being, if Albie don't mind, I'll stay here with you and help out with the beasts. No one can say I haven't got enough knowledge of animals, can they?'

Emily subsided in her chair. Josh was going to have his way: he would ruin things between her and Albie, she could see it coming. But for now she would have to keep her eyes open and her mouth shut.

Non stood outside the smouldering embers of her old shop and stared in dismay at the jagged stonework. A black and gaping hole showed where the window had once been.

'Oh Gawd,' Ruby clutched her arm, 'the men have just told me there's a body in there. You don't think it's that Carrie, do you?'

'Oh my God!' Non put a hanky to her nose to keep out the awful smell of burning. 'Carrie didn't deserve to die like that, whatever she'd done.'

'It's bleedin' terrible, all right, but Carrie must have started the fire deliberate to get rid of your stuff, Non, don't you see? Non, the fire has taken all your books and recipes – things you spent years gathering.'

'That doesn't matter,' Non said. 'Not now.'

'I'm sorry you were troubled with all this,' said one of the men when he spotted Non. 'Everyone thought you still owned the shop, so we sent the boy to fetch you from Ruby's. Good of you to come, but you'll have to get out of the way now and let the boys bring out the body of the poor lady who got burnt in the blaze.'

Non watched in horror as two young men manhandled a charred door through the ruins with a covered body lying on it. She shuddered and turned away. What was the loss of her notes compared with the loss of a human life?

'Come on, Non,' Ruby said, 'come on home. There's nothing we can do here.' She took Non's arm and guided her away from the smoking ruin and through to the little courts leading back to the boarding house.

Non allowed herself to be led; her strength seemed to have deserted her. She felt empty. All the fight had been knocked out of her and now, with her notes and recipes burned, all seemed hopeless and dark.

'What you need is a good strong cup of gin,'

Ruby said, feeling her despair, 'and then you're going to bed to rest, my lady.'

'All right, Ruby,' Non said listlessly. 'I think I need a rest – I'm so very tired.' She hardly saw the narrow courts and dark alleyways; all she wanted was to get back to Ruby's house and fall into bed to sleep her pain away.

Morgan was glad when the last of the shoeing was done. He rubbed his hands on his leather apron and took a deep breath – and immediately regretted it as the stink of Smithfield market filled his lungs.

Beads of perspiration ran from his forehead onto his cheeks; he was tired, but soon he would wash the stink of horses away and then he would go to Ruby's lodging house and find Non. Never was there a better time to see her. It was the talk of the drovers that Caradoc Jones had deserted his wife in favour of another woman and Morgan intended to take advantage of the situation and make one last bid to woo Non.

They couldn't marry, at least not at once, and that grieved him, but he would take Non away to the land of plenty, to America, where a man's talents were recognized. There he would set up a smithy, work in the trade he loved and where folk would take Non and him for a married couple.

It would mean selling the tools of his trade – he could hardly carry anvils and braziers halfway across the world – but those things were easily replaced. He would sell off his stock and close down his shops, including the one he'd set up in the Wye Valley. It would be a wrench, but he was confident he could set up one large smithy shop in America, the land of opportunity. For the first time in ages, Morgan felt real hope. Non wouldn't reject his advances this time, he was sure of it.

Evening was drawing in, bringing with it a London Particular that swirled around the gas lamps, making eerie shapes against the pavements. Morgan would be glad to leave the town behind him, leave everything behind him, and start a new life with Non. She would bear him sons, strong sons, he just felt it in his gut.

Ruby let him in and her face was troubled. 'If you've come to see Non, then you're bleedin' out of luck. She's shut herself in her room.' She opened the door wide. 'I can offer you a drink of cordial though. Come on in.'

It was good to be in the warm kitchen of Ruby's lodging house. The kettle was singing on the fire and a tray of freshly baked cakes stood on the scrubbed wooden table.

'Hungry, Morgan?'

'Aye, though I didn't realize it until now.'

'Sit down, then: take the weight off those big feet of yours.' She made the tea and then pushed a skillet onto the fire. 'Bacon and eggs do you?'

'I don't want to put you to all that trouble,' Morgan said, looking round, hoping for a sight of Non.

Ruby read his thoughts. 'She's had a terrible shock.' The sizzling of the bacon in the fat drowned out her voice.

'What was that?' Morgan leaned forward in his chair, his big arms resting on his thighs. He wasn't aware of how strong and self-assured he appeared and Ruby's next words came as a surprise.

'Why ain't you married, Morgan, a handsome man like you?'

'The only woman I'll ever love is Non,' he said. 'I'll love her till my last breath is spent. What's wrong with her? Why is she in her room? Is she sick?'

'Sick at heart, more like.' Ruby cracked an egg into the pan with deft fingers. The fat sizzled as she slipped a thick chunk of bread alongside the solidifying egg.

'Let me just do this meal for you and then we can talk.' Ruby was silent while she slid the bacon, egg and fried bread onto a plate. She put the plate in front of him and sat down. Then, 'Everything is going to the bad for poor Non,' she said. 'Her man has left her, did you know?'

Morgan picked up his knife and fork. 'Aye, I know. That's why I'm here.'

'Well, what you're hoping for I don't know, but

if ever there was a time for a good-looking man to show Non some feeling it's now.'

She pushed a mug of strong tea towards him. 'The old shop she used to rent 'as burned down and that girl Carrie was in it. She was cheating Non blind and some might say she had her comeuppance, but Non is very upset about it.'

Morgan nodded, his mouth full of delicious bacon. He waited for Ruby to go on. It was clear she had a need to talk.

'All Non's notes is gone, burned in the fire. How she'll make a fresh start now, I don't know.'

Hope filled Morgan's heart. 'I can offer her a fresh start,' he said, and just then the door was pushed open and Non came into the room. He looked at her white face and saw the dark circles under her eyes and his heart leaped with love and pity. He got up at once and took her in his arms. She clung to him for a moment and then sank into a chair.

He felt a burning sense of anger. If Caradoc Jones were here right now, he'd get the finest beating of his life.

'Why has he done this to you?' he asked, taking Non's thin hand in his. 'How could he just walk away from his marriage? The man must be mad.'

'Don't talk about it,' Non said quietly. 'There's nothing to be said. He chose another woman and there's nothing I can do about it.'

Morgan pushed his plate away. Suddenly his

342

appetite had gone. 'I've got something to say to you.' He stroked the back of her hand with his fingers. 'I'm going to America, to make a fresh start, and I want you to come with me.'

Ruby shook her head at him but slipped out of the kitchen, leaving him alone with Non.

'I know we can't be married but we belong together, we always have, Non. You know that as well as I do.'

She looked at him and her beautiful eyes were filled with tears. 'Thank you for your offer, Morgan, but it's impossible for me to go with you. Whatever Caradoc's done to me, I love him and I'll always love him.' She touched his cheek gently. 'You know I care for you. I really do love you in a way, but not in the way a woman loves her man.'

'I can make you love me in time.' Morgan's voice was thick with emotion. He felt her nearness and her vulnerability and it tore the heart out of him. 'What's here for you now? You've no business to run, no husband to go home to.' He pushed back a stray curl from her forehead. 'We can both make a fresh start in a new country. You would do so well in the Americas with all your herbal knowledge.'

'I can't go away,' Non said. 'I still have a hope in my heart that Caradoc will come back to me. I love him so much, I just can't let him go.'

Morgan heard the pity in her voice and his last hope vanished. 'You are sure, then?'

'I'm sure. You go to America, Morgan. You're a fine, handsome man and you'll soon meet a beautiful American girl just longing for a husband like you.'

He took a deep breath. 'Of course I will.' He stood up. 'I'll never forget you, Non.'

'And I'll never forget you, Morgan. God go with you.'

He forced a smile. 'Thank Ruby for my supper.' He stood lingering for a moment in the doorway as though even now he might be able to persuade her. He saw her eyes look into his pleadingly and he left her quickly, unable to bear the profound sadness in her face. As he walked away from his dreams and into the fog, unashamedly he felt tears course down his cheeks. It was over. Non did not want him. There was nothing to keep him here now. First thing in the morning, he would book his passage to America and try to build a new life out of the ashes of his old one.

CHAPTER THIRTY

Gwenllyn knew she should be the happiest woman in the world. She had her precious son in her arms and her man sitting on the opposite side of the fire, his long legs stretched out to the flames. Why, then, did she feel so uncertain, so restless? She studied his handsome face. He was still the same Caradoc she had lived with, and loved ever since she had met him, and yet she felt in her bones that she wanted Harry to be sitting there opposite her, not Caradoc. She wanted to talk to Caradoc, tell him of her doubts, but his eyes were closed and she wondered if he was asleep.

'Are you content, Caradoc?' She spoke softly, unwilling to disturb him and yet longing for re-assurance. He opened his eyes and what she saw there unsettled her.

'Contented enough.' His voice was hoarse with

sleep and she wished she'd not spoken, not seen in his eyes that he was anything but content. He was missing his wife but he was too kind to say so.

Fear sped through her. She was missing Harry, she couldn't deny it to herself any longer. But Harry had gone: he'd given up on her; he'd had enough of her fickle ways. What if she was left alone? What if Caradoc decided to leave too? What if Caradoc went home to his wife? So many questions, so many doubts and fears.

Gwenllyn sighed. She wasn't happy with Caradoc and it was clear he wasn't happy either. She knew deep in her being that the dream was ending and reality taking its place.

Caradoc sat up straighter in his chair and looked steadily at her. 'What's wrong, Gwenllyn?' The sleep was gone from his face. 'Just tell me truthfully how you feel. Are you worried about Harry coming here to make a scene?'

A dart of anger made Gwenllyn's voice sharp. 'I think Harry has more to do than think about me all the time,' she said. 'He's struggling to make a success of his business. The last thing he wants is an errant wife.'

Caradoc took a deep breath and Gwenllyn knew the time had come to hear the truth from him.

'You want to go home, don't you?' Her voice was firm. She knew this was coming – the signs had been there for some days now. As the droves passed through the Wye Valley she'd seen the look on his face and knew the cloistered life at the cottage just didn't suit him.

'It's no good, Gwenllyn.' He rubbed his eyes. 'I can't stay here. I don't pretend to understand my own feelings. I thought I wanted you, and I do in a way, but most of all I want Non, my wife. What sort of fool am I to mess up the lives of the two women most dear to me?'

Gwenllyn swallowed her fear. 'Then perhaps you should go away, right away, be alone for a while, think things over.'

'I suppose you're right.' He gazed into the fire and, as she saw the fleeting expressions on his face, pity replaced her fear.

'One thing I must say,' she said softly: 'we are not meant to be together.' She paused. 'I think we both know that now.' He was silent and so she spoke again. 'I should have been loyal to my husband and I shouldn't have let you come to live here. I've been a weak and foolish woman.'

His eyes met hers. 'You are right, Gwenllyn. We both know this is wrong and we both need time to sort out our true feelings.'

Outside, the wind was rising. Gwenllyn could hear it singing through the trees. 'Well, we can't do anything tonight.' She forced a smile. 'You go to bed – there's one made up in the spare room. We'll sort everything out in the next few days, you'll see.'

He rose to his feet. His hair was tangled over his brow and he'd never looked so handsome and so vulnerable.

She put out her arms to him. 'We tried our best to make a go of it together but we failed. I'll always love you but we can't be together.'

Tears came into her eyes and Caradoc wiped them away with his fingers. 'I know, Gwenllyn, I know exactly how you feel, because I have the same feelings. We are more than friends but we must be honest. We are not in love with each other, not any more.'

He released her and she heard him cross the hall towards the stairs. She sank down in a chair and covered her face with her hands. She had lost everything. She'd failed her husband, betrayed him, and now she knew it was all for nothing. Caradoc was right: the love, if it ever was real, was gone. They would always be connected because of the baby, but that was the only bond between them now. Caradoc loved her but not enough to give up everything for her. She couldn't stop shedding tears for her lost dreams. It was over, the great romance was over, and what was she left with?

'Oh, Harry,' she whispered, 'what a stupid fool I've been. I had love, real love, with you and now I've lost it all.'

It was a long time before she went to bed. She paused outside the door of the spare room and then, after a long moment, she went to her own bed.

Non had planned to go home to Swansea. She felt stronger now, her head was clear; she would set up business again in Swansea, work the markets as she'd done as a girl, and if it was without Caradoc she would just have to live with that. But even as Non was busy making her plans, Ruby had fallen sick and was lying in her bed, moaning in pain.

Non fell back on her old remedy, a mixture of angelica. It was all she had left of her stock. She stayed in Ruby's room all day, bathing her face and hands in cool water, but it seemed to do no good. Ruby tossed and turned in the bed, her eyes open but glazed, her body convulsing with the fever.

Non pushed aside the bedclothes and felt Ruby's stomach. It was distended and, as her fingers probed, Non knew that her friend had a sickness that couldn't be controlled by herbs.

She searched her possessions and managed to find the last of her money. 'Ruby,' she said, 'I'm going to fetch a doctor. I won't be long, I promise you.'

She pulled on a shawl. The air outside the lodging house was chill with the dying of autumn and she shivered. Bad things were happening to her and Non was powerless to change the course of her life.

The doctor recognized her. 'Of course I'll come, dear lady. Just lead me to your patient and I'll do what I can.'

'I've taken the liberty of having a cab ready outside. The driver will bring you back home after your visit.'

'Very thoughtful. You're the herb lady, aren't you?' he said. 'What do you think ails your friend?' He settled opposite her, his case on his plump thigh.

'I believe she has an infection in her stomach, Doctor Stevens,' Non said nervously. 'She's feverish and it seems my herbs are unable to cope with the sickness.'

'Well, sometimes a real doctor is needed. I know you've done some good work in the past, Mrs Jones, but, as I say, a real medic, a man who knows his business, can't be bettered.'

Non sank back in her seat and the leather creaked. 'I hope you can help Ruby, Doctor Stevens. She's very dear to me.'

When Non led the doctor upstairs to the bedroom, Ruby was still feverish. Her face was flushed and beads of perspiration ran down her face. Her eyes were closed and she was moaning in a low, hoarse voice.

'Let us take a look.' The doctor examined Ruby without taking off his coat. He pressed on Ruby's right side and nodded. 'Yes, I can feel the source of the infection. The good lady has appendicitis. I'm afraid she needs surgery.'

It was exactly the diagnosis Non had made for herself and she shivered. Ruby was very sick. 'Can we get her into hospital?'

'No time for that.' The doctor was removing his coat. 'I'll have to operate here if her life is to be saved.'

'But, doctor, we're not equipped for surgery here. Are you sure we can't take her to hospital?'

'Look at the condition she's in,' the doctor said. 'Don't look so worried, dear lady, I'm a very good surgeon and, what's more, I'm the best chance your friend has got right now.'

He rolled up his sleeves and gestured for Non to bring the bowl of water for him to wash his hands. He smiled ruefully. 'My friends think I'm a little eccentric to care about cleanliness, but I find the patient's survival rate is better if the attending doctor is careful about his person.'

'I couldn't agree more, doctor,' Non said. She watched as he selected a blade from his bag.

'You'll have to hold her arms, Mrs Jones,' he said. 'She might heave about as I remove the appendix.'

Non took a deep breath. She was in an agony of fear that Ruby might die. She took her friend's hands and closed her eyes. She couldn't watch as the doctor made his incision, but she held on tightly to Ruby, knowing this was her only chance of survival. Softly, in a low voice, she began to pray.

* * *

Harry couldn't stop thinking about Gwennie, and yet he was torn with indecision. His first impulse had been to rush up to the cottage and beat Caradoc senseless, but he knew that would only turn Gwennie against him.

Why had he walked away from his wife and left her in the hands of that man Caradoc Jones? Was he mad? He couldn't bear to think of them together and yet what should he do? If Gwennie wanted Caradoc, not him, perhaps he should give her a chance to be happy. And yet he knew in his heart she would not be happy. Gwennie was a respectable woman: she wouldn't like living over the broomstick with any man.

He roused himself and pulled on his coat, looking round the empty rooms of the house he had rented. He was doing well for himself, he was a man who could read and work figures, he had everything he wanted except the woman he loved. He berated himself for being a fool. He would make up his mind later whether to go after Gwennie, but first of all he had to get some work done or his business would be short-lived. And having a business of his own was what Harry had always wanted.

Today one of the farmers was bringing two of his beasts to be serviced by the bull. In exchange Harry would receive two heifers, young animals not yet put in calf. It would be another step on the way to having his own herd. He was getting steadily nearer to his plan to run cattle from Carmarthen to Smithfield and he should be happy, yet there was a big gap in his life that beasts and business profits couldn't fill.

Still, he owed it to the farmer to be businesslike. ''Morning, Farmer Davies,' he said, smiling at the red-faced man approaching his gate. 'It's a fine sunny day, though a little cold, mind.'

'Aye, 'tis that.' Farmer Davies was a man of few words. Taking the hint, Harry led him to the paddock at the back of the house. The bull was trampling the ground, his nostrils quivering as he scented the cows: he was eager to do his work. Harry led the beasts into the paddock and turned to the farmer.

'Let's go inside. I'll get us a mug of beer. It will be a while before my bull makes sure he's done his job right.'

In the kitchen, Farmer Davies sat beside the fire, relaxing a little now that the reason he'd come to the paddock was being dealt with.

'Good stock, that bull?' he asked.

Harry nodded as he poured some beer from the jug. 'Aye, the best. Came from the Jones herd, did that fine animal.'

'He looks eager for the mating. Should get a calf from each of my cows for my dairy herd, with a bit of luck.'

The two men fell silent and Harry became

aware that the farmer was looking at him closely.

'Wife and babba out getting the air, are they?'

Harry hesitated, not knowing what to say. He poured more beer to give himself time to think. 'She'll be with me before too long. She'll have to leave her home, you see, the only home she's ever known, and it takes a bit of organization.'

Farmer Davies nodded sagely. 'Aye, there is that, but a wife's place is at her husband's side, mind.'

'Well, as I say, she'll be joining me once I've got this place tidy enough to house a family.'

'Old Martha's granddaughter, isn't she?'

Harry looked up in surprise. 'How did you know that?'

'Used to travel the drovers' roads, see. I was a fine young buck in my time and I well remember old Martha. 'Course, she wasn't old then: a bright young lady, she was. I think half the men in the Wye Valley was in love with her.' He shrugged. 'But she had her sights set higher than a lowly farmer from Swansea.'

Harry was uncomfortable. He didn't like the way the discussion was going. 'Well, Gwennie's a real lady. Married me good and true, she did.'

Farmer Davies looked at him with knowing eyes but chose not to say any more. Harry clenched his fists. Everyone must have heard the gossip the drovers brought to the town. Farmer Davies probably knew that Caradoc Jones was living with

Gwennie in the house above the Wye valley, perhaps even knew that David was Caradoc's son.

Later, when Harry led Farmer Davies to the paddock, the bull was docile and Harry knew that the job was done.

'What do I owe you?' Farmer Davies asked, putting his hand in his pocket.

Harry shook his head. 'I'll just have some of your heifers as we agreed,' he said. 'I want to build up my herd until I've enough beasts to take the trail to Smithfield.'

'When you go you can take my beasts with you.' The farmer adjusted his hat. 'Good herd I've got, see. Needin' only a good bull. Not thinking of selling him?' He gestured towards the bull. 'I could give you seven pounds. Good price, that.'

'I can get more than that in Smithfield,' Harry said.

'Aye, I know, but there's many a slip, see. Lot of things happen on the trail, as you well know.'

'Still,' Harry said, 'I'll keep my bull. He's a good 'un and I'll get many a calf out of him yet.'

He watched from the gate as the farmer led his obedient cows back down the lane. Harry stood there long after the farmer had disappeared and then he went back indoors. He stood for some time staring into the fire and then at last he squared his shoulders. Gwennie's place was with him. Was he a man or a mouse to leave his wife in the arms of another man? It was time he asserted himself and went back to the Wye to claim her.

'Damn and blast!' He slammed his fist on the table. 'I'll fetch you home, Gwennie, if it's the last thing I do.'

CHAPTER THIRTY-ONE

Albie looked across the table at Emily. She seemed subdued; her normally smiling face was creased into a frown. He glanced towards Josh and Albie knew he was behind Emily's strained manner. Since he'd been staying with them Josh had disturbed the quiet of the house with his constant comings and goings. He was dealing in something shady but Albie couldn't quite put his finger on what it was.

'When will you be moving on, Josh?' he said bluntly. 'I'm getting a bit fed up with keeping you in food and shelter. You don't even do a hand's turn about the bleedin' place so, I ask you, why should I put up with an unwelcome lodger?'

'Unwelcome, am I?' Josh flared up at once. 'And is my little sister unwelcome too? She does most of the work around here as far as I can tell.'

'Take her home with you, then,' Albie said, 'but

I want you out of here by the end of the week.'

He saw Emily's startled look but didn't meet her gaze. He had come to know Josh well enough by now to realize the man had no real interest in his sister: he was just using the situation to suit his own ends.

'All right, then! I'll go if that's what you want. Come on, Emily, pack your things. We're not wanted here.'

'But, Josh, Albie, I don't want to go. I've got no home except this one. I can't leave London, I just can't.'

Josh stalked out of the room ahead of Emily and she stood nervously in the doorway, looking pleadingly at Albie. He squeezed her shoulder.

'It will be all right, you'll see. That brother of yours is bleedin' bluffing. He ain't going to support you as well as himself; he'll soon realize he's taken on more than he can chew and then you can come back to me.'

He saw the relief in her face and put a warning finger on her lips. 'Just be patient, Em – you'll be back with me sooner than you think.'

'I hope you're right, Albie.'

'Go now, get your things, see how far that brother of yours will take you.' He smiled grimly. 'Not more than a few miles I'd say.'

He watched with a feeling of pity as Emily packed up her few belongings, wiping the tears from her eyes as she pushed her pathetically few clothes into her bag. He should have been more generous with her wages, made sure Emily was adequately dressed. Josh was right about one thing: Em did an awful lot of work about the place and for very little reward.

Josh was ready at last and he threw Albie a venomous look before charging out of the door without even a word of thanks.

'Go with him, Em, and just be patient. I'll be keeping an eye on things, so don't worry.'

Emily nodded but her eyes were still full of tears.

As he watched her go, Albie felt a sinking feeling. So far, Emily had provided a barrier against grief and loneliness – why hadn't he realized that before? Of course he had bad times when he could think of no one but his dear wife Jess, but being with Emily, talking to her about the milking trade, had taken the edge off his pain. Still, she would be back with him soon. At least that was something to look forward to. In the meantime, he would hire another hand, an older woman perhaps, who would act as chaperone when Em did come back home.

He put the kettle on the fire and took out two cups before he remembered that he only needed one. He sank down into a chair and put his hand over his eyes. 'Oh, Em, I didn't want to send you away but I had no choice.' His words rang hollow in the empty room and Albie felt salty tears run down his face and into his mouth.

★ ★ ★

Non sat at Ruby's kitchen table, a pen in her hand and a blank piece of paper in front of her. She was trying to remember some of her herbal remedies but it was all so confusing. The roots of some plants were pulped and used as an ointment and some leaves were made into infusions, but which ones?

She put down her pen in despair. She would never remember all her recipes and did she really care any more? She heard the chinking of cups and saucers and moved her papers as the new maid pushed open the kitchen door. After her sickness Ruby had admitted she needed more help in the house. Ruby came behind her, still pale but anxious as ever to see that her guests were all looked after.

'Gawd! I thought that lot would never finish the meal.' She sank into a chair and stretched her feet out towards the fire. 'I'm glad I took on that girl – she's a real gem,' she said as the maid hurried from the room. 'I should have more help in the place. I'm not getting any younger.'

'You're not getting old either. You mustn't think like that,' Non said.

Ruby sighed. 'You know something, Non? I feel like a dried-up old woman. I know I'm lucky to be here; I thought I'd never get over my fever but the doctor worked a miracle and I'm glad to be alive.' She paused. 'But it's made me think about my life: do I want to be waiting on folk all day and every day without a special man to care about me and love me and . . . well, you know.'

Non did know. She felt the same. She wanted Caradoc back in her life, back in her arms.

'I wait on men all day long and yet no sweetheart comes calling at my door, not ever,' Ruby continued. 'What have I done with my life when you bleedin' think about it?'

Non forced a smile. 'You've been a good friend to me for a start, and as for men wanting you, well, maybe you haven't looked at the people close to you.'

'What the 'ell do you mean by that?'

'I mean there's always Mr Jameson. He never stops giving you the eye but you're always too busy to notice.'

'Frederick Jameson is just a lodger,' Ruby said, but her colour was high and she made a great fuss about poking the fire.

'Ah, so you have noticed him?'

''Course I've *noticed* him – he's one of my best lodgers. He always stays with me when he's got business in town.'

'I know he does,' Non said, 'and I've seen the way he looks at you. He makes cow eyes at you all the time, but you don't give him any encouragement.'

'Well, it's just business, isn't it?' She patted a stray curl into place with an almost coquettish glance at Non. 'In any case, he's no doubt got a wife tucked away somewhere.'

'I don't think so – have you seen the way he packs his bags?'

'I can't say I've noticed.' Ruby rubbed at her red cheeks, making them even redder.

''Course you've noticed. You do his washing: have you ever seen a sign of a woman's hand arranging his clothes? He mixes up good shirts with threadbare socks and it's not as if he can't afford to buy whatever he wants. No, he just needs taking in hand by a good woman, that's all.'

'But he's seen me at my worst, sweatin' like a bleedin' pig over the cooking. How can he think of falling for a woman like me?'

'That's all the more reassuring, Ruby. Shows he loves you for yourself, just as you are.'

Ruby shook her head. 'You must be mistaken, Non. Frederick 'as never hinted that he likes me.'

'Why would he, when you practically ignore him?' Non smiled. 'I can tell you have a special liking for him by the way you get flighty when he's around you.'

'I don't get flighty!' Ruby protested. 'I'm not the flighty sort. I'm a practical woman and I run a lodging house, a respectable house, mind, and there's no time for romantic ideas in my life.'

'Make time,' Non said. 'Now, sit down while I make us a cup of tea with plenty of sugar in it – good for shock, you know.' She smiled ruefully at Ruby. 'Don't waste this chance. Don't make a mess of your life the way I've done.'

'Well, we'll see.' Ruby sat down obediently, dabbing at her face with her apron. Her eyes were alight and she looked like the girl she had once been. Gone was the tired droop to her mouth and her shoulders were straight as she sat upright in her chair, a mingling of disbelief and hope chasing the expressions across her face.

'Do you really think he likes me?' she asked quietly.

'I really do,' Non said. 'Now take a rest, for heaven's sake: you're still not back to your full strength yet. The place won't fall down about your ears if you learn to delegate.'

'Oh dear, what posh words, Non! But, dull though I am, I get their meaning and you're right, it's time I took it more easy, like.'

'Thank goodness you're seeing sense. I'll expect to see you dressed like a well-to-do landlady from now on, just presiding over the lodging house without burdening yourself with all the work.' She touched Ruby's hand. 'And I expect you to pay more attention to Frederick. Seriously, he does really care for you – I can tell.'

'Perhaps you're right. It's time I sat back and enjoyed myself. The lodging house is doing well and I've got a little nest egg from it.' She smiled. 'I like the idea of being like a posh landlady and sitting at table for meals with the guests.'

'That's exactly what you should be doing,' Non said. 'Tomorrow we'll start on your transformation.

I'll style your hair and choose some decent clothes for you to wear – how do you feel about that?'

'I feel bleedin' good, that's what I feel.' Ruby looked at her steadily. 'Now, how about you making a move to get your man back? You've sorted out my life – what about your own?'

'The minute I know you're on your feet,' Non said, 'I'm going to see Caradoc, ask him what he really wants out of life. It might turn out to be what he's got, Gwenllyn and the baby, but that's a chance I have to take. Then again, maybe he wants me back. I won't know unless I go to see him.'

'Good girl,' Ruby said. 'In the morning we can make our plans. You can help me to look like a lady and I can send one of the lodgers to book you a place on the mail coach, but, for now, let's just have another cup of tea and relax.'

Emily sat in the snug room of the Farmer's Arms and tried to fight back her tears. She was missing Albie sorely, even though it had sometimes felt as though he had taken her presence in his life for granted.

She became aware that the farmer Josh was talking to was looking her over as if she was one of his heifers. She felt uncomfortable, wishing Josh had grown tired of trailing round with her as Albie had predicted.

She saw him take a bag of gold from the farmer

and then he left the inn without so much as looking in her direction. She looked down at her hands. Why was Josh taking money from a stranger and why did he leave without her? Well, the exchange of money was his business. He must have left to sort out a room for the night. Though he begrudged spending money on lodgings, he complained sometimes that he was tired of sleeping in hedgerows, so he might book them a comfortable bed for the night.

The farmer tilted up his tankard and drained it and then made his way towards her, weaving through the throng, his eyes never leaving her face. She was uneasy as he sat down beside her and she moved away from him as she smelled his beery breath.

'Nice evening.' He held out his hand. 'I'm Eddie Dobson. I've got you a place for the night.'

Emily sighed in relief. 'That's very kind of you,' she said, drawing her skirts away from his leg. 'Is my brother paying you?'

'Aye. Don't worry about paying. Come on, we'd best get back to the farm.'

He got up and walked away and Emily had no choice but to follow him. He had a pony and trap outside the inn and as he helped her into the seat his hand brushed her back. She shivered and sat down, covering herself demurely.

'Where's Josh?' she asked as Dobson took his place next to her. 'Has he gone on ahead?'

'Aye,' Dobson chuckled, 'you could say that.'

Emily looked at him uneasily. 'What do you mean?'

''E's gone on his way – that's what I mean.'

'Gone where?'

''Ow do I know, girl?' He glanced at her. 'But you needn't worry: I'm looking out for you from now on.' He paused and looked her over with probing eyes that made Emily cringe away from him. 'You're my property now, girl.' His hand touched her knee. 'You're mine.'

'How do you mean, I'm yours? If you think I'm going to work on your farm, you've got another think coming.'

'Aye, you'll work, my girl, but you'll be warming my bed as well.' He squeezed her knee. 'I can do just as I like, see? I bought you fair and square and from now you'll do exactly what I tell you to do.'

A feeling of horror swept over Emily. Josh had sold her to this man as if she was nothing more than an animal. For a moment she thought of leaping from the cart, but it was moving too quickly over the uneven ground. She looked round in despair. What could she do? 'Oh, Albie,' she whispered, 'please help me.' But Albie was back in London, in the warm house, no doubt waiting for her to come back. Would she ever see him again?

CHAPTER THIRTY-TWO

Harry was ready, at last, to leave Swansea and go to the Wye to try to win back his wife. It had taken him longer than he thought to organize the small drove through the Welsh countryside. He was used to the actual trail and used to driving the animals over the rough terrain, but he'd no experience of arranging provisions for the journey. In the end he'd worked out he'd need a loaf a day, some cheese and some water.

It was late in the year for a drove to take the road, but instead of bedding down in the fields, he would spend the nights at the inns along the drovers' route, paying halfpenny a head to the farmers for his animals to eat their fill and bed down somewhere safe and snug.

He'd sold all but two of his horses, keeping only one to ride and the other spare in case one of the animals threw a shoe. But now, at last, he was leaving Swansea and his heart was thumping as he went out into the fresh morning air. He took a deep breath. He didn't know if he would ever have the heart to start again; the dream of being a rich drover was not as important to him now. All he wanted was Gwennie, his true love, his wife.

He mounted his horse and looked back at the green fields, frost-rimmed now with the onset of winter, and felt a lump in his throat. He loved Gwennie more than he thought he could love anyone. She had changed him from an illiterate devil-may-care drifter to an honest hard-working man and he was not going to throw it all away.

What if she refused to send Caradoc on his way? She might be happy as she was with no thought in her head for saving her marriage. Harry cracked his heels against the horse's flanks and began to ride. The cold air caught in his throat, and as his breath touched the air it turned into vapour. He realized he might be throwing aside everything he dreamed of being, but it would all be worth it if only his wife wanted him back.

''Ere, get up on the cart before I whip you soundly.' Dobson frowned, his beetle eyebrows forming a hard line above his steely eyes. 'You've tried to run once but I won't give you a second chance to make a fool out of me.'

He hauled Emily into the well of the cart and took out a length of rope from his pocket. ''Old your hands out, girl. Come on, I 'aven't got all day.'

Emily began to cry as Dobson tied her wrists. 'Oh, don't start sniffling. Tears will get you nowhere, my girl.'

Emily watched as Dobson climbed into the creaking cart, which dipped as he settled his large weight on the seat. 'Now, stop bawling or you'll feel the back of me 'and.'

He'd been like this since they'd left London early that morning, treating her like a slave, talking to her as though she had no more sense than one of the beasts he sold at Smithfield.

So far he hadn't touched her, but she was dreading the night, when they would stop at one of the wayside inns. He would insist on her sharing his room if for no other reason than he was mean with his money. Emily dreaded being alone with him. He'd made it plain she was his property now and she knew she would have to run away from him if she was going to escape his unwelcome attentions. She shivered. She was a maiden still – how awful it would be if Dobson had his way with her.

'Oh, Albie,' she whispered. 'Please come and rescue me from this awful man.'

But her words were taken by the wind and she knew with a sinking of her heart her pleas would never be heard.

★ ★ ★

'Tell me where she is, you bastard!' Albie caught Josh by the throat. 'You'll tell me, if I have to beat it out of you.'

'I haven't done anything with Emily,' Josh said angrily. 'I don't know who's told you a cock-and-bull story about me selling her to Farmer Dobson but it's all a pack of lies.'

Albie shook him. 'Talk to me, you scum!' he said. 'There were at least three witnesses to what you did with Emily, and you bragging about it in the taproom afterwards as cheeky as you like.'

'What's up with you?' Josh stuck out his chin pugnaciously. 'Missing your little whore, your willing bed-warmer, are you?'

'Emily is a good girl,' Albie said, shaking Josh fiercely. 'She's still a child and you've sold her like a slave. How could you do such a thing to your own sister?'

'So you're trying to tell me that Emily is innocent after living alone with you? You must think I fell off the last apple tree.'

'I've never touched Emily, I tell you – she's as virgin as when she came to work for me.'

Josh gave an unpleasant laugh. 'Well, with old Dobson randy as a goat she won't be a virgin for long.'

It was then Albie hit him. Josh fell back into the mud of the road, his arms and legs flailing. Albie dragged him to his feet and took his time before hitting him again. Josh reeled under the blow.

A crowd of men had gathered outside the Drover's Rest, happy to be given a few moments' entertainment.

'Go on, belt him in the mouth, he's a scoundrel,' one of the men called. 'Got rid of his little sister like she was no more than a dog.'

'Where is this Dobson taking Emily?' Albie's fist shot out and connected with Josh's nose. There was a cracking of bone and blood gushed over Josh's face.

'How the hell do I know?' Josh gasped. 'Stop hitting me; I've had enough. There's nothing I can tell you.'

Albie began to beat him in earnest and Josh crumpled under the barrage of blows. He tried to run but Albie was too fast for him: he stuck out his foot and Josh went spinning over onto his back.

He held up his hands. 'All I know is that Dobson lives somewhere near the Wye Valley.'

Albie stood back. 'Is that everything?'

'Aye, it is.'

'And how much did Dobson pay you?'

'Eight pounds,' Josh said, glowering at Albie. 'And there's no point asking me for the money: I've spent it. If you want to play the hero and save my little sister you'll have to pay up yourself.'

Albie wanted to hit the man again but Josh was bleeding badly, his eyes were swollen and rapidly turning black and a few of his teeth were missing. Albie looked at him in satisfaction. 'You won't be so pleasing to the girls now,' he said. 'You look as though you've been kicked by a horse.'

'I'll get you back for this,' Josh said, 'you just see if I don't.'

'Aye and pigs might fly.'

Albie left him lying in the street, still cursing, and hurried along the streets towards Ruby's lodging house. He would need some money, his own all being tied up in the business; he doubted if he had more than three pounds at his immediate disposal. He would have to pay Dobson the eight pounds he'd spent on Emily and he needed a good horse and some provisions. He would also need someone to look after the servery, but he knew he could rely on Ruby and Non to bail him out when he needed help.

By the time he reached Ruby's house, his hands were stinging and there was blood oozing from his knuckles. Still, the pain was worth it. At least he knew where to go to find Emily and when he found her he'd take her home, look after her, treat her like the little sister she was to him.

A pretty young maid let him into the house, though she looked at his dishevelled appearance with an expression of alarm in her eyes. 'I don't know if Miss Ruby is in,' she said nervously. 'I'll go and find out.'

'No need,' Albie said: 'I'll find her.'

He went straight to the kitchen and, to his satisfaction, found both Ruby and Non seated at the table. Ruby was still a little pale – she'd had very little time to recover from her illness – but she smiled when she saw him and rose to give him a kiss.

'What's happened to you, boy? You look as if you've been run over by a horse and carriage.'

Non tipped her face up to his and touched his bruised cheek lightly. 'I can see you've been in a fight. What was it all over?'

He told them briefly and both women listened to him in silence. At last, he sat at the table with them and held out his hands. 'So, you see, I'm going to need help. I haven't got the eight pounds to hand and as for a horse and provisions, well . . . will you help me?'

Ruby got to her feet. ''Course we'll help you. What are bleedin' friends for?'

Non spoke slowly. 'I haven't got any money but I can give you a horse. He's a cross-breed and no one wanted him except me, but he's eager to please and he'll ride as fast as you want him to.'

Albie smiled. 'I knew I could depend on you good friends.' He put the keys of the servery and the house onto the table.

'I'll see to your provisions, Albie,' Ruby said, 'and I'll get someone to see to the milk business until you get back.' She paused and looked at Non. 'If Albie's going to the Wye Valley, why don't you ride with him? I can get hold of a good horse.' She smiled wickedly. 'My Mister Jameson keeps a very fine animal at the stables round the back.'

Albie felt a momentary dart of unease. Would Non hold him up? It was imperative he got to Emily before that monster Dobson laid a hand on her.

Non saw his dilemma. 'I can ride as fast as any man,' she said. 'Don't worry about me.'

Albie smiled. 'Come on then, my dear friend, let's get ready to travel. If God is willing, I'll find Emily and you'll find ... well, whatever it is you're looking for.'

CHAPTER THIRTY-THREE

Josh sat in the Tradesman's Inn, wrinkling his nose against the smell from the Thames. 'What a bloody awful stink.' He ground out the words, looking at his companion, Bennett, as though everything that had gone wrong lately was his fault. Josh was not in a good mood; he was still filled with resentment about the way Albie had treated him. Why did the man poke his nose into business that didn't concern him? It was nothing to do with him what happened to Emily.

Josh burned to get his revenge, but now, according to his customers, Albie had gone away. Josh could guess where he was – chasing after Emily like a love-struck schoolboy. Well, he wouldn't escape Josh's wrath that easily: he'd find that running away wouldn't do him any good at all. Josh was confident he knew every inch of the drovers' roads and he would find Albie however long it took.

He clenched his fists as he thought of the way that bastard had made him look like a prize fool in front of the other men, but he would pay, oh, yes, he'd pay. Josh wanted Albie to suffer and he needed to see the bastard suffering for himself.

'So how do I get my hands on these explosives, then?' He turned to Bennett and forced a genial note into his voice. 'If you help me I'll pay you well.'

'I know you will.' The old quarryman sitting opposite him spoke with a gloating gleam in his eye. 'You'll pay me the eight pounds you got from old Dobson.'

Josh swallowed his rage: no good antagonizing the man. 'Aw, come on, Bennett, I got to keep some money to see me through. I'll need to get hold of a horse for a start. I tell you what, I'll give you three pounds – take it or leave it.'

'Make it five and we got a deal.' Bennett grinned cunningly. 'In any case, you'll need a pack-horse as well as one for riding. And don't be a fool: why buy animals when you can just as easily steal them? It's five pounds or you don't get the goods. That's my last word.'

'And what goods will I be getting exactly?'

'You'll need two Pins for a start.'

'Pins? What the hell are Pins?'

'Barrels to you, filled with a mixture of saltpetre, sulphur and charcoal. Mix the stuff in with some tar and a load of nails, and just light the fuse on the damned thing. Your enemy will be gone, and everything around him as well.' He stared at Josh for a long moment. 'I won't ask why you want the stuff. I 'spect it's better not to know.'

Josh nodded briefly. 'That's right. Now, when are you going to fetch me the powder?'

'You hands over the money first. As for the powder, you come and collect it. I'm not lugging that muck all over London for nobody.'

Josh sighed. 'You're not an easy man to deal with, Bennett, are you?'

'Well, just think, you got the benefit of my years of experience. That sort of thing don't come cheap.'

'Well, that's true,' Josh said. 'So at least you can buy me a mug of beer with my five pounds.'

He sat and watched as Bennett waved his hand at the landlord. 'Two beers, if you please.'

Josh leaned back in his chair. He'd spend the night in London and in the morning he'd go to Bennett's shack and pick up the powder. After that, who knew? When he'd evened the score with Albie he'd think about the future.

He might wait until spring and join the droves again. He would need to work to get some money. For a time he'd been well off, with eight pounds in his pocket and the world at his feet, but now, by the time he'd paid Bennett, he'd be left with a few measly pounds.

A thought struck him: what if he got Emily back

from Dobson? Perhaps Dobson had been too poor to pay a good price for the girl. He gloated silently. He could sell her to some other fool for a higher price; he could claim she was a young untouched maid, whether she was or not, and she'd be worth more than eight pounds.

Dobson was heading back to Wales but he would be travelling slowly with Emily to drag along. Catching him up would be no trouble, and then the matter of knocking the man unconscious and taking Emily from him would be easy enough.

He took the beer Bennett ordered and sucked on the rim of the tankard. The taste of the alcohol hit his palate and he belched loudly. Bennett added his own belches and, with a sigh of satisfaction, Josh leaned back in his seat, prepared to enjoy the rest of the evening.

Gwenllyn put the baby into his bed and tiptoed from the room. She prayed David would sleep well: she wanted this last night alone with Caradoc to be one she would remember for the rest of her life. The two of them had spent the last few days talking things through. They had agonized about the course they must take but in the end both of them agreed they had to part.

Nonetheless, when she saw his bag standing in the hall by the door, her heart fell. It was a symbol of their last night together.

Caradoc was sitting in his usual chair in front of

the fire and he looked up as she entered the room. Shadows from the lamp played across his face and she wondered if she imagined the tears that seemed to gleam in his eyes.

He held out his hand to her. 'Come here, Gwenllyn.'

Obediently she sat on the floor at his side and rested her head on his knee. She felt him touch her hair, his fingers moving gently in a caress. He loved her, she knew he did, and yet it wasn't the all-consuming love a man felt for his wife.

'You know it's best if I go,' he said gently. 'We should be doing our best to mend our marriages, shouldn't we?'

There was a note of uncertainty in his voice and Gwenllyn felt her heart lurch. She believed that in another time and another place they were meant for each other, but for now it was simply impossible.

She turned to look up at him. 'Just one more night together,' she said softly, 'but when we go to our beds it will be to separate rooms. Our days of sleeping together are over, Caradoc, but one more night as friends isn't too much to ask for, is it?'

He put his hand under her chin and kissed her gently, without passion. 'No, it's not too much to ask. I'll stay for one more night and then, when daylight comes, I'll be on my way.'

He drew her up in his arms and sat her on his knee. Her head fell naturally into the hollow of his neck and she kissed his cheek, forcing back the tears, determined that she wouldn't spoil the short time they had together.

'I'll never forget you, Gwenllyn,' Caradoc murmured.

'And I'll never forget you, my darling.' She closed her eyes, felt the warmth of his arms around her, felt the touch of his skin, and for the moment she was content.

Josh cursed as his horse stumbled yet again on the rough ground. The nag was old, flea-ridden, and the pack-horse was no better, but at least the creature had the strength to carry a couple of barrels.

Josh knew he was not far behind Dobson now – he'd checked in the inns on the way down country. He smiled. He'd gained plenty of information from the last landlord, whose palm he'd greased with a few shillings. It seemed Emily had slept alone in one of the tiny bedrooms while Dobson had spent the night on one of the benches in the taproom of the inn.

Dobson had told the landlord that Emily screamed like a banshee whenever he went near her and that he would beat her into submission once he got her home. But Dobson was not going to get that chance.

The little serving wench at the inn was good to him. She had an eye for young men and, as he was flirting with her, Josh was craftily getting her to talk about the customers. A man matching Albie's description had arrived at the inn shortly after Dobson had left with Emily and Josh knew he was hot on the trail of his quarry. He would kill two birds with one stone: he'd get Emily back and teach Albie a lesson he would never forget.

Josh was nearing the Wye Valley now and he knew Albie would have to book into an inn somewhere near the village. When the right moment came, Albie would die in a horrible accident and Josh wouldn't have to worry about the man interfering in his affairs ever again.

He saw the gleam of the river and sat up in the saddle. He would have to go into the local inn and find out how far it was to Dobson's small farm. He sighed in satisfaction: it was all coming together now and what he hadn't worked out would be more easily solved over a couple of mugs of beer. Soon he would be in the money and then he could do anything he chose: rear a herd of his own, or perhaps – he smiled unpleasantly – open a shop . . . There would be a vacancy in the milk trade once Albie was out of the way. The world was his oyster and it was all down to his own cleverness.

CHAPTER THIRTY-FOUR

Emily lay on the lumpy bed, then sat up and dried her eyes. There was no point in crying: it was time for action. She would have to get away from the inn tonight and make her way to Swansea or be a slave to Dobson for ever more.

He'd left her in her room with a sigh of exasperation after failing to kiss her. She'd slapped his face hard and at last he left her alone and went to join the men downstairs in the tap-room. By now he would doubtless be regaling them with the story of how he'd bought a woman from her own brother. And boast that once she was under his roof he would tame what he called her 'vile temper'. Well, she wouldn't give him the opportunity. She would never live with him: she couldn't stand the sight of him, he stank worse than a pig, and his breath, when he came near her, was foul.

Tonight was the last night they would spend in an inn before they reached his home and it was time now for her to make her escape. She could hear the sound of the men in the taproom below, their loud, raucous voices raised in laughter. It would be no use appealing to any of them for help – they were all too well into their cups to think clearly. In any case, what was the importance of a girl bought for money? They believed she belonged to Dobson and that was an end to it.

When she was sure that enough time had passed for Dobson to have drunk a bellyful of beer, she crept to the door and strained her ears to listen. She heard Dobson's loud voice shouting above the chatter of the other men. By now his head would be fuddled with drink and he would think her safely asleep in her room. It was true she'd tried to escape at an earlier opportunity, but that was when she was still in London. Once they took to the trail Dobson believed she'd given up trying to run away from him – and she had allowed him to think that, so he might be less vigilant.

She was still dressed as she'd been on the day Dobson had taken her from London; she must now stink as badly as he did. She tiptoed towards the stairs, fearing every creak of the floorboards, and stood on the landing, listening with bated breath to the sounds of merriment from below.

As though she was treading on eggshells, she

made her way down the wooden stairs towards the front door, praying no one would spot her. She could see she would have to pass the taproom door, but by a stroke of luck it was half closed against the chill of the night. She could smell the beer and the stale odour of pipe smoke as she made her way across the hall. She held her breath as she passed through the door, slipping like a ghost into the darkness of the night.

Outside, the freshness of the air was like wine to her senses. She began to run. The darkness was deeper as she plunged towards the drovers' road and she stumbled and almost fell, but strong arms closed around her, gripping her tightly. With a cry, she tried to struggle. She could tell by the clean scent of the man it was not Dobson holding her but she saw any man as a threat to her now.

'Bleedin' 'ell, is that you, Em?'

The voice was warm, familiar, and she stopped struggling at once, peering eagerly into the face of the man she loved. 'Albie! What are you doing here?'

'I've been following you, Em. Lost sight of you and Dobson a few times but I was never far behind.' He held her away and looked down into her face. 'Has he, well, hurt you in any way, Em?'

She shook back her hair. 'He hasn't had the chance! Every time he came near I screamed like a banshee and scratched at his eyes.' She took a deep breath. 'But tomorrow it would have been a different story: he'd have taken me to his home and then I'd have had no chance to escape.' She shivered. 'But I'm all right, Albie my love, I'm all right.'

'That's my girl.' He ignored the endearment and began to lead her away from the inn. 'Non is waiting for me in the paddock with the horses. The inn is full and in any case we want to be as far away from Dobson as we can be. Don't worry, though, we'll find somewhere to lay our heads tonight.'

'I don't care if I sleep in a field so long as I'm with you, Albie.'

He led her to where Non was waiting, holding the reins of the two animals, her face a white oval in the darkness.

'You've found her!' There was a note of relief in her voice as she saw them. 'I was beginning to get worried.'

'We'll have to think again about where we're to sleep. Dobson's at the inn and we don't want a running battle with him. Local folks might agree he 'as a bleedin' right to Emily,' Albie said.

Non shivered. 'Well, it's too cold to sleep out-doors, and the next inn is half a day's ride away. Look, we'll have to go to Gwenllyn's cottage. I might as well face my husband tonight and get it over with.'

'You go on ahead then, Non. You can ride faster than us; me and Em will take our time. You'll want a bit of privacy when you face your man, I'm sure.'

Emily watched as Non, her skirts billowing, headed away towards the cottage in the hills. Albie helped her into the saddle behind him. She felt absurdly happy: Albie had come to rescue her and there was nothing in the whole world better than that.

'Hold on tight, Emily,' Albie said. 'We don't want to lose you now we've found you, do we?'

As Emily snuggled close to Albie, her arms around his waist, she felt relief and happiness surge through her. She was safe now – Dobson couldn't harm her. Albie had come to her rescue as, deep inside her, she'd hoped he would.

Josh was in a foul mood. He'd stopped at the inn, expecting to get himself a room, but the landlord was drunk and in no state to bother with a late traveller. 'You're out of luck, *butty*,' he said. 'I've just turned away some young fellow who came all the way from London, so you got no hope of getting a bed here tonight.'

'A man from London, did you say?'

'Aye. Good trade, that would have been, with him willing to fork out for a decent meal and a bed.' He looked Josh over with disdain. 'As for you, well, you don't look like you got two half-pennies to rub together.'

Josh saw he had to tread warily if he wanted to

get any information from the man. He moved a step forward and spoke in a conciliatory tone. 'This man from London, did he give you a name?' Josh immediately suspected that someone travelling from London could be Albie, come running after Emily. But Emily was still there at the inn, she had to be, because he'd seen Dobson in the taproom, heard him amusing the men with tales of what he was going to do with her once he got her home. Well, he would deal with Dobson later.

'Didn't get no name. What the heck, what did I want with the name of a man I'd never see again?'

'Which direction did the man take?' Josh jingled some coins in his pockets and the landlord became more amiable.

'Saw him heading up towards the hill, though he won't find a bed up there. Not much up in those hills, mind, except old Martha's cottage.'

Josh let the coins fall back into his pocket. The landlord would get nothing out of him. He mounted his horse in a thoughtful mood. Something was going on here: it looked as if Albie had other things on his mind apart from running after Emily. He was up to something, that was sure – something that might well prove valuable to himself. In any case, he had to get even with the devil. Before sunrise Albie would get exactly what he deserved. And then Josh could go back to the inn, sort out Dobson and take Emily away from him.

He rode his horse gently up through the hills, leading the pack-horse on a loose rein. The animals were tired, heads drooping, and he leaned forward and patted his horse's neck. 'Not far now, girl,' he murmured. He was in no hurry. He'd catch Albie up soon enough and then the bastard Londoner would get just what he deserved.

At last, the cottage came into view and Josh saw lights spilling from the doors and windows onto the pathway outside. He reined in his horse, dismounted and crept up to one of the windows. Peering in, he could see Albie standing in the candlelight, blocking the other people in the room from view. Josh didn't know who else was in the cottage, but in any case that didn't concern him: Albie was there and now the man was going to pay for crossing him.

Hatred boiled inside Josh. He still felt the blows on his head, the way his nose had split across his face as the bastard Londoner had kicked him. Well, now the man would get his just deserts. He wouldn't live to strike anyone else; nothing was more sure than that.

He went round the side of the house, walking carefully; he didn't want to be spotted. In one of the outhouses he found a brazier with some old tar still in it. He smiled unpleasantly. The tar would catch alight and if the explosion didn't kill the Londoner then the fire surely would.

At the rear of the cottage, a small window was

open and Josh congratulated himself on his luck. He climbed inside and found himself in a large, cold room where milk and cheese and butter were stored.

He looked around and his eyes alighted on an empty milk churn. He examined it. The tall, narrow opening was just perfect: he could ram the chunks of tar down into the bottom, pour in the gunpowder and add some horseshoe nails for good measure. All he had to do then was to set a fuse running through the window to the garden outside. If Bennett had told him the truth, the whole house would go up and Albie and his friends would find themselves in hell. But first he would take what money and valuables he could find; he'd leave the cottage a richer man and with his honour satisfied.

The back door opened easily and Josh stared inside. It was dark and silent; there was no danger of anyone hearing him do his work. Quietly he led the pack-horse across to the door and quickly untied the barrels of gunpowder. He was jubilant: tonight he would see his enemy wiped from the face of the earth; and then tomorrow he'd begin his new life as a man of means.

Non drew a sharp intake of breath as she saw Caradoc come out of the sitting room. His hair was tousled and it was plain to see he'd been woken up from his sleep. Before Non could speak,

Gwenllyn came hurrying down the stairs and Non breathed a sigh of relief: they hadn't been sleeping together, not tonight anyway.

'I had to see you,' Non said. 'I'm sorry it's so late.' She felt foolish for apologizing but she stumbled on. 'There was no room at the local inn so I thought I might as well come here straight away.'

'So you want to see me, do you? I thought you were never going to speak to me again.' Caradoc's voice was edged with pain.

Her anger evaporated. 'I had to come. We need to talk, Caradoc. I said awful things to you but I'm sorry and I want you back.'

Caradoc's face softened. He turned to Gwenllyn, who was standing at the foot of the stairs, looking down at her feet.

'Leave us alone, please, Gwenllyn,' he said gently. 'Look, Albie and Emily arrived a few minutes ago and I took the liberty of sending them into the sitting room. Perhaps you'll join them?'

Gwenllyn didn't move and the silence seemed to go on for ever. Non was the first to speak.

'I'm sorry I had to come here.' She appealed to Gwenllyn: 'I just had to see my husband. Please try to understand.'

Gwenllyn nodded, but Non wasn't looking at her. 'Caradoc, I love you; I've never stopped loving you. Please believe me.'

'Are you sure about that, Non?'

'It's true, as God is my witness.'

Gwenllyn sighed. 'I'll leave you and your husband to talk.' She made her way across the hall and into the sitting room and Non stood looking pleadingly into Caradoc's face.

'I'm sorry, my darling, so sorry.'

Caradoc took her hands. 'I know and I'm sorry too for all the hurt I've put you through. I love you, Non; I've always loved you. Do you think we can repair the damage I've done to our marriage? Can you forgive me?'

'I'm willing to try if you are,' Non said softly. He held out his arms and, hesitantly at first, Non went into them. 'I'll do my best to put all this out of my mind, Caradoc,' she whispered. 'I'll try not to think of you and her together. All I know is that I love you and I want to be with you for the rest of my life.'

He kissed her then, a gentle lingering kiss, and Non began to cry. 'How I've missed you, my darling,' she said. 'I felt as if part of me had gone with you when we were parted.'

'We're together now and nothing will ever come between us again. I promise you.'

With shocking suddenness the explosion ripped through the house. The building seemed to lift from its foundations as a roaring sound like an animal in pain tore through the rooms. Non clapped her hands to her ears as the noise seemed to fill her senses. A thick layer of dust burst through the hallway, blinding her eyes, and she was swept off her feet, her head cracking against the crumbling staircase as she fell.

She reached for Caradoc's hand as the wall seemed to cave in on her and the last conscious thought she had was that, if she was going to die, at least she and her darling husband would be together for all time.

CHAPTER THIRTY-FIVE

As he neared the top of the hill leading to the cottage Harry heard a terrible rumbling noise. It was as if the earth was cracking asunder beneath him. He urged his mount into a gallop, his heart thudding in fear, and as he crested the hill the cottage came into sight. As he rode towards the house the roof seemed to rise in the air as if lifted by a giant hand. Then it crashed down again, crushing the walls, shattering glass, spilling debris everywhere.

A cloud of choking dust came billowing towards him and his horse reared in fright, throwing Harry to the ground. He shook his head, trying to clear it, and staggered to his feet. He rubbed the dust from his eyes and began to run towards the cottage. As the dust cleared a little he saw that only a few walls of the building were standing; the back of the house was nothing more than rubble.

'Gwenllyn!' He called his wife's name, but the sound was drowned out by the rumble of masonry creaking like a soul in torment. Harry's heart thumped in his chest as he began to pull at the rubble with bare hands. 'Gwenllyn, for the love of God, answer me.'

Then Harry heard a cry and turned towards the sound. He clambered over the pile of rubble, almost losing his balance, masonry still moving beneath him. The cry was repeated, a cry loud and piercing on the night air. A baby's cry.

He found David's crib marooned like a ship on top of a heap of stones. 'It's all right, boy,' he said softly, 'you're safe now.' He carried the baby away from the ruins and set him down a safe distance from the house.

Along the brow of the hill Harry saw the gleam of torches. The villagers must have heard the explosion and come to help him. His heart warmed: with more hands to dig into the rubble, he had a better chance of finding his wife.

'The good Lord has saved this little mite,' one of the village women gasped as she drew near, her hand on her breast as if to calm its beating. 'I hope his mother is as lucky.'

Harry returned to his digging. The men were with him now – Morton from the inn and some of the local farmers with him. They were lifting the stones, passing them back along a line of outstretched arms, so calm, so collected, as if an explosion was an everyday event.

'Gwennie, where are you? Call if you can hear my voice.' There was nothing but a sudden still silence as the dust settled over the ruin of what had once been a home. He pulled at the rubble, unaware that his hands were bleeding.

The men from the village worked silently with only an occasional call to chart the progress of the digging. The time seemed to pass in agonizing slowness, but then one of the men called out, 'Silence, I can hear someone calling.'

Non Jones was the first to be pulled free. Her face was coated in dust, and it was in her mouth and her eyes, but she was alive.

'Oh, Harry, thank God you've come to rescue us. Find Caradoc for me, please find him.'

She sank onto the ground and one of the women-folk bent over her. 'You hurting anywhere, love?'

Non shook her head. 'I'm just shocked, that's all.' Her teeth were chattering. She put her arms around her knees and stared at the wrecked house as though by sheer will power she could bring her husband out of the rubble.

'Where was Gwenllyn when the explosion happened?' Harry asked urgently.

Non looked up at him with wide eyes, a small smear of blood beginning to show on her cheek. 'She was going towards the sitting room.' She rubbed her eyes. 'I don't know, I just don't know where they are, Harry.'

'They?' Harry leaned towards her. 'Who else was there?'

'Emily and Albie. Oh, Harry, just find them.'

Harry hurried back to the ruins. Where was Gwennie? Was she in the hall or in the sitting room, the walls of which were still standing?

He felt tears burn his eyes. The dust was caked on his face and in his eyes, blurring his vision, but he had to find his wife. His life would be over if she was lost. He heard Non give a cry of joy and looked up to see her husband being pulled free from under the masonry.

He paused for a moment and saw Caradoc fold Non in his arms and was ashamed that he wished it was his wife, not Caradoc Jones, who was alive and safe.

Small fires were springing up and Harry realized he would have to move fast if he was to find Gwennie before the fire took hold and engulfed the remains of the building.

He stopped where he thought the sitting room lay and began to tap one stone on top of another. There was an ominous silence and with his heart in his mouth he tapped again, but there was no response. He moved his position and began tapping again, frantically beating stone upon stone.

Morton caught his arm. 'Wait, I'm sure I heard something over there where the kitchen was.' He called some of the other men and they began to work on the rubble, pulling the stones carefully aside, wary of causing a movement in the ruins.

Harry scarcely recognized the still, lifeless body as it was laid on the ground. He wiped away some of the dust from the man's face. 'Josh! Oh hell and damnation, what's been happening here?'

'Looks like this was done deliberate,' Morton said. 'I can smell gunpowder on this man's clothes. Looks like the poor sod got caught in his own trap.'

'Do you mean Josh was blowing up this place deliberately?'

'That's exactly what I mean,' Morton said.

A young girl was being pulled free from the ruined building. Her eyes were wide with shock and her clothing was hanging on her in rags but she seemed unhurt.

'Emily! Are you all right?'

She nodded and put her hands over her face.

'Emily, look at me. Have you seen Gwennie? Where was she when the explosion happened?'

Emily made an effort to calm herself. 'She was in the doorway of the sitting room. Albie was at my side: he must be all right if he was standing next to me, mustn't he? Please get him out as quickly as you can.'

'Don't worry, girl,' Morton said, 'we'll get him free.' It took another hour before enough masonry was moved to find the floor of the once grand sitting room. Albie was lying on the blackened carpet, moaning in pain.

Emily crawled towards him. 'Albie, are you all right?'

Morton pulled her away. 'Don't touch him: you might do more harm than good.' He wiped Albie's face. 'Looks like he got a few injuries, girl, and perhaps some broken bones as well, but I reckon he'll live.'

'My darling boy,' Emily said softly, 'I'm here. You're going to be all right.'

Albie opened his eyes and looked at her. 'Don't worry about me, Em,' he croaked. 'I'm as tough as a bleedin' old boot. I'll be around for a long time to look after you.'

Harry knew he should be glad for them. Non and Caradoc were together, wrapped in each other's arms, and Emily and Albie were both safe, but what about his wife? 'Where's Gwennie?' Harry asked despairingly. 'Dear God, where's my wife?'

'She was standing by the table.' Albie winced as he raised his head. 'Look, you can see the boards jutting out of the ruins, just over there.'

Harry's heart was pounding as he carefully negotiated the rubble to where the table-top lay like a coffin lid among the ruins. 'Gwennie,' he said, 'Gwennie, can you hear me, my love?'

Like a whisper on the wind came a faint cry for help.

'Morton, come here,' Harry called urgently. 'Help me get these boards away. I think Gwennie's underneath them.'

Like a madman, he tore at the rubble, uncaring that his hands were bleeding badly now, blood mingling with the grey dust between his fingers. All he could think of was that Gwennie was alive and needed him.

'Take your time, Harry,' Morton said, 'take your time.'

Harry took no notice. He scrabbled away at the rubble with frantic hands, sweat streaming down his face.

'The place is going to go up like an inferno,' Morton cautioned. 'Come away, for God's sake, Harry.'

The flames of the fire seemed to take hold, moving closer towards him. He felt the heat on his face but he didn't care: if his Gwennie was going to die, he would die with her. With a last frantic effort, he levered the boards away.

'Gwennie!'

She was lying quite still and for a moment he feared she was dead. Then her eyes opened and they brightened when she saw him.

'Oh, Harry, my love.' Her voice was little more than a whisper. 'Thank God you're here. Is my baby all right?'

'David's safe – he's with one of the villagers; don't you worry about him. Let me get you out of there.' He lifted her up and held her close in his arms, his eyes wet with tears. 'Oh, Gwennie, I thought I'd lost you, I really thought I'd lost you.'

'I'm all right, Harry, I'm just a bit shaken. Oh, my darling, I want to be with you always. Hold me tight, just hold me.'

'My lovely Gwennie.' He took her in his arms. 'Don't you know you're the very air I breathe?'

'You've become quite a poet, Harry my darling.' Suddenly, she burst into tears and clung to him, her cheek against his. 'I realized as I lay there in the ruin how much I loved you, Harry. I think I've known it for some time but I . . .'

'Don't try to talk. We're together: that's what counts. I'll take you and little David home to Swansea and we're never going to be parted again.' His heart was full as he bent and kissed his wife. 'Gwennie,' he said, 'I love you.'

She reached up and put her soft hand on his cheek. 'And I love you, Harry, so very much.'

His heart was filled with joy as he carried his wife away from the rubble and across the grass. 'You'll soon be able to hold your baby in your arms, Gwennie.' He paused. '*Our* baby: we're a family now.' As he looked at the love in Gwennie's eyes, Harry knew that from the ruins of his marriage had come joy and peace. He bent over her and as their lips touched he felt joy flood through him. He murmured softly against her lips: 'I'm taking you home, Gwennie, I'm taking you home.'

THE END